$2

Winner of the National Book Award

Also by Jincy Willett

Jenny and the Jaws of Life (stories)

Winner of the National Book Award

A NOVEL OF FAME, HONOR, AND REALLY BAD WEATHER

JINCY WILLETT

THOMAS DUNNE BOOKS

ST. MARTIN'S PRESS 🙣 NEW YORK

Just in case the reader may feel that the title of this book means it actually has been nominated for the National Book Award, let us be clear: This book has not been nominated for or won the National Book Award. It has not been prepared, authorized, or endorsed by the National Book Foundation or anyone else associated with the National Book Awards. Which is not to say it may not one day be nominated for said award, or the National Book Critics Circle award or the Pulitzer. Time will tell.

—The Publisher

THOMAS DUNNE BOOKS.
An imprint of St. Martin's Press.

WINNER OF THE NATIONAL BOOK AWARD. Copyright © 2003 by Jincy Willett. All rights reserved. Printed in the United States of America. No part of this book may be used or reproduced in any manner whatsoever without written permission except in the case of brief quotations embodied in critical articles or reviews. For information, address St. Martin's Press, 175 Fifth Avenue, New York, N.Y. 10010.

www.stmartins.com

Design by Phil Mazzone

Library of Congress Cataloging-in-Publication Data

Willett, Jincy.
    Winner of the National Book Award : a novel of fame, honor, and really bad weather / Jincy Willett.—1st ed.
        p.   cm.
    ISBN 0-312-31181-8
    1. Triangles (Interpersonal relations)—Fiction.   2. Eccentrics and eccentricities—Fiction.   3. Women—New England—Fiction.   4. New England—Fiction.   5. Sisters—Fiction.   6. Murder—Fiction.   7. Poets—Fiction.   I. Title.

PS3573.I4455W56 2003
813'.54—dc21
                                                            2003054966

First Edition: October 2003

10   9   8   7   6   5   4   3   2   1

For Ward and Joanne Willett

Fame and honor are twins; and twins, too, like Castor and Pollux, of whom one was mortal and the other was not. Fame is the undying brother of ephemeral honor.

–Schopenhauer

Winner
of the
National
Book Award

Prologue

August 15, 1983

Lightning sought our mother out, when she was a young girl in Brown County, Indiana. Licked her body up and down, so she said, with a long scratchy cat tongue. She smelled the ozone, which she described as indescribable. "Not a smell at all, really, but a new and horrible sensation of the nose." We used to beg her to elaborate. She said it didn't smell like animal, vegetable, or mineral, or anything else in the world. Then how did you know? we asked. "It had," she tried again, "a tactile pungency. Every hair on my body stood out straight and vibrated. I wanted to drop flat on the ground but I couldn't move. It licked me like a big cat! Girls, I was an idea in the mind of a charged cloud!"

Then the lightning dismissed her, and demolished a dying elm across the street. "You always look so disappointed," she'd tell us, when she came to the end of the story. "You wouldn't be here, you know, if it hadn't let me go." But both of us truly *were* a little sorry she wasn't struck. It reflected badly on our mother, that she was tasted and found wanting. Fate had jilted her. "Where would we be?" Abigail always asked, and Mother would answer, variously, In heaven, In deep space, Nowhere, Who knows?, A twinkle in your father's eye. When I was twelve, one of the last times we talked about it, I said, "Maybe we'd be an idea in the mind of a charged cloud." Mother was terribly pleased.

As it turns out, I have never been an idea in the mind of a charged cloud. I have never, with the one grotesque exception, been an idea in the mind of anybody at all. I'm earthbound, of course, but not grounded. My sister is the family lightning rod.

Mark Twain was right: New England weather is a literary specialty, not a science. He gave a more reliable forecast in 1876 than those boobs on channel ten.

Probable nor'-east to sou'-west winds, varying to the southard and westard and eastard and points between; high and low barometer, sweeping round from place to place; probable areas of rain, snow, hail, and drought, succeeded or preceded by earthquakes and thunder and lightning.

I woke up this morning with a hurricane headache and turned on the stupid TV and there they were, one of each sex, babbling in front of a huge weather map. "We're going to get it," the man said, and the woman added that "the only question is how hard it's going to hit. Pandora is on the way." Last night these same people were promising she'd miss us by a hundred miles.

A hurricane headache is no guarantee. The big one is out there somewhere, that's all, eyeing your neighborhood. You're on her list, and the atmospheric pressure plummets, skyrockets, some damn thing, and the air is humid, smelly, ominous, and your head feels caught in a padded vise. You want to crawl right out of your skin.

We had a bad one here, in Rhode Island, in 1938, the year of our birth, and another bad one in '54, which I remember, and that's it. Rhode Island is not Key West.

Many have noticed this.

Hurricane headaches make you feel antsy and doomed, but they can be gotten around, like the premenstrual whimwhams. You just remind yourself that your emotions are physical in origin, and ignore them. I'm good at that.

"How bad it's going to be is anybody's guess." The man in the red blazer, Ernie, was unable to act convincingly as though this were bad news. "We're going to get it for sure."

"The main thing right now," his partner added, "is not to panic."

"And remain calm. I repeat. Hurricane Pandora is on the way. I repeat. Pandora is coming."

"And not just her tail."

"Nope. Head to toe!"

"Full body slam!"

"She's got us in her sights!"

"We're staring right up her gun barrel!"

"She's made a shambles out of Cape Hatteras!"

"Heading straight for us at thirty-seven per!"

"But don't panic!"

From my bay window in the living room I could see at least two people dutifully panicking already. Old Mrs. McArch had just about covered all her windows with masking tape, and John and Marie Bucci were squeezing children and beagles into the station wagon.

The Buccis always head out. They headed out in '68, when we were supposed to get the race riots. I asked John then where he was going, and John stopped and thought and said, "Burlington?" I pointed out (I was only thirty; I had more energy then) that (a) we weren't going to get any riots, and (b) if we did they'd be in Providence, where Negroes actually live, and not way out here in Frome. John shrugged. "Yeah, I know," he said, reddening, staring down at two bulging suitcases, "but hey." John's a nice guy. I always wish him luck. John is my bellwether, and John was heading out.

Today was supposed to be my day off. I had scheduled my Saturday crew, T. R. and Gloria, to man the library without me, and particularly to catalogue that three-foot pile of new books standing on the floor beside my desk. Usually I do these myself, the new books. Usually I want to. Of all my duties, opening brand-new books is the most pleasurable. When it comes to books, I am a sensuous woman. Usually. But not today, and so, naturally, today is Panic Day, and the Saturday people have flown away home, and I have had to come in myself and face it. The new book pile.

I knocked on Anna's door and told her about the forecast, and asked, did she want to come with me. She was already awake, listening to her clock radio, and said she'd stay here by herself. "I've always wanted," she said, "to batten down the hatches." How a twenty-year-old could have "always wanted" to do anything was a puzzler, but her decision was just as well. Today I didn't need the company. I poured some scotch in our father's old silver flask, put on jeans and a white shirt, filled three grocery bags with towels, and drove out to the Star for cold cuts and bread.

I'm not a drunk, by the way. It's going to be a long day, that's all.

I waved to John and Marie as I backed out the driveway. John shouted that they were heading up to Portland. "But the storm is moving north," I said. "I know," Marie said, and John said, "We know. But hey." We all had a nice laugh, and I wished them luck.

It was six thirty A.M. and twenty people stood outside the locked glass doors of the Star, watching the manager and a couple of checkers shuffle around inside. When I joined them they greeted me like a family member. I had forgotten about this. Rhode Island gets so few near misses, so little natural drama, that I forget from one time to the next about this phenomenon: what Conrad Lowe called "the disaster factor."

Rhode Island natives, including those born overseas, are under ordinary circumstances so shy and mistrustful around people they don't know as to seem almost deranged. They never look a stranger in the eye, or if they do, they unfocus their own eyes. I don't mean a stranger you pass in the street, I mean a stranger who's lived next door to you for twenty-five years, or a stranger you ask directions from or hand his dropped wallet to or knock down with your car.

This probably has something to do with the tradition of overcrowding, of living cheek by jowl for two hundred years. Whatever the cause, we have no stage presence at all, no Southern theatrics, Midwestern irony, Western hyperbole, New York cynicism. We don't even have the famous and overrated Maine understatement. We have instead an Un-fortunate Manner.

We literally don't know how to act. We have no roles to

play. We are the nakedest of Americans, and when native strangers, themselves naked and ashamed, make even innocuous demands of us—How much is this? Would you please get off my foot?—we panic and writhe, we shamble and fumble with our buttons, we mutter even as we back away. We make inappropriate noises. I've seen man-on-Weybosset-Street interviews on TV, and they're really too painful to watch. A stout woman with anxious haunted eyes, asked for her New Year's predictions, blurts, "I think we're going to have World War III!" and giggles like a toddler. She stands for all of us, an awkward cipher, silly or rude, or silly and rude, and inside, clearly glimpsed in the frightened eyes, some poor trapped soul screaming for help.

Our body language, of course, is wonderfully complex. We know a thousand different shrugs.

We are so lonely here, with only our loved ones for company. We kill, maim, insult our loved ones, or dream of doing so, to keep from going mad. And then disaster strikes. God, how we love disaster.

Let the storm come and flatten us, please, let the poor riot, let our houses burn (we have a terrific arson rate), let our president fall, our spaceships explode. What we wouldn't give for an LNG holocaust or a freeway sniper. Anything. I used to think we were just a big bunch of cowards, but that isn't it. We panic early, and we panic hard and long; but we love every minute of it. Rhode Island: The Panic State.

Panic frees us, to look around openly at one another. Disaster makes us friendly, in a demented opportunistic fashion all our own. We stumble toward one another, hilarious with terror, crazy with all the possibilities, like hibernating grizzlies injected with speed and shoved out into the light. We go berserk with candor. We lose it, big time, and oh, what a sweet relief that is.

. . .

Except for us Yankees, true and false (us Yankees do have stage presence), everybody waiting outside the Star was burdening the stranger on his right with the intimate details of his private life. The running theme of the conversation was "We're really going to get it now," and around us the wind picked up, and green maple leaves, plucked before their time, eddied in the parking lot, batted around in the smelly air as though by a bored child who, though already strong enough to rip down tree branches, had only leaves to play with for the moment.

The stranger to my right, a squat wide-rumped blonde in turquoise bermudas, asked me if I had filled my tub this morning, and I said yes, to take a bath. "You're not saving water?" I shook my head. "You tape your windows?" No. "You here for candles? Batteries?" "I'm here for my lunch."

Her face fell, and I felt bad about ruining her good time. She looked back up at me in a bold, speculative way. "I seen you someplace," she said. This is what passes for polite inquiry around here.

"I'm the head librarian at Squanto," I said.

"Nah," she said, shaking her head. "That's not it."

She was distracted then when the manager opened the glass doors. We wished each other luck, my new friend and I, and then we all squeezed through the single door in discrete lumps of ten. It took great effort not to panic along with everyone else. Men and women grabbed carts and began cruising down the aisles, like contestants on that old game show where you had five minutes to load up and the one with the biggest total won.

I concentrated so hard on strolling that I got to the deli counter second, behind a ruddy, big-chested yachting type, probably from Little Compton and somehow stuck inland, who had obviously decided that cold cuts were the way to go in the coming apocalypse. Soon there was a small crowd around him, and he gave them a big show, ordering corned beef, prosciuttini, smoked turkey, even olive loaf, in thinly sliced two-pound units. No one but me resented the way he was hogging the counter and showing off his money. I ended up buying a jar each of dried beef and mayonnaise, a package of stale burger buns, and an old head of iceberg lettuce.

By the time I got to the checkout the two lines were twenty deep and festivity was at its height. Shoppers sighting bare acquaintances across the way abandoned their lines to embrace one another; and when they returned, their places remained open to receive them. Most people were giddy and riotous but here and there stood someone badly frightened by all the excitement. A tiny old woman cried and was comforted by a family of Portuguese; a pregnant teenager with a Cro-Magnon forehead and hair bleached to the color of driftwood bellowed like a steer every time someone bumped into her cart, "Quit hittin' me, you retard!" Joe Hiltebrand, retired Frome Junior High School principal, turned around in line in front of me and addressed us. "This lady," he said, pointing to an old woman whose elbow he held, "just has two boxes of candles. Surely we can let her in ahead of us." We all nodded except for the cave-preggo, who said, "Fuck huh." The line turned toward her as one. "Fuck all a youse."

The woman in back of me, who had been talking in my ear, an academic type Not From Around Here, probably a Brown University wife, spoke soothingly to the girl, as though she were a zoo animal. "We're all scared, dear," she said, and so forth, carefully using monosyllables, but she didn't get far. "Fuck you," said the girl, and the woman Not From Around Here turned away without losing poise and whispered in my ear. "Two eloquent arguments for abortion rights, right there." Academics always spot me for an educated woman. What is it? How can I avoid it? "I'm a nun," I told her. She laughed unconvincingly and turned to the woman in back of her. "Isn't it fascinating," she said, "to see what other people buy in times of crisis? I see you're loading up on packaged mixes. An interesting choice." "Yeah, I guess so," said the humiliated housewife From Around Here, who obviously wanted to shield the contents of her cart with her body. Even during Panic Time it is inexcusable to comment on someone's groceries. We all stared rudely into the academic woman's cart, which brimmed with wheels of cheese and bags of whole wheat flour. Miraculously, the woman sensed hostility. "Brie is the perfect hurricane food!" she said, in her too loud Midwestern voice. "It can't spoil! It can only get runny and smelly and yummy!" "Fuck huh," said the preggo. Indiana, Illinois, Ohio. Somewhere out there. Well, we all have to come from someplace.

I come from Rhode Island.

When I got to the library, a pane in one of the back windows was already broken, and not by flying debris, because across the double doors in front was chalked a fresh message:

Dork From Ork

By "fresh" I mean of course "new." Some variation on the DORK theme has been scrawled on the door or the brick face every week for the last ten years. For a long time I thought it was the same kid, and all I had to do was wait for him to grow out of it. This cracked Abigail up. "It's not one kid, silly," she said. She said the graffiti were a local tradition, that the pink chalk was passed like a baton from one grubby little hand to the next one down. That my vandal would always be ten years old. "If you had a child, you'd know," said Abigail, shamelessly affecting modesty, doing her famous Virgin Mother imitation.

My vandal is a tradition, like those parodies of defunct TV commercials that children sing. Kids born in 1978 chant:

> *It's Howdy Doody Time*
> *It isn't worth a dime*
> *Let's turn to channel nine*
> *And watch Frankenstein.*

Somewhere in Frome even now a chalk-stained lad, forced indoors by panicking parents, stares wistfully out at the bruised sky and the dancing leaves and entertains himself with the sensuous memory of tiptoe stealth and the rugged feel of chalk on oak, and wonders, briefly, why he did it, and what DORK FROM ORK means. Who is Dork? Where is Ork?

Well, you little wretch, my name, for what it's worth, is Dorcas Mather, Dork to the likes of you, and I come not from Ork but From Around Here. And while it's thoughty of you to use chalk instead of aerosol auto paint, if I ever catch you breaking another of my windows and letting the weather in on my books, I will personally give you the sensuous memory of your unexamined young life.

First thing when I got here, I patched the window with the front cover of one of our older discards. *Forever Amber.* They don't turn them out like that anymore. The cover is nice and thick, wrapped in good fabric, and just fits the pane.

When I was twelve, and *An American Tragedy* was my favorite summer book, my sister thrilled to *Forever Amber,* especially the scene where Amber, trying to rekindle the passion of Bruce Carleton, her first rapist, appears at the King's Ball in a beaded gown that makes her breasts stand out "like full pointed globes." I had to call Abigail "Amber" all that summer. She had been "Scarlett" the previous spring. Already Abigail was coming down in the world.

I spent my next hour reshelving, and the next thirty minutes straightening out the Mc's and Mac's. Nobody on God's earth understands the Mc/Mac principle anymore. In order to do that, you have to be willing to think about something other than your genitals for a full minute. Nobody appreciates the horror of a good book dying on the wrong shelf. We have limited space here. We have to discard books that haven't been checked out in four years. Four years!

What I was really doing, of course, was avoiding the new books, piled on the floor next to my desk. If T. R. hadn't stampeded, along with the rest of the sheep—if she had catalogued the goddamn thing and put it on the new book shelf—I would have managed to avoid looking at it, until, dog-eared and shabby, it had been relegated to the 600 stacks and duly misshelved and swallowed whole.

Because then I could have looked away forever. Christ knows I am a disciplined person.

But today Pandora is toying with us, and so here I am, behind my desk, and in front of me is the world's saltiest sandwich, a Styrofoam cup full of spiked coffee, and a brand-new copy of *In the Driver's Seat: The Abigail Mather Story,* by Hilda

DeVilbiss and Abigail Mather. Wrapped in fresh thick plastic, bordered in Squanto Brown.

My sister's book is no longer a threat. It's an object, with weight and color. Like my sister.

The cover is a ludicrous, unimaginative collage: the front grille of what looks like an Edsel, a pair of smashed glasses, the lower half of a screaming face belonging to a woman who bears no resemblance to my sister, and a "Police Report" of which only the first line (*Comments: battered wife*) is legible, although, having stared at it now for some time, I swear I can make out the first sketchy report of a Japanese sneak attack on our naval forces at Pearl Harbor.

The back cover confronts me, not with a snapshot of my sister's big face, but with a list of advance raves from log-rollers in the wife abuse exposé biz. Here is a truly squalid practice for you, but it will work. It'll sell, and not just locally, although God knows it'll do good business here. In hardback even.

I was up all night reading this, literally riveted to the page. A true-life shocker which grabs you and never lets you go. Abigail Mather is a heroine for our times.

—Marj Wysocki, author of *Black Eye*

... you will weep, you will tremble, you will cheer, and yes, you will laugh ... incredible, horrifying, nauseating, and, ultimately, life-affirming and empowering. Abby Mather's triumph is our triumph.

—Victoria Fracas, author of
Rape, Rape, Rape

Abigail's story is by no means atypical. The only special
thing about her marital horror is that she did something
about it. This book should be required reading for every
bride. . . .

—June Bessette

Would you like to know who June Bessette *is?* June Bessette
is *nobody.* June Bessette is Abigail's *therapist.* The only reason
her credentials aren't listed is that she only has a *bachelor's
degree.*

Move over, Joan of Arc! Step aside, Charlotte Corday!
There is a newcomer to our pantheon of world-class heroines, and she is

I believe I'll have a drink.

I don't have the guts to read the blurb on the inside cover.
The L of C cataloguing is mildly interesting: First of all, no
index, since that's the kind of slob Hilda DeVilbiss really is.
Then:

> 1. DeVilbiss,   Hilda.   2. Conjugal   abuse.
> 3. True-life crime. 4. Biography—Lowe, Abigail
> Mather. 5. Regional—Frome, R.I. 6. Title.

I sort of like that. Regional—Frome, R.I.
Then we get the author's modest encomium thanking

everyone in Frome and New York City for enabling her to blah blah blah, especially my courageous, wonderful, funny sister. "Working closely with Abigail this past year," Hilda gushes, "has been the most fulfilling learning experience I could possibly have had." This I can believe.

There are three hundred and seventy-six pages here, which I will not read.

Yes I will.

There are sixteen pages of photographs, half in the front, half in the middle. There is our mother, recognizable only to us until this shameful moment, standing in the deep shade of the porch of the New Bedford house. You can see peeling paint, dusty ground. It looks like a slum. Whereas it's really just an ordinary amateur snapshot of an ordinary house *which was never intended for mass ogling goddamn you Abigail you rotten old babyfat bitch!*

Beside her there's Jabez, our father, a nice picture, his college picture, taken before he even met our mother, and running underneath them both, yoking them nicely, an educational caption informing us that "Jabez, whose mother died of tuberculosis when he was only five, grew up in an all-male world. His wife, Mattie, produced only the twins, and so his own family was all-female. The inevitable tragic results are all too predictable."

The inevitable tragic results. I grow numb.

There I am on the porch swing with Abigail. We are six and complementary, as always. Her hair was so light then that you couldn't get a shot of us together without one of us being poorly exposed. This is the one where I am a wizened gypsy in a navy collar middy and shorts, and Abigail beside me a white nimbus with eyes and a wide, camera-mugging smile, and some sort of flouncy dress, though even the dress pales into a dream cloud. How eloquent I look. How terrible to see irony clearly in the gaze of a six-year-old. A gypsy indeed, I look out into the future and give surprising comfort to my middle-aged self. *This was always going to happen,* says the child. *You've had a lifetime to get ready for it. Don't whine.* I won't. Even when I read the caption.

Dorcas remains a cipher. According to Abigail, "She knows me better than I know myself"; but Dorcas refused, categorically, without explanation, to cooperate in the writing of this book.

It's not such a great trick to see into the future. Take the next eight hours. I shall sit here and torture myself with this wretched artifact, and methodically self-medicate, which medicine should run out around noon. Before that, at approximately ten thirty, I shall start to feel its effects, and by eleven I shall have reached that stage where everything seems absurdly delightful and I have sudden cause for cheer. The cheap olive wall-to-wall indoor-outdoor carpeting they put down here last month will become *interesting* in texture and the colors of all my books, new and old, will sharpen up and give out a welcoming heat. The wind outside will pick up and sing to me in an enchanting way, and the sky will darken, brightening my lamps and overhead lights and it will seem, for a time, so *fortunate,* so, well, *wonderful,* to be alone on this day of days, riding out the storm in my beautiful little library. The whole show will seem to have been arranged for me. And if a window breaks, why, how exciting that will be. And if I trip and stumble, or spill booze on my desk, how droll. And as for the Book, the Excrescence, the Abomination . . . well, really, what the hell. Good for you, old girl. Pretty amusing, when you look at it the right way. Ha ha ha.

This ought to last for thirty minutes.

After that, depression, nausea, disgust. The basement will flood, ruining the bottom shelves of the children's books and stinking up the whole building for weeks, and I'll be down there slogging through rank water rescuing what I can, with a pounding skull and a lucid wish to die.

And Pandora! The promised apocalypse! Well, Pandora will send regrets, the sadistic bitch. Pandora's just tasting us, like Mother's lightning. Pandora will spin away laughing, leaving all of us, even me, especially secretly me, red-faced at having been duped yet again. There will be a big mess to clean up, that's all. No one will die. No great big thing will be destroyed. Lives will not be blasted. Heads will not roll. Come the new dawn, the cleansing, life-renewing dawn, here we'll be, every one of us in his assigned seat, eyes averted, smiles inappropriate, thumbs up our butts. Oh, hell.

DEDICATIONS

—for Guy DeVilbiss
husband, genius, admirer of women,
in whose robust imagination I dwell secure,
and who could not imagine me ever failing

—Hilda

—for Dorcas
who knows
and won't tell

—Abigail

An Ordinary Birth

Chapter 1

An Extraordinary Birth

Abigail Mather was special from the very beginning.
A fraternal twin, she had her birthday all to herself.
Abigail was born, to Mathilda Wallace Mather, in the
Providence Lying-In Hospital, on the thirty-first day of
December, 1938. Six hours later, in the New Year, her
twin, Dorcas, was born. Doctors and nurses exclaimed over
this phenomenon, which had never before happened in the
history of the hospital.

Here's oral history for you. Here's folk tradition.
Hilda obviously didn't bother with any pesky, prosaic research. Why go down to the actual hospital and rifle through
moldy files when you can get it from the horse's mouth?
Well, our filly has a convenient memory. We got this
story, about the two distinct birth dates and being a legend
in our own time, from Mother. Mother lived in a magical
world, where the unbearable was blinked away even if it was
ululating and pointing and hopping up and down in front of
you, and the past was always rosier than actual experience.

There was nothing wrong with Mother's mind, or her intellect, either. She was just, like her first daughter, remarkably good at fantasizing.

Abigail and I were born within fifteen minutes of each other on the last day of 1938. It says so on the certificates. We learned this, at the age of twenty, after having bragged for years about our unusual debut. I suspect the story started with Mother amusing herself, in a relatively innocent way, with alternate, more exciting versions of the great event, imagining different ways it could have happened, eventually hitting on this one, the most dramatic. After that it was a simple trick for Mother to forget that the story wasn't true.

Doctors and nurses did not "exclaim" over you, Mother. I wish for your sake they had. You never did get enough attention in this world. You weren't as good at it as some.

There was, in fact, something rather special about our birth, but it won't be reported in *In the Driver's Seat*. Abigail came first all right, and she was a breech. They had to knock Mother out, so intense was her prolonged agony, and rummage around inside her like a cow, but no matter how often or how firmly they turned Abigail, she wiggled herself back into her preferred position.

Ass first. That's how she finally came out. My sister mooned the world for two hours while, behind her, I choked for air and sustenance. My sister blocked the light with her pinchable, Rubenesque behind while I groped, disoriented and blind, for the exit. All I wanted was to breathe and see. *Just let me live.*

My sister emerged with a list of complicated, interdependent demands. They pried her loose, with infinite patience, a pair of strong, hairy, male hands gently cupping her loins and hindquarters, pulling, releasing, in a pleasing tidal rhythm. When they got her out she held her breath, deliberately I have no doubt, so that they held her upside down and spanked her and generally made such a fuss that when I, the afterthought, emerged (on my hands and knees, I picture it, like an old ragbag crawling across a cartoon desert), I was given only cursory attention. And they told Mother, who briefly fought her way through the ether to get the vital stats, that she had a child of either sex: "A beautiful little girl"— holding Tubbo aloft like the Wimbledon Cup—"and a boy"— smiling in a kindly, commiserating sort of way, giving her just a glimpse of my homely little face, swaddling me like a hideous burn victim.

I was not a remarkably homely child. It was just the comparison. All things being *relative.*

This story, the one about my being a boy for the first half hour of my life, is probably true, unlike the other old wheeze. Mother told it often, but not with cruelty, and certainly not to aggrandize herself. Years later she was still outraged about their carelessness. "I don't *want* a boy," she had told them. "Now, now," they said. "I do not want a boy, and I have not made a boy, and that's all there is to that." The doctors, unwrapping me to prove their point, stared at her, she said, as though she were a witch and had changed my sex after the fact.

Mother favored Abigail in character, and me in sympathy. Mother *admired* me. That was nice.

Unadulterated Yankee Crap

Hilda had two basic organizational choices open to her with respect to chronological events, both real and imagined. She could simply start at the beginning, wherever she decided that was–the Garden of Eden, say–and go through to the end. No one does that anymore. It's unfashionable.

Or she could take the low road, beginning with Abigail's "savage act of assertive self-realization" and then segueing back to the Garden, or whatever. I think this is what she should have done, considering the vulgarity of her subject. So we could open with the killing itself. Something like

February 13, 1979. The Eve of Valentine's Day. Chopmist Hill, Rhode Island, on Route 6, east of the 102 intersection. Moonless night. 11:30 p.m. Conditions: snowing lightly, temperature barely 32°.

No one happening to spot the ancient '56 Plymouth plowing west at a sedate pace could have guessed that inside a man and woman were playing out a primal struggle for survival which could only end in death for one of them. Emotionally the temperature inside the car was 211° and climbing.

The woman was softly crying, her gentle, defenseless body shaking. Somehow she had enraged him. Somehow she had set him off again. If only she could understand how. *Maybe,* she thought, *if we get home in one piece, he'll go right to sleep. Dear God, let him sleep.* The man's right hand left the steering wheel and backhanded her savagely, without warning, across the face. "I'm going to kill you, Abigail," he said, in a terrifying new voice, a low silky purr. "I'm finally going to kill you."

————————————

And so on. Nice and junky. And then, after . . . *again and again, forward, reverse, forward, reverse, and all the time screaming, with every sickening thump, "No more! No more!"* . . . we could cut to the beatific birth, and all the attendant ironic contrast.

Here's my guess: Hilda's editors pleaded with her to do it this way, but our Hilda would never pander to the baser instincts. Guy would never forgive her for it. What we get, instead, is careful, plodding evidence for Abigail's ultimate canonization. Hilda starts, of course, with what she thinks is the beginning: the pedigree.

Chapter 2

Solid Yankee Stock

So we learn that Abigail's first American ancestor was one of the "First Americans"! See, this is the thing about Abigail. She has just as much contempt for Hilda as I do, if not more. My sister is not stupid.

. . . descended not, as might be supposed, from Cotton Mather, but instead from one J. Herkimer, of Bristol, England, who booked passage on the *Mayflower* in 1620. Though there is no further record of Herkimer in the colonies, he does not appear on the list of the dead, and apparently, in 1625, he married one Mary Willett . . .

Mother paid a cut-rate genealogist to come up with a *Mayflower* ancestor, and he obliged, but all he would tell her was that Herkimer disappeared from view upon his arrival at Plymouth. Mother made up that stuff about Mary Willett, probably to amuse herself and us. Mother was not a snob. She just liked a good story.

We believed in J. Herkimer, First American, for about the same length of time we believed in our different birth dates. As I recall, accidentally discovering the truth about our birth led us, or rather me, to look into the other matter. After a great deal of correspondence, much of it transatlantic, I learned that J. Herkimer, who really *was* our ancestor, was also the only passenger on the *Mayflower* to return to Southampton with her crew in the spring of 1621.

. . .

If you ask me, here's what happened. Herkimer, *my* Herkimer, a threadbare, desperate, misanthropic little loser, uneducated and unfit for any aspect of life, arrived in the New World, took one good look around, announced, to an empty hall (people had stopped listening to him weeks ago), "This place isn't worth the powder it would take to blow it to hell," turned on his heel, and stalked off.

Of course, the ship had to wait for winter to pass before leaving for England, so that while he didn't have the opportunity for just this dramatic crispness, he did have plenty of time in which to harangue the miserable settlers with variations on his prophecy of doom. J. (for Jeremiah) Herkimer had quite a time for himself that winter harassing the frost-bitten, alarming the exhausted. For a few months he managed to preserve, just, the fiction of compassionate concern, confronting the beleaguered pilgrims with looks of such elaborate pity that they could not stand to look at his face, and many a good man turned to his goodwife as Jeremiah glided out the door and muttered, "Jesus, I hate that guy."

Eventually he dropped all pretense, and while Squanto patiently explained to the ragged circle of survivors the principles of corn-planting, Herkimer rolled on his back on the soggy spring ground, hooting and slapping his thighs, and if he hadn't been about to sail away he would have been beaten to death.

He got off one parting shot—"So long, suckers!"—as the stiff sea breeze mussed his thinning hair, and the creaking tub carried him toward the eastern horizon and the one sure thing which lay beyond.

He died penurious and bitter, or at the very least confused, in 1635, in Cheddar, England (twenty miles west of the original Frome), leaving a wife and ten living children. I have no idea how he had supported himself or them, but I like to imagine him as a speculator, in futures of some kind.

Eventually, as they will, Herkimers turned into Mathers, and one of them, Alfred, made it back here, in 1893, to work as a textile machinist. Alf was part of the *other* wave of English immigrants, which wave has never, to say the least, achieved the cachet of the first. Alf's people were garden-variety wretched refuse, and for a time, and despite the fact that they didn't have to learn a new language, they managed to be an embattled ethnic group. The Portuguese, who had been there far longer, looked down their noses at them, and made fun of their awful food and their strange ways. They told English jokes.

Between Alf's people and the children of the first wave, the Real Yankees, lay an unbridgeable class gulf. And while I've always found the distinction hilarious, Alf apparently didn't. When he was forty-five he married a visiting school-teacher from Indiana, and, soon after the birth of Jabez in 1923, Alf quit his job and moved his family to Indianapolis, where he could masquerade successfully as a Real Yankee, and school his offspring in their bogus heritage. When Jabez reached his majority, Alf sent him east, to claim his cultural birthright.

So much for Solid Yankee Stock.

This was the third and final blow in the trinity of our disillusionments, and it affected us just as deeply as the news about our ordinary single birthday and J. Herkimer, First Un-American, which is to say, not in the least. My sister was born knowing she was special, and so was I. We both knew she was special, and that this had nothing to do with her being a potential member of the DAR. It made us a bit sad on Father's account, until we realized that he never knew about the fraud, and died believing in it, taking comfort from a relatively innocuous lie, which makes him lucky, really.

Your True Yankee died out long ago, anyway, in the collective American imagination; which is to say you never come across him in a movie. The Redneck lives and thrives, and the Western Loner, and the Stoic Farmer (Solid Pioneer Stock), and so on. These are archetypes, but they stand for extant individuals, who really *are* Ethnics, with their Ethnic ways, like fiddle-playing Cajuns; and the people of Minnesota and the Dakotas really *do* embody something, with their musicality and their plain-spokenness and their Scandinavian lilts. And even though every human being has an inalienable right to be judged by his own actions, it does seem to me that every American but the Yankee comes from some still-living subculture which gives him a starting point to do with as he will.

Of course these groups vary enormously in vitality, and it may be that the Yankee is only the first of many inevitable casualties, as we all homogenize. Whatever the cause, the Yankee has become a pure Idea, an abstraction, and because nobody really knows one, none of us can ever agree on just what the Idea is. We talk about Yankees, but without a great deal of coherence, since we have lost our ostensive definition. They turn out movies about "Yankees," and they never, never get the accent right (even though we can't all agree on what the right accent *was*). All you have to do is show some raw-boned moron sucking on a pipe and muttering "Ayah" and audiences of all regions outside of ours will thrill to the stereotype; but nothing much follows the "Ayah." Your Hollywood Yankee is either (a) implacable, taciturn, darkly mysterious, fatalistic; or (b) righteous, taciturn, deadpan, gently cynical, mythically decent. In either event, your Real Yankee is the world's furthest thing from a fool, which may be why we won't bury him no matter how badly he stinks.

Abigail claims that there are Real Yankees still, up north in Maine and Vermont. But those are a lot of slow-talking, full-of-themselves Yankee impersonators, in my view. Of course, there are plenty of Country People up there, as there are still everywhere, but they're just Country, and Country is the same all over.

Whatever the truth, it's a fact that the Yankee in southern New England is a shmoo, a leprechaun. An Idea. Rhode Islanders with English names talk in hushed tones about so and so being a Real Yankee and with the same reverence with which Arizona people talk of ghostly Indian tribes, who are out there somewhere, but whom no one has actually seen. Just watch their faces when they talk about old Mrs. Sprague, down the road and up the hill, watch their delighted smiles when they say "real Yankee." How badly they need to believe.

The people with English names, that is. The clear majority of Rhode Islanders, who do not have English names, couldn't care less about Solid Yankee Stock.

Our bogus heritage did influence us as children, but not in any way intelligible to Hilda. Our parents left Indianapolis in 1938, deciding to settle here in the Plantations rather than New Bedford. We were born in Providence, in the Lying-In, but to Hoosier parents dedicated, for two different sets of reasons (Father, out of obligation to his father; Mother, for sheer love of romance), to seeing that we were always mindful of our roots. We were raised on tales of the *Mayflower* voyage and the legendary deprivations of that first winter, but we were also raised by people with flat Indiana accents, which both of us picked up and still retain today. They sent us off to public school with weird speech patterns and imagined, I think, that our blood superiority would be tacitly recognized and acknowledged.

There was nothing tacit about it.

They called me Dork from the first day of first grade. I have been called Dork all my life. I don't run home crying anymore. I used to beg Mother to change my name, and she would remind me of how special it was, and strong, my Solid Yankee Name.

Abigail, who had a much easier time of it, punched Nick Pappas in the mouth for tormenting me. And then he jumped on her and ground her face into the snow and I had to pull him off. We were seven. I remember it clearly because I was so surprised and impressed by my sister's championing me, and then confused by how easy it was to pull Nick off her. I had thought her overpowered, in trouble. But she was twice his size and could have thrown him off any time.

That night was the last time I tried to get my name changed. Abigail backed me up. I even had a new name picked out: Stella. Stella, for the prettiest girl in class, a slender child with olive skin and hair the color of milk chocolate. "Stella is a Greek name," Mother said.

"I want to be Greek," I said.

Our parents laughed and explained that "we can't just be everything we want to be."

Oh, really?

"Besides," Mother said, "you don't realize how lucky you are to have a nickname already. Not every child receives one. You didn't, did you, Jabez? And you both have been given yours already. Abby and Dork."

Abigail and Father snorted, at the same instant, and their faces turned pink.

"What's so funny?" Mother asked. "It's no sillier sounding than Hank, or Jack, or . . . Gert. I think Dork is a nice—"

Father covered his eyes with his hand, and Abigail pounded the table with the handle of her spoon.

"What is going on?" They shrugged and shoveled food into their mouths and would not look at her or me. Mother was really angry. She took a slow breath and resumed eating in silence, and finally said, "We think you're both rude. Don't we, Dork?"

Ha ha ha ha ha.

Later that night Father must have explained things to Mother. Abigail explained them to me. Abigail at seven knew what a dork was, and quite a few of the other names by which it is called, and something of its function. Well, I did too. I could hardly help knowing, since in our inseparable preschool days I had accompanied her on her fact-finding missions. We went with little neighbor boys into garages and basements and behind bushes and under card tables tented with sheets on rainy days. She had an old flashlight Father had given her, and she made the battery last. She always invited the boy to inspect her, and he was always too scared, or too smart. She always invited me to join in, and I was always too scared, or too smart.

My sister's face at such times became entirely opaque to me. I could never tell if she was in control or not. It seemed that something was in control, of the three of us, especially Abigail. What strikes me about it now is the total absence of nervous giggling. Abigail was never, never embarrassed by sex, and so it was impossible to be embarrassed about it in her presence. Which was, in a way, quite horrible. What do you do if you can't laugh?

I bowed out of these sessions shortly after, on our sixth birthday, on which I got my little nurse's uniform and she got her doctor's kit. (We had not asked for these. How did they know? Why did they help us?) The whole thing became too frightening then, the possibilities too threatening. It was bad enough when she operated on me, or on the boy, or the other girls. (We didn't use other girls much; they giggled.) There was never enough oxygen in our rainy-day tent, in our dusty attic, in the sunny open air. It was too soon, too soon. And when she lay beneath my hand, with her eyes softly shut, and did not move . . . We could do anything. Anything. We did nothing. But we could have done anything.

I told her I wasn't interested anymore, and that it was a stupid thing to do. This was the first time I ever really hurt my sister, and she surprised me with the generosity with which she let me know it, her disinclination to hide her sorrowing face. But she never argued with me about it, or needled me.

When she lay in bed beside me and explained what a dork was, she was being kind.

Dirty girls have piggy faces and shifty eyes. Dirty girls always look unwashed, whether they are or not, and only other dirty girls will befriend them. Dirty girls always look cornered, desperate, as indeed they should, with their lives just begun and their backs already to the wall in a dead-end alleyway. My sister never was a dirty girl. She has been known about and talked about all her life, and when she got in trouble no one who knew her was surprised; but no one who knew her was happy about it, either, in the way we are reassured by the self-destruction of dirty girls. She was, from the beginning, just too powerful to be dismissed like that.

Also, as I said, she wasn't a giggler. She didn't find dirty words intrinsically funny. She found dirty words intrinsically *interesting*. When she laughed at the dinner table she was laughing at Mother's ignorance. She adored Mother—we both did—but she always thought Mother's innocence funny, whereas it plain worried me.

Mother was always giving us terrible advice. For instance,

kids used to ride us about our Indiana accents. "Are you from the South?" they asked.

"We're real Yankees," we would say. This confused the issue, considerably.

"Why do you talk like that?"

"Like what?"

"Say *summatime*."

"Summertime."

"Summerrrrrtime." Laughter. "Say *byank*."

"Bank."

Hilarity. "Say *gool*."

"Goal."

"Steer."

"Stir."

"Draw."

"Drawer."

"Drawrrrrrrr. What part of the South do you come from?"

"Our parents are from the Midwest."

"What part of the South is that?"

They weren't being cruel. Just skeptical. They were trying to figure things out, same as us. And though we were never hated, they always kept us somewhat apart from them. They suspected, I think, that we belonged at arm's length. They suspected we thought ourselves better than they. This is because Mother was constantly warning us not to.

When we complained about feeling left out because English was spoken in our home, and our grandparents didn't come over on a boat, and we didn't have an Old Country, our mother instructed us to the effect that "all Americans are the children of immigrants. Yours just happened to emigrate a very long time ago. The fact that the boat your ancestors came over on was the *Mayflower* does not make you better than anyone else."

Naturally we repeated this speech many times, to the children of people who just happened to emigrate twenty years before.

Dorcas: "The name of the boat just happened to be the *Mayflower*."

Abigail: "They came over in 1620 instead of 1920. Big deal."

Dorcas: "We are all the children of immigrants."

Abigail: "Ours just happened to speak English."

Dorcas: "We're no better than anyone else."

Child of recent immigrants: "No shit."

Mother was always sending us out into the world with instructions on how to win friends, and it didn't take us long to figure out that she didn't have a clue. "When the other children call you by . . . that name," my mother said to me (after the night Father explained to her about dorks), "you just look right at them and say, 'Do you know that when you call me . . . that name . . . you hurt my feelings very badly?' Just look right at them and say it straight. You'll be very surprised at how quickly they change their ways."

Mike Callahan, my nemesis, couldn't believe his luck. "Awwwww. I hurt your feelings. You gonna cry? HEY EVERYBODY! THE DORK IS GONNA CRY, BECAUSE HER *FEELINGS* ARE HURT . . ."

"All right. When they call you . . . that name . . . just answer to it, as though it didn't bother you at all. Don't give them the satisfaction of reacting to it. You'll spoil their fun, and in no time they'll get tired of teasing you and begin calling you by the right name."

Again I delighted the bullies and their sycophants, who, after two weeks, showed no signs of boredom with their magical ability to make me acknowledge at their every whim that my name was a dirty word. In one way Mother was right: they *did* tire of using "dork" to get my weird, obliging attention, and soon they began calling me "Ass Hole."

"When they call you . . . that word," advised my dear mother, "you just look right at them and say, in a voice clear as a bell, 'Sticks and stones may break my bones, but names will hurt me not.' "

The next day Mike Callahan called out to me in the playground during recess. "Ass Hole! Yeah, you! Watcha doin', Ass Hole?"

I walked over and stood in front of him and his semicircle of snorting admirers, and I said to him in a voice clear as a bell, looking right at him, "You are a stupid, ugly little boy, and an Irish Catholic, and when you grow up you'll belong to a labor union and live in a tenement and have ten kids and turn into a big stupid drunk."

Mike Callahan looked as if he had been axed in the center of his forehead. His face turned red and his eyes filled and he was apparently struck dumb. This was one of the happiest moments of my life.

My mother hung up the phone. "Did you call Mike Callahan an Irish Catholic?"

"Yes," I said.

"Why?"

"I wanted to hurt him," I said.

When Abigail came up to bed that night she brought me some supper. "Mom's still mad," she told me. "She keeps saying to Dad that she can't understand deliberate cruelty in a child of hers. Dad just laughs." Abigail watched while I munched cold chicken and carefully wiped my greasy fingers on the napkin she had brought. "Why did you do it?" she asked.

"I already said. To hurt him. He's been hurting me forever."

"I know that. I mean, why did you admit it?"

It was my turn to stare at Abigail. It was the first time we ever regarded each other across the Ethical Divide.

"Okay. Pretend you're Mom. Say, 'Why did you call Mike Callahan an Irish Catholic?' "

"Why did you call Mike Callahan an Irish Catholic?"

Abigail wiped the conspiratorial expression off her face and assumed the piercing innocence of a child martyr. "Did I do something wrong, Mother? Is it bad to say that someone is an Irish Catholic? Isn't that what he is? I was just saying what you and Father say all the time." A plump tear appeared in the inside corner of each eye. "I'm sorry, Mother," she said, "and I'll never, ever do it again."

What strikes me about it still is not how good she was at it, moving me almost to tears of pity in spite of everything, but how strange she was to me at that moment, and from then on, really. I know Abigail better than anyone else in the world, and if I were asked to explain this or that particular thing, I could probably give a fairly accurate account of her motivations. I can report that duty has never played an even minor part in her decisions; that she is moved solely by the desire for pleasure and the avoidance of pain; that she derives pleasure from an astonishing variety of sources, and pain from astonishingly few; and so on. I can even predict her behavior, with a respectable success rate.

But I don't understand her at all. To understand you have to do more than predict and explain. You must feel some degree of empathy. I have a greater understanding of cats and internal combustion engines and Iranians than I do of my twin sister, Abigail.

CHAPTER THREE

Jungle Drums

Chapter 3

Coming of Age

Adolescence came upon Abigail Mather like a bad dream. She woke up one morning with agonizing, cramping pains, the white sheets of her childbed *[!!!]* awash in blood. What was happening to her? "I thought I was dying," she says now. "That I had done something terrible, and that God was punishing me..."

Scotch in coffee really isn't as awful as it sounds. Abigail really despises Hilda. I always knew she thought Hilda was a fool, we both do, but I never before realized the depth of her contempt. This is really a surprise, and not as unpleasant a surprise as it should be. When I first learned that this book was being written, I knew that Abigail would manipulate the truth, as she always has, but I assumed that her sole purpose was to attract the attention of the world, as if she hadn't had enough of that already. But really, already this stuff is so ludicrous, so trite, that I can see my sister winking, like the cynical old bawd she is. Who is she winking at? Me?

Abigail's adolescence came upon the *rest* of us like a bad

dream. We woke up one morning with jalopy tracks across our front lawn, outsized footprints in the flowerbeds, squashed to-matoes from our father's garden piled in a telltale smelly heap beneath my sister's tomato-fouled bedroom window, and the air, outside and in, tangy and gross with musk. When I say that from that time on, in the black of night, I sometimes heard outside the house the howling of animals who run in packs, the yowling of animals who hunt alone, I am not, strictly speaking, kidding around. This is actually how I re-member things.

When she was out on bail and holed up with me, and the press besieged us night and day and camped out on our porch and we couldn't use our own telephone, I felt rather as if I had gone back in time, to the familiar nightmare world of Abigail's adolescence.

The implication that Mother did not prepare her daugh-ters for the fact of menstruation is an actionable lie, or would be if Mother were still alive. But this is how my sister works. She loved our mother as much as I did, but Mother is gone now, and so, in Abigail's mind, incapable of being wronged.

Mother prepared us by sending us to talk to Father, who prepared us by drawing diagrams on manila paper with a number two pencil. The picture he drew, again and again, was an excellent rendition of that cross-section of the female reproductive system that we see everywhere, in gynecologists' offices and on tampon boxes, the one as familiar to us as the Bambi face in the "Famous Artists" ad.

I have never had a head for maps. I remember thinking it was interesting, and understanding that it was important, without being able to relate the map to any portion of my body. I still have great difficulty following maps. Spiritually I always face north.

We sat on the couch on either side of Father while he told us about our wombs and the little nests our bodies would soon begin to build and then discard. My mind kept wan-dering. I would have missed the whole thing except that Abi-gail's attention was so thoroughly engaged that I couldn't help homing in from time to time. She never took her eyes off the diagram and our father's hands elaborating, shading. Her mouth hung open and she kept forgetting to breathe out, just like a three-year-old child, so that his lecture was punctuated by her explosive little sighs. She was rapt. "This is the egg chamber," our father said, "and this is the long passageway leading from that chamber to the Great Hall . . ."

I don't know. Maybe he didn't actually say this. The way I remember it now, he spoke, really, to Abigail, while I hung around and eavesdropped in a desultory way. But that is unfair and, I believe, untrue. I believe he addressed us both, and turned to me as often as to my sister. Both our parents were scrupulous in the division of their attention. But of course he was really, really speaking only to her.

And she was listening as intently as a son would have listened to his father explain, for the first time, the mechanics of the rifle. *Today we have naming of parts . . .*

Not that it matters in the least, but I got mine first. I hid it from Abigail for three months. I don't know why I did that. Partly self-protection, I suppose, because I expected her to be jealous and angry; partly the pleasure of secrecy, or, I should say, a twin's pleasure in secrecy. Something you have to be a twin to appreciate.

When she found out about it she behaved, briefly and strangely, like a handmaiden, honoring me for it, and ex-pecting me to honor myself. She ran and told Mother. I think she hoped we would hold some sort of ceremony. "Well," Mother said, looking at me, smiling. "Dorcas is a woman now."

"I am not," I said.

"You are too," Abigail said.

"No I'm not." I was still small—I hadn't begun to get my height yet—and scrawny. I didn't even look like a girl, much less like a woman. I looked like a child, which is what I was, and knew it well. My body was built for running and climbing, not for having babies.

Abigail, in contrast, looked ripe when she was green. She was taller than me by a head and outweighed me by twenty pounds. At ten she was as moist and plump and dimpled as she had been as a baby; as she has been all her life. She still used baby talc. She still does. She has always had a baby smell, a sweet and intoxicating scent that makes you yearn, in an immediate, objectless way, and underneath the sweetness you detect the sour; and over the years the sourness grew more complex, jungly, powerful, and the sweetness stayed the same.

At ten she had the breasts of a plump man. You could tell they wanted to be real breasts, and would become real breasts if given half a chance. Mine were just pink disks stuck on a bony little chest, with no promise or inclination to become anything more. They looked like the suction cups of two toy arrows.

As to how I felt about this, I felt very little. I didn't dread "becoming a woman." I expected it to happen. But somehow it just didn't seem very important. To put it baldly, I felt, and was, redundant.

But not sad, or left behind. Having Abigail for a sister made my "becoming a woman" *unnecessary*. Not impossible: just unnecessary. I could not have become Abigail's sort of woman, but, after all, there are other sorts of women. Stella Mylonas, the chocolate-haired girl, was going to be a woman, and she was lithe and watchful, like a deer, and a sprinter, and the boys loved her. She got all the valentines in the Valentine Box. Abigail actually got very few. Stella had a collection of toy horses, wooden, plastic, bronze. Stella would be a beautiful woman. (I was wrong about this. She became a nice-looking woman with a trim figure. She was beautiful only as a child.)

And there were other girls, not pretty like Stella, but plump like my sister, who did not, like my sister, look purely *functional*; who were able to blush and giggle around boys, and give off their own weak, intermittent signals, and still operate on some level apart from the sexual. They were going to be women too.

But not like Abigail.

The Universal Choking Sign

Chapter 4

Jabez

By the standards of their day, Mathilda Wallace Mather and Jabez Mather had an excellent marriage. Jabez was a "devoted family man," which is to say that when he wasn't working he was at home, with his family. There is no evidence that he was ever unfaithful to Mattie, or literally [!!!!!!!!] abusive to his daughters. Visitors to the Mather bungalow must have envied this happy man, the "king of the castle," the object of devotion for no fewer than three females. "The sun rose and set on my father," Abigail says now.

I'm going to skip the next few pages. Clearly Hilda is about to depict our father as some kind of pampered, vaguely perverted, pleasure-swollen sultan, lolling and rolling about on tasseled hassocks while "no fewer than three females" scurry through the "bungalow" fetching sweetmeats and aphrodisiacs. With all *the inevitable tragic results.*

Our father worked for the northeastern division of International Bean. He stocked the grocery shelves of Rhode Is-

land and southeastern Massachusetts with bags of dried
legumes. He was able, just, to make a living this way. At least
one meal per week was meatless, and centered around a vat
of some kind of pasty goop. We ate them all, since we got
them for free: lentils, navy beans, great northern whites, li-
mas, chickpeas. Mother did her best, but to this day neither
Abigail nor I can bear to take our protein in this form.

I think Father enjoyed spending fifty hours a week pushing dried legumes just about as much as most reasonably
bright people would. To compensate, he became a dedicated,
though fickle, hobbyist. Over the years, and without disci-
pline or any kind of overall plan, he educated himself (with *the
inevitable tragic results*). He got on what Mother called "kicks."

He was a gardener of erratic brilliance, working pitiful
wonders with the tiny bit of land we had, and the miserable
Yankee soil. One of his longest kicks was rose-grafting. He
tried to perfect a new rose for each of us—a "Mattie-Lou," a
miniature "Baby Pilgrim" for me, a "Honeysuckle" for Abigail (respectively scarlet, blue-tinged white, and coral, as I
recall)—but he never could sell the AARS judges on any of
them. They were always, in my opinion, beautifully shaped,
but they would fall short in "vigor" or "foliage" or succumb
at the last prequalifying moment to some ignoble disease. Abigail's rose, the biggest and loveliest of all, had none of these
flaws, but gave off an offensive perfume, a cloying, hypocritical scent. It smelled like a cologne-drenched Bourbon princess six months after her last bath.

He would get on reading kicks, bingeing on one subject,
reading everything he could get his hands on about it, like
the Boer War or the Roman aqueducts or the Gadsden Purchase, and for weeks he would talk of nothing else, until,
inexplicably, he would stop talking about it altogether.

I remember him telling Mother about the Battle of Rorke's

Drift. I must have been pretty young at the time, because I got the impression that he was reporting to her the events of his working day, during which a handful of stalwart English troops, commanded by an engineer, held off an army of warring Zulus. This wasn't pure naïveté on my part, for there really was an immediacy to his prandial book reports, such were his excitement and enthusiasm. I think now that he was as suggestible to books as a hypnotized subject, so eager was he to be taken out of his humdrum life.

Business reverses, the protracted death of ambition, perhaps even the postwar anxiety which afflicted most Americans on a subliminal level . . . these are at least some of the possible causes of Jabez's perceptible withdrawal from Abigail just at that time of her life when she most needed him. At the age of ten, at the brink of womanhood, she sensed a growing coldness in him. "He didn't want me to be affectionate with him anymore," she says, with sorrow surviving in her voice. "I felt as though I had done something unforgivable, so bad that no one would tell me what it was."

Abigail Mather's great sin was, of course, in growing up. Her father, likely out of his own inchoate sense of guilt, precognizant of his own incestuous desires, withheld from Abigail the male approval necessary to her erotic self-esteem. Just when she had the greatest need of him, he declined to validate her sexuality. . . .

. . . with

THE INEVITABLE TRAGIC RESULTS.

———————————————

I'm staring at the wall in front of me. I have been reduced to that already. Happily, the wall is not blank. There's a black and white poster on it spelling out the Heimlich maneuver in a series of cartoon vignettes. The Board made me put it up. T. R. thinks it's a Good Idea.

T. R. is one of those people who apparently believe that if you are sufficiently cautious you stand a real chance of living forever. A hypothetical disaster—"I could have been killed!"—is as horrible to her as a real one would be, has been, to me.

The centerpiece of the poster is the central metaphor for our times. A middle-aged woman, mute, imploring, grimacing, clutches her own throat with one panicky hand. Underneath is the caption:

THE UNIVERSAL CHOKING SIGN

T. R. doesn't think this is funny. I had seen these posters before in restaurants, but had never studied one closely until T. R. put it up across from my desk. We had just the one conversation about it, which became absurdly heated and hateful, and I have not mentioned it since.

"You can laugh," she had said as she taped down the last corner, "but I personally can't think of anything worse than choking to death. I'm haunted by the idea of asphyxiation."

"You're haunted by the idea of death," I said. "Last week you said you couldn't think of anything worse than Alzheimer's disease."

"Alzheimer's can't be avoided. Choking can."

"Well, now that we have this poster, anyway."

T. R. blushed and zipped her lip. She is a resentful youngish woman, unfunctionally fat, and will do just about anything to throw a fight in her opponent's favor. She was not born to lose: She has been conditioned to prefer it, the disadvantaged position, like so many of her generation. (She is a child of the sixties; I am a child of the fifties.) She is happiest when sullen, most assured when outnumbered, most peaceful in defeat. The high point of her life came and went long ago, when a policeman's horse stepped on her foot and smashed her big toe during a peace demonstration in South Kingstown.

She was busy now figuring out ways to lose her argument with me. "All right," she said, "tell me what's wrong with showing people how to perform the Heimlich maneuver. It's not intuitive, you know. If you plant your fist in the wrong place you can break the guy's ribs."

"I'm not talking about the Heimlich maneuver. I'm talking about the damn sign. What is the point, T. R., of this picture? Is it supposed to familiarize us with the *appearance* of a choking person? So that the next time we see someone turning purple and grabbing his throat and gagging we won't assume he has a tension headache and pass by in discreet silence? Or . . . maybe it's to give us some idea of how to act when we ourselves are choking to death, so that we won't make the common mistake of doing nothing and waiting for people to guess?"

"You're always making fun, Dorcas. Well, it's easy to make fun."

"I'm not having fun here. I'm serious."

T. R. was slightly mollified. "Of course you're right," she said, "that ninety-nine out of a hundred people don't need to be reminded of what a choking person looks like. Probably nine hundred and ninety-nine out of a thousand. But think about that exception, that one in a thousand, and the life he could have saved if he'd seen this poster."

"I am thinking about him. I can't stop thinking about him. Where's he from, Neptune?"

"What harm does it do, for God's sake?" T. R. whined. "Even if it doesn't actually save anybody, you're totally disregarding the spirit in which it was conceived—"

"No, no, no. The spirit of the thing is exactly what I'm complaining about. This . . . artifact," I waved my hand at the poster, "is not a flash in the pan, or the work of a single demented soul.

"Committees turn these things out. They probably had some kind of poster contest, and *this won.* A group of educated adults decided how many tens of thousands of these things to create, and how to disseminate them, and of course the government's in on it, and it's a federal offense not to put this up on a restaurant wall, and every day millions of people look at it, whether they realize it or not, and the real message comes through, sinks in, we absorb it like trees absorb carbon dioxide, and the message is:

THERE IS NOTHING SO OBVIOUS
SO NATURAL
SO INSTINCTIVELY RIGHT
THAT IT CANNOT BE SPELLED OUT
AND MADE SIMPLE ENOUGH
FOR A MORON
LIKE
YOU

T. R. surrendered then, needlessly of course, as I was just flailing around, and she smiled her triumphant loser's smile. "I'm not going to go through this again with you," she said. "You're just going to start trashing Ralph Nader."

"It's sinful to treat adults like children. It's sinful to insult the intelligence of any sentient human being. It's unpardonably sinful to do these things for the person's own good." Every time I said "sinful" T. R.'s smile grew thinner and more obnoxious. First off, the antique notion of "sin" amuses her, and secondly, she knows that when I stop wisecracking she's got me, and I had gotten onto a subject about which I have very little sense of humor, because willful stupidity on this scale is criminal, abominable, and giggling at it is an act of capitulation.

The Universal Choking Sign is not funny, it is tragic, the product of a culture *in extremis,* choking in a moral vacuum, and I will not laugh at Hilda DeVilbiss either, and poke easy cowardly fun at her psychobabble, except to make the obvious, yes, brain-numbingly obvious point that if Father had failed to "withdraw" from Abigail when she entered "that time of life when she most needed him"—that is, when she started to sweat like a bad rose, carry herself like a tubful of liquid gold, thicken the air around her into honey, menace the innocent world with her delirious, half-lidded stare—if, that is, Father had undertaken to

VALIDATE HER SEXUALITY

he would have ended up at the

ADULT CORRECTIONAL INSTITUTION AT HOWARD

doing

TWENTY TO LIFE.

CHAPTER FIVE

The Death of Marilyn Monroe

I tiptoed, or belly-crawled, past the fifth chapter, the one about Mother. It is entitled, unless I am hallucinating, "The Third Sister," and the term "role model" pops up on every page. I assume that Mother is shown to be deficient in the role model department with *the inevitable tragic results.* "Child-bride" and "child-woman" also pop up a lot, along with "dream world" and "denial mechanism." The stark, minimalist beauty of this sort of writing is best revealed when we highlight the clichés and blank out the lines connecting them, which are just filler anyway. Only the clichés themselves, particularly spaced, are required. It's like those children's connect-the-dot puzzles. The dots alone reveal their true configuration to the patient, discerning eye. You don't have to connect them at all.

Hilda's idea, that Mother was our "sister," is just stupid enough to be original with her, and not part of our terrible, post-celebrity mythology. Mother, for all her softness and vulnerability and innocence and maddeningly cavalier attitude toward the truth, was in no sense our sister. That she had given birth to us, and would precede us in death; that she had come before us, and made us possible; these were the central facts of her life, I think. More important to her, even, than her marriage, which was affectionate and enduring.

When she would tell us our birth-story, the true part about my being mistaken for a boy, she would always end by saying, "I knew you were both girls. I always wanted daughters." She loved the phrase "my daughters," and referred to us whenever possible, to the most casual stranger. She didn't bore people with snapshots or cute stories. Often she didn't even refer to us by name. Just: "my daughters." Never "my children" or "my kids." Her only sorrow was that there weren't more of us. Now that I think of it, she was a modern mother. She said "my daughters" with exactly the sort of proprietary, foolish pride with which mothers of boys say "my sons." Mother felt herself special, I think, because she had produced girls.

And though she wasn't the sort of mother you could turn to for teenage guidance, for sensible maternal advice, she never wanted to be our girlfriend, to stay young with us, and when her modest beauty faded she took it cheerfully, as though it still existed, instantiated now in Abigail. She passed her beauty on to Abigail, and her love of books to me.

She was the oddest reader I've ever known, and in my line of work I've known quite a few. She had absolutely no taste. She would read everything, everything fictional, anyway. One week it would be *The Cloister and the Hearth* and the next week *Claudia*. She thrilled, really thrilled, to *Moby Dick,* and read passages aloud to us in a sonorous voice, a deep register unfamiliar to us, and as I remember it—we were eleven or so at the time—she didn't skip over anything, and the chapters she found the most moving were the very chapters traditionally given the most attention by academics. And then, overnight, she was thrilling to *King's Row* or *Kiss Me Deadly* or *Leave Her to Heaven*.

Mother and I talked about books. It was our way of loving each other, and the reading of the same book was our principal shared experience. The worlds we inhabited were very different; here we had a common text. Even after I grew up and became aware that Mother did not discriminate between art and trash, and that I needed to, I remained, forever, willing to read any piece of garbage she wanted me to, just for the pleasure, the cocoa-in-bed, Christmas-Eve pleasure, of sharing it with her.

And she didn't like any old thing. She found depressing books depressing, horror stories unnerving; she was particularly critical of novels with uninteresting or inconsistent characters. "People don't act like that," she would say, and she was frequently right. But no matter how egregious the writing, she would always finish the book.

Reading was not an escape for her, any more than it is for me. It was an aspect of direct experience. She distinguished, of course, between the fictional world and the real one, in which she had to prepare dinners and so on. Still, for us, the fictional world was an extension of the real, and in no way a substitute for it, or refuge from it. Any more than sleeping is a substitute for waking.

When we were twenty-four I lived away from home, mostly. Abigail was a widow then, at home with baby Anna, and I was away at Amherst getting my degree in library science. That summer, though, the summer of '62, I came home. It was the last time we four were together as a family. It was the summer Marilyn Monroe died.

I got up before Abigail one morning. (I got up before Abigail every morning.) I took my coffee outside, to the tiny gazebo Father had designed and built in the backyard.

Barely ten feet in diameter, it dwarfed his little lawn when he first set it up. Soon he dispensed with the lawn altogether and extended the garden borders up to the base of the gazebo, so that the structure appeared to rise like an island in a lily-choked pond. He set down flagstones so that we could get to the gazebo without trampling the dahlias, but his gardens were so lush that the flagstones were the devil to locate. Getting out to the gazebo was like a child's game, and reduced you to a child no matter what your age.

The gazebo itself was beautifully constructed, ingeniously designed—to ludicrous effect, because of its scale. Father was an excellent craftsman, with no sense of proportion or perspective. The gazebo still stands, in what is now my backyard. It has weathered twenty-five years absurdly well. Professional office buildings have crystallized and disintegrated in Frome during that time; a major section of the interstate highway has been constructed and duly condemned and now partially rebuilt; in Providence an entire hotel has evolved from Platonic ideal in the minds of the city council to whorehouse and eyesore. And still my father's gazebo stands, like the pyramids of Cheops, weathered to the bone and white with age, but too solid even to creak and sway.

Anyway, that morning I picked my way through the snapdragons and sat up on the railing, watching the bees, listening to the others stir within the house. I heard toilets flushing, and the sound of the *Today* show on TV, and a woman's cry, "Noooo!", I couldn't tell whose, and the crash of breaking glass. Someone had dropped a china cup on the kitchen floor. After a long time Father came out the back door with his mug of coffee, and stood sipping it in the shade from the eaves. Usually he came right out to the gazebo on nice days, and took his breakfast with me. When he did emerge from the shade he walked deliberately toward me. There was a portentous hunch to his shoulders, and intuitively I braced myself for terrible news, although I couldn't imagine what it could be. The telephone hadn't rung. (It's an indication of my youth and the youth of my country that it did not occur to me, that morning, that bad news could have come through the TV. Kennedy was still alive.)

He sat down in one of the painted wooden chairs, and I sat beside him in the other, and for a time we didn't say anything. I was very frightened by whatever it was but in no rush to hear about it. The air smelled particularly good to me as I waited for him to speak, and the coffee tasted fine. A door was closing, and everything behind it was beautiful. Good-bye, snapdragons! Good-bye to simple animal mornings, to the life I've led. I'm needed at home, at childhood's end.

Father's voice when he finally spoke was pleasant, but there was a husky, nasal quality to it, as though he had a cold, which he didn't. He said, "Marilyn Monroe is dead."

I held myself perfectly still.

"Suicide," he said. "She was all alone, poor thing."

I gripped the broad, flat arm of the chair with one hand, and covered my mouth with the palm of my other hand. Covering my mouth was an instinctive act. I didn't know whether I was doing it to hide my mouth, or hold it shut, or both.

"Abigail's with your mother," he said.

I was trying to abstract the things Father was saying: to get beyond the apparent non sequitur, to whatever awful thing had made somebody scream and drop a teacup. I made a geometrical problem out of them:

1. Marilyn Monroe is dead
2. Abigail is with Mother
          Therefore:
3. What????

I tried algebra.

$$(M.\ M.\ is\ dead) + x = Childhood's\ end$$
$$x = (Childhood's\ end) - (M.\ M.\ is\ dead)$$
$$x = What????$$

All my life I had yearned for responsibility, for someone to need me, to require me to do some hard service, so that I could begin the business of my life. I yearned for duty the way Abigail yearned to show her ass. And here it was, my first assignment. Horribly, and for the last time, I burst into tears in the presence of one of my parents.

He covered my hand, the one gripping the chair, with one of his. "You surprise me, Dorcas," he said. "I've never known you to be sentimental." He squeezed my hand. "She was special, though, wasn't she?" He was smiling sweetly at me, a father comforting his daughter, in control of the situation.

I blew my nose and took a few breaths. "Of course I'm not sentimental," I said, "and I never knew you to be either, especially about movie stars. What's happened here? What's really wrong?"

"Nothing's 'really wrong.' " Father laughed, in a maddeningly fond way. "You don't have to be ashamed, honey. Lots of people loved Marilyn Monroe."

"Well, not me! You're the one who's making a big deal

out of it!" As the tension drained away, humiliation rushed in to take its place.

"You know," he said, "that there are only three women in the world I care about, and they're all right here. I was just upset on your mother's account. It seemed to hit her pretty hard, and Abigail, too."

I couldn't imagine why. Mother was a reader, not a fan. "Did she know her in high school or something?" Mother had gone to high school with Red Skelton.

"Mattie looks just like her," Father said. "I've always thought so."

"She does not," I said. Although I knew what he meant. Mother had the baby-blond hair and a real sweetness, an innocence that made us all want to protect her. But she had a long, horsy face and an angular body. She gave the impression of softness because of her personality. Actually, she looked like a cross between Marilyn Monroe and, well, Arthur Miller. I said so, and it gave me no small satisfaction to see Father wince at my infliction of this sharp little truth.

"She's Marilyn Monroe to me," he said. "Prettier."

"Excuse me," I said, without looking at him, and went into the house. Mother was changing her bed and humming. "Mother," I said, "are you all right?"

She nodded brightly, unable to more than grunt, with one corner of a pillow in her mouth as she coaxed it into its case.

"About Marilyn Monroe?" I said.

"Isn't that sad," she said. "Poor thing."

"Does it especially bother you?"

"No." Mother sighed. "But your sister is taking it very hard."

Abigail was feeding baby Anna in the sunroom. She held the bottle carelessly, tilted slightly up, so that the baby had to work hard for her meal, and Abigail's face was pale, her eyes red-rimmed. I took Anna and the bottle away from her and sat down to do the job properly.

"I know it's crazy," Abigail said, with her lower lip quivering, her big myopic blue eyes swimming in fresh, easy tears. "She died with a telephone in her hand. She was trying to call someone." She sobbed freely, like a baby on its back. "Don't you say it, Dorcas. I know I'm being dumb. But she was so . . ."

". . . much prettier than you," I said, "and now she's gone."

Abigail blew her nose. "Bitch," she said. "She had a special quality, which I don't expect you to appreciate."

"And what quality is that?"

"Oh, you know." She gestured impatiently toward Anna. Even in youth Abigail was profoundly lazy. She loved to make me finish her sentences for her.

"Infantilism? Baldness?"

"Innocence, you boob. But it wasn't just that. She was . . . a pure tramp."

"Takes one to know one."

"Come on, you know what I mean. She was pure *and* a tramp. She had this way of making the whole world . . . I don't know . . . what?"

"Salivate. Ogle her breasts. I give up."

"Gosh, you're hateful today." Abigail threatened to cloud up again. "You wouldn't appreciate this, but she had this special ability to make the whole world feel responsible for her. That's it. She wasn't *supposed* to watch out for herself. Everybody else was supposed to do it for her."

I just let her run on. The bare idea of my sister feeling responsible for anything or anybody, including Marilyn Monroe, was beyond comment. She was quiet, finally, for a long time, and then she looked up at me and asked, shrewdly, without artifice, "Do you think I look like her at all? Do I remind you of her in any way?"

This was the sister I knew best, and loved, over my severest disapproval. Hard as nails, absolutely shameless. She had never hesitated to expose her worst self to me, or pretended to feel guilt, or even the justification for guilt, about anything.

She was, on this very day, the day of the dreadful news about Marilyn Monroe, a two-week widow, her shotgun husband, Everett Esser, having died of a heat stroke during basic training at Fort Gordon.

I had been with her when she got the news. She put down the telephone and told me, briefly, what had happened. She sat still for a while, without expression, absently hugging her fatherless baby. She sucked me in for a few minutes. I averted my eyes from the spectacle of my sister thinking, for perhaps the first time ever, about something besides herself. It was, for me, a holy moment. She cleared her throat. "Dorcas? Do you think we could hold off the funeral until Monday? Is there some law that says you have to do it right away?"

I was a little slow, but I got it. Country club dance on Saturday night. She had bought a dress for it, a Monroeish scarlet taffeta thing cut low to just about her nipples, stretched tight across her high waist, her appalling rump and thighs, flaring out with brilliant irony at the knees, allowing free movement now that none was possible. A 1962 version of the dress Amber St. Clair wore to the King's Ball. The dress my sister had dreamed of wearing since she was twelve.

I told her she could wear it to the funeral, which, of course, would have to be held on Saturday, and that in any event if Everett's parents caught wind of her cavorting at the Agawam Hunt Club dance they would cut her and the baby off without a cent.

"Shit," she said. "You're right." And grieved, visibly, for her missed opportunity.

Abigail showed me everything. Only me. She cried at the funeral, and got her money, but she never pretended to me.

The only grief she has ever felt was for our parents, whose deaths were a year off, and for Conrad Lowe, whom she murdered and, in her own horrid way, loved. She cried with pleasure at the death of Marilyn Monroe.

"You are like her," I said, "in that you are an amoral exhibitionist."

"If I killed myself," she asked dreamily, "would people feel responsible?"

"If you killed yourself, pigs would fly."

Abigail laughed. "I'd be missed, though."

"Sure. Every flag at Quonset Point Naval Air Station would be lowered to half staff."

She smiled still, and closed her eyes, and slept like a cat, leaving me with the baby and the bottle. You are like her, I had refused to tell her, though she already knew it well, in that you make a man out of everybody.

Diminished Responsibility

Chapter 6

After the Game

Nineteen fifty-three, just after Abigail turned fourteen, was the year Frome High won the state football championship. On the night of January 10, at 9:00 P.M., the winning touchdown scored, setting in motion a number of traditional rites. The ritual tearing down of the goalposts. The ritual beer bacchanal in the woods behind the stadium, beside the frozen Assonocket Reservoir. The ritual human sacrifice.

Abigail Mather, giddy with drink, was the only female remaining at midnight in a stronghold of brutally healthy young men. When the beer was gone they moved out on the thick ice, sliding, at first cautiously, then with increasing confidence. They formed a long hand-linked line, which became a circle, with Abigail at the center.

She flew across the starry night with her feet tucked up under her bottom and her head thrown back, held up by the steely arms of the young men. There was laughter, and then there wasn't, and Abigail was alone, in the middle of the frozen lake, at the center of a rough circle of men. . . . No one was to know what was done to her that night. Ever. Until now.

Which was my fault, as I had refused to listen to her when she climbed into my bed at three in the morning, her hair filthy, reeking of dried beer, her body rank and strange. She smelled of copper and hops and fear and horses lathered by a killing run.

"Dorcas," she said. "It's wonderful." My sister was trembling, in the grip, for the first time in her life, of something more powerful than herself. She squeezed one of my hips in her hand. "They'll love you," she said, laughing, as I tried to jerk out from under her. "They'd love you just as much. You can make them do anything! I know you're not ready yet, but Oh, Dorcas, I wish I could show you now. . . ."

I punched her soft stomach with all my strength. "Get out of my bed, you pig," I whispered through my teeth. I hit her again. "Get away from me. Wash yourself. Get off me." It was enraging not to be able to scream, to have to protect her from our parents, our parents from her. For the first time I saw my sister as a burden, and understood that I would have to carry her, in some sense, for the rest of my life. I kept punching her, and she made no move to protect herself, and everywhere my fist sank in, its small force was muffled by her flesh.

I kept hissing at her to get off me, although, literally, I was on top of her, kneeling on her thighs, wobbling precariously, and her dirty nightgown was bunched and twisted around her waist, but still she was on me, really, with her bullying musk and her appetites, and I stopped hitting her only when I saw, through the stars of my rage, that she loved it, with her eyes shut and her mouth jagged in a sow's pink grin. I slapped her hard across the face, drawing a tear from one eye, making no difference, and then leaped away from her, hugging myself with fright.

The only effective weapon against her was indifference. I

had always instinctively known that, but had not, until that night, begun to know just how horrible that was. She thrived, she prospered, on any sort of attention, like a plant on light. Even horror, disgust. Even fear. Love, disapproval, clinical interest, curiosity, outrage, hate, cold, and warm—no matter how you regarded her you were already lost, for the mere fact of your regard became her nourishment. To look at Abigail was, is, to feed the beast. To look at her with strong emotion is a kind of suicide.

She drew a bath for herself in the basement tub, so that our parents would not hear. She came back clean and cleanly dressed and got into her own bed. I lay awake until daylight with burning eyes, worrying at my parents' innocence, my duty to preserve it, my duty to Abigail, my crippled sister, my monster, who slept deep. At one point during the night she rolled up onto her knees and slept the way she had when she was very young, with her face mashed into her pillow and her bare rump in the air. My innocence was gone forever. Hers returned, and always would, settling upon her in the night like dew. My sister manufactures innocence, like adrenalin, or sweat.

So I never learned What Happened That Night until last year, when Abigail was at the ACI and I couldn't raise bail because it took all the money I had to retain a decent lawyer. Frank Calef was a great help to me at that time. Frank's a banker, probably more responsible than any one other individual for the Wampum Factory Mall, and one of the City Council Yankee Impersonators who stand fast against the Italian Menace. But Yankee impersonators, like their Platonic ideal, have some virtues, the greatest of which is devotion to duty. Frank helped me out with money and made his shoulder discreetly available should I want, in an uncharacteristic (but permissible in the extreme circumstances) moment of weakness, to sag against something. I suppose he was motivated by a notion of solidarity, and if my name had been Squillante or O'Malley or Fishbein (especially Fishbein) he might not have been so willing to stand by me. Although I suspect he would have anyway, but would have missed a beat between hearing the news and offering assistance.

In any event we spent a lot of time together the first few months, drinking coffee in my parlor and talking, like characters in an old soap opera; not the new kind, with all the sex. Frank is a soap opera man, with a regular, handsome, sober face, and a ponderous, stolid tolerance for voluble females. He is sexless, too, like soap opera men. (I am as unlike Abigail as possible, but my instincts have never been in doubt. I share, along with my imprudent sister, and all imprudent sisters, a bawd's contempt for sexless men.) Needy females made him unctuous. "I know," he would murmur, nodding. "I know." Organ music up and out. I remember him as a handsome boy, self-assured, twinkling, clever in a modest way; always bound for Brown and Harvard Law. What I forgot, until he reminded me one evening, was that he was first-string quarterback for Frome High in 1953, their championship year.

I went to one game in my life, when I was twelve. The boys looked robotic and stupid with their padding and their helmets. And the cheerleaders . . . It seems now, though this can't be true, that I pitied them even then. I remember how pretty they were, how professionally they filled the space in which they crouched and leaped. It seems to me now that they smiled like airline stewardesses, unexcited, in control; and that in their generous, graceful display of frost-reddened thighs and pure white underpants was an unflinching awareness that this, now, was the high point of their lives and beauty; that all that remained was decline, disappointment, a lifelong footing of the bill. They smiled like the retiring Miss America. They were icons, and in my memory they always knew it. Abigail was no icon; she envied and hated the cheerleaders for their beauty and popularity. But she was happier than they were even then, and her life has had no high point, nor required one, and the only reason she bothered to envy them was her own bottomless greed.

I assumed that Frank was acting out of loyalty to his head librarian. He said, one early evening, that the town owed something to Abigail, and I laughed and said I couldn't imagine what. Until she married Conrad Lowe she had been an embarrassment and a nuisance, everywhere at once in her mailman's uniform, an absurd and unflattering outfit that made her look even hippier than she was, with those trousers cut for men, stretched across her buttocks and thighs, the hip pockets gaping wide, and her mailman's hat set way back on her head, held on with long pins, framing her round wicked face.

And like Cain's postman she was Fate itself, and when she rang the bell on Saturday the husbands came to the door, and sometimes their wives were out at Food Land, and once in a while, according to Abigail, they were just down the hall in the kitchen, scrubbing the linoleum. She poisoned half the marriages in her territory (and she covered a lot of ground) and a good many outside it, where she was only legend.

I said that if the town owed something to her, it was tar and feathers and a one-way ticket to Worcester. Frank failed to nod and murmur "I know," but stared into his cold beige coffee and blushed. "I knew her when she was just a kid," he finally said.

"Everyone did," I said. "You mustn't let it make you sentimental. Abigail can take care of herself. She'll be all right,

Frank. I don't know how yet, but she's going to get out of this without a scratch."

"You don't understand," he said. "I was her first lover." He shivered.

I laughed without knowing I was going to, shocking and hurting him. "Frank, someone was her first lover. Maybe it was you. You ought to know, though, that my sister has always had a love-hate relationship with the truth, and an eccentric sense of humor."

"I know what I'm talking about. I was *there*."

There's no arguing with people who cite experience. He was becoming agitated, and his face was transformed by genuine emotion, his skin slack and dry, and I could see the skull beneath, the old man's face.

"I'm going to tell you something, Dorcas, something I've never told another living soul."

Why? "Frank, please don't. If you've never told another living soul, chances are there's an excellent reason. You'll just regret it. I regret it already, and you haven't even done it."

He closed his eyes. "Dorcas, your sister was . . . your sister was . . . when she was fourteen . . ."

"I know," I murmured. "I know."

". . . gang-raped by the football team, and I was the first." He spoke with his eyes closed and held his breath afterwards. I couldn't speak because he had taken me by surprise. First, I had forgotten he was on the team; and second, I had forgotten That Night, having shoved it viciously so far back in my mind that his saying this acted on me like those phony revelation scenes in psychiatry movies. And third, I had never considered rape, or imagined my sister as a victim. Gang rape.

"We were all out on the ice and drunk as skunks. She had her coat off and she was laughing. We were all so snockered that we weren't cold at all, although it was below freezing that night, and my fingertips were still numb the next morning. She was laughing and she took off her hat, one of those wool stocking caps, and her hair tumbled down to her shoulders.

"We had just been carousing, you know, whooping it up and full of . . . well, booze, obviously, but also joy. Real joy. I was never that happy again. And your sister stayed with us, like a mascot. She was fun. It was fun to get her drunk and she was a good audience. She laughed at our jokes. We were easy with her at first. It was like she'd always been with the team. And then, I don't know, we were horsing around on the ice, and then she was standing there, and we are all standing around her, in a circle, watching.

"She wasn't afraid then. She was laughing so hard, she lost control. Even when she saw we weren't laughing anymore she kept it up, forcing it. It was like she loved the sound of it. It was like a song, or a chant. She whirled around and around, looking into our faces, laughing. Not afraid.

"Your sister wasn't stupid, you know."

"I know."

"She wasn't some bimbo, some retarded girl. We weren't that bad. Or maybe we were worse. She said, 'What happens now?' Her voice wasn't scared. We didn't say anything. We didn't know! She said, 'What do you want me to do?' And somebody said, 'Take off your sweater.' *I* said it. And she did. And someone else told her what to take off next, and so on. Every time she took something off she got bigger. She kept smiling and we could hear her breathing. We didn't look at each other, or move.

"She stood there naked on the ice, under the moon, with just her shoes on, and then she took them off, although nobody told her to. We weren't *that* cruel." Frank laughed, an awful, barking laugh. I don't often pity people. I pitied Frank. "I think she took them off because she knew they looked wrong. Halloran, lineman, laid down his jacket for her to stand on.

"She danced.

"She didn't dance like a stripper or a whore. She didn't move her hips around. She raised up her arms and turned, around and around, with her head thrown back and her legs apart, but not being obscene, just showing us. I have never in my life seen anyone as happy as she was then.

"All the guys threw their jackets down. She thought they were giving her a bigger dance floor. She thought that this was what we wanted. To watch her dance."

"No," I said. "Abigail was born knowing everything."

"You're wrong about that, Dorcas. I know what you mean, but this time you're wrong. She may have known the, you know, about the birds and the bees. But she didn't understand that she couldn't stop it. She was frightened when I touched her, and when I entered her, I'm sorry, Dorcas, she cried, and I hurt her. She was just a kid. I didn't hit her. I didn't need to. She could see how it was. And by the time I was through, she was talking back to me, complaining even, 'Where you going, Frank? What's your hurry, Frank?' I can still hear her voice in my ear. And after me came Lawson, and Siniscalchi, and Halloran—"

"This is not necessary," I said.

"And she stopped crying, and, I swear, got into it. She wasn't in shock or anything, I'm sure of it. And finally came the place-kicker. McAdoo. Henry McAdoo. Runty little red-headed guy, died at the Yalu. We were all zipped up again by then, and turned away. We left them on the coats, on the ice, and walked away to wait for McAdoo to finish. We weren't watching, except when McAdoo started yelling 'Stop it! Let go of me!' and we looked over and he was trying to push himself off her and she wouldn't let him go. He was pushed up on his straight arms and you could tell he was really trying—which was funny-looking, and we started razzing him—because she had both hands on his butt like claws, clamping him on top of her; and anyway, even if his head wanted to go, his dick wanted to stay, I'm sorry, Dorcas. He was still humping away, which is why he looked so funny, like two different men joined at the waist.

"So we couldn't figure it out, why he was acting like this, and then he started shouting to us for help, really sounding terrified. He was maybe fifty yards out, but you could hear him clearly, *Jesus! Jesus!* McAdoo was hysterical, and we were razzing him from the shore, and then I heard it, the slow cracking of the ice, like branches snapping, only electrical, and you could just see under the surface blue bolts like lightning shooting out from them in every direction. It was like a meteor was landing in slow motion exactly where they were.

"It looked like they'd both had it. It looked final. I suppose we were . . . disposed to think along those lines, considering what we'd been doing. Somebody would pay for what we'd done." He was lost for a moment; disappointed, maybe, about the failure of divine retribution. "McAdoo died within the year."

"You see a connection?"

"No," he said immediately, surprising me, "of course not. I tried to imagine a connection at the time. You know."

"I know."

"We were yelling across the ice at them to get the hell off. We didn't have to tell McAdoo. He could hear the ice break. She couldn't or didn't care. She was crazy. When she finally let him go—when she was through with him—the ice wasn't solid anymore, although it still held together. It wobbled like Jell-O, especially around the two of them. We were all frozen on the shore. I kept thinking that any minute I'd get brave and go out there. I was so sure I was going to do it that the shock hit me only much later." The shock of his own cowardice.

"McAdoo slithered away from her on his stomach, which of course you had to do. He didn't even get up on his hands and knees. He swam across the ice, and made it. She didn't move. She stayed on her back, with her arms out and her knees up, and when we yelled at her to move, she laughed. She sounded so strange when she laughed that I was afraid she was going to do something nuts, like stand up and dance, or something worse. She was wild. Somebody had to go out and get her, and every guy there was terrified. Of her. She had the power to ruin us all, literally. She could stay out there and die and we'd go to jail for life, and then to hell. She could take any of us down with her to the bottom of the lake if we tried to rescue her.

"Sippy Siniscalchi was the one who got her back. He crawled out there while I was dithering and dragged her back on the coats, on her back, laughing, while we all watched and couldn't breathe. When he got her on shore he went crazy and tried to slap her in the face, but we stopped him. He called her names. I remember he said, 'Get your clothes on! Show some respect!' But she wouldn't even do that, and we had to dress her, like a doll.

"She just flopped against us, worse than drunk, while we jammed her back into her underwear and blouse and skirt and sweater. And her shoes! It was a nightmare getting her feet into those shoes. When my kids were little I could never dress them. That same looseness, that way they have of *letting* you . . . always brought it back to me. I called her a stupid kid, accused her of being childish. Nothing I said, nothing anybody said, affected her. She was so *happy*. It's grotesque, but she was happy.

"I took her home. I dropped her off at your house. We'd

all split up without saying a word. When we got to your house, she said, 'You're worried that I'm going to tell. I'm never going to tell.' I believed her, but the awful part was, I hadn't even thought of that yet, I was so worried about the other thing, the responsibility. The sickening way her ankle wobbled when you jammed her foot into the saddle shoe.

"We owned her now, or she owned us. We could have done anything we wanted with her. I don't expect you to understand this, but we could have left her to die, or killed her and buried her in the snow. We could have brutalized her, I mean much worse than we did, far worse. She was ours, she was mine, I'm sure every man there felt she was his. It was horrible. See, it has nothing to do with guilt, really. I'm sorry, Dorcas, but no matter what we did, we didn't rob her of anything. We didn't take anything away from her."

"I know, Frank."

"We did something very bad, but I don't know even now what it was. See, when I say she was passive, she wasn't a zombie . . . she was alive. It was her show. She handed it to you, the responsibility, for her life, for her safety, for her character, her future, her past, she just handed it over." Frank was crying. "You could see her do it. Your sister is . . . we let something loose that night, and if it hadn't been us, it would have been somebody else, but it *was* us.

"I owe her. She knows it."

I couldn't shake the image of Abigail naked on the ice, revolving at the center of a circle of men. I asked Frank if that had really happened, and happened the way he had just described, and he said that it was honest to God true, every bit of it.

I said that if he owed her anything, then or now, it was a bill for services.

He left, offended as hell. Although the next time I saw him he was, of course, solicitous and correct, as ever.

. . .

I mentioned him to Abigail the next visiting day. She was tired and slow on the uptake. It took her a while to remember who he was and what he was to her. "He tell you everything?" she asked me. She smiled. "He spilled his guts, didn't he? What an asshole." This was unusually hard-edged of her, and I said so.

She was quiet for a minute and then sighed. "I never thought I'd come to this," she said.

"You didn't? Really?" I was astonished. "Where did you imagine you were going to end up?" I got up and started to pace. The guard didn't like that. I had to sit back down. "Did you imagine," I asked, "that you were going to wind up supporting yourself? Raising your own child? Ministering to the needy? Did you imagine that I, for instance, would have a life of my own? Does it surprise you to find me here every day of the week, and off raising money in your sorry behalf when I'm not here, and generally devoting twenty-four hours to you?"

"Poor kid." That's it. *Poor Dorcas.* "Is there any chance, do you suppose," she asked, "that Frank would tell that story on the stand? For the defense? For me?"

I said yes, there probably was a good chance, but that it would ruin him. I said I didn't see the point of asking him to jeopardize his standing and his family life for so little. I asked what causal connection there could possibly be between That Night and the death of Conrad Lowe.

"They're working on a scenario," she said. *They* being Minden & Wayland, and specifically the Old Man, Miles Minden himself. "They call it a 'hypothesis' but it's a scenario, really."

Too bad. I loved the idea of Miles Minden saying "scenario." I loved it almost as much as the idea of Miles Minden himself, Son of the American Revolution, thirty-second-degree Mason, defender of insurance companies and banks, Grand Old Gentleman of Weybosset Street: a white-maned, apple-cheeked, baby-soft anti-Semite anti-Catholic racist, who tipped his hat to everyone he met, treating bag ladies as royalty, construction workers as peers, so that a simple lunchtime stroll down the street would turn into a parade, and he would leave his inferiors dazed and grateful and babbling about "breeding," which, according to Minden, was something he and his family had, and that the rest of the world should refrain from doing. Miles Minden, the twinkling Nazi, he of the "rockbound principles" and the "ironclad convictions," as the *Providence Journal-Bulletin* always puts it.

That this lovable, deeply evil old man would allow himself to be personally involved in my sister's defense just illustrates the extent to which your false Yankee will go in aid of his diminishing kind. (Miles is himself a pale shade of his father, an almost real Yankee, Russell Minden, who served one term in the U.S. Senate. Russell, a truly Grand Old Man, is often cited in modern American history books, having been the only legislator in the twentieth century to introduce a bill disenfranchising the poor. The old man's love of principle ran even deeper than his love for the Constitution. Also, he was insane. Miles still speaks of him with awe.)

It was Miles Minden's brilliant idea to have Abigail spend the last few months before trial in the Big House rather than home with me. He achieved this by responding in muted fashion to the prosecution's half-hearted "flight risk" bail-revocation request. In prison Abigail is bored and restless and complains bitterly about the food, but she trusts Miles. He has established her, in the local and national imagination, as a martyred saint.

"Mr. Minden says—" Abigail closed her eyes and concentrated. "That everything in my life, my reconstructed life, should point to the tragedy. Like an arrow. Like a great big blinking arrow that a four-year-old child couldn't miss. The jury must be convinced that everything that happened was inevitable. That I never had a chance. That it was always going to happen. The tragedy. If we can get them thinking along those lines, he says, there's no way in the world they can convict me." She grinned. "He calls me Little Lady."

"Let me get this straight," I said. "What happened that night, the night of the gang bang, was the first involuntary step on the road to 'the tragedy'? I don't get it. *Quel* non sequitur! I mean, that night on the ice you had quite a time for yourself, as I understand it. Is that the point? You acquired a lifelong taste for debauchery and lawlessness? Well, I'll drink to that! I can't see winning a jury over that way, though."

"Rage," Abigail said, suppressing a belch. "All these years I've been carrying that rage with me, locked up inside."

"Oh, come on!"

"Don't blame me. It's not my idea. Oh, and self-esteem. They destroyed my self-esteem."

"How?"

"I don't know." Abigail chewed her thumbnail. "How's Anna?"

"How does this contribute to the self-defense idea?"

"It doesn't. We're partly scrapping that, see? We're going to say, number one, she killed him to save her life, and, but, number two, she killed him because, I don't know, hell, everything in her past was one great big flashing arrow—"

"Insanity? Good Lord. How are you going to act like an insane person? That's the most ridiculous thing I ever heard."

"Uh-uh. Not insanity. Diminished responsibility." She saw the appalled look on my face. "That's a real defense. He says it's our best shot."

For a second I was derailed by the thought of Minden saying "our best shot." "That's an actual *defense?*" I asked.

"Yup."

"Diminished responsibility." I started to laugh. "Kid," I said, "you've got nothing to worry about." Abigail got the joke—we've always laughed at the same things—and we became rowdy and the guard made me leave.

Two Creepy People

Chapter 7

The DeVilbiss Circle

Here, Readers, I must step out from behind the curtain and admit my small part in this tale. For Abigail's story cannot be told without extensive reference to my husband, Guy DeVilbiss, whose fondness and deep admiration for Abigail Mather played no small part in what was to happen to her. And how terribly ironic, how grotesque this connection is. My brilliant, tender husband, who wished for Abigail—for all his friends, students, readers—only the richest joy. *O God! that one might read the book of fate . . .*

———————————

Indeed.

Guy DeVilbiss, the poet, husband of Hilda, lover of women everywhere, is not a local poet but an actual, internationally acclaimed poet who happens to live in Frome, Rhode Island. He has always talked of how fond he is of the Community, and the Community itself is actually fond of him: they regard each other, Poet and Community, with fond incomprehension. When reporters from the *Journal* interview him at his home, which they do every four or five years, there is always a great deal of forelock-tugging, and an obeisant display of awed confusion on the reporter's part, humility on the part of the Great Writer. Guy is the sort who "gazes kindly out at you through rimless glasses with a curiously childlike innocence," for which read *vacuity*.

He is shiny bald, short, and pear-shaped. His skin is as white and blue-veined and paper-thin as that of an anemic young girl. His eyes are watery gray, myopic. He has an asymmetric, sensual mouth, one side of the lower lip permanently swollen, bee-stung, the upper lip thin and cruelly, subtly curved. His mouth is the only noticeably masculine aspect of him. His hands are plump, the cuffs of his long-sleeved flannel shirts always too tight, as though Hilda, who dresses him, were trying to cut off his circulation slowly over time. There is something particularly repulsive to me about the way his hands swell, wristless, painful, at the ends of his short arms, like ugly fruit.

Guy is an authentic genius artist, read by almost no one, revered in lit-crit circles. "The only postwar poet," according to the *Times,* "certain to survive the millennium." He writes about sex, and he writes about God, and he fuses the two. Sex is altar, pit, eternity, theology, the single worthy object of worship and subject of art.

He is a confessional poet. Critics call him instead the Poet of Analysis, or sometimes just The Analysand. In other words, he confesses not to a priest, not to an audience of gossip-hungry voyeurs, but to an Ideal Therapist. To say that these confessions are "intensely personal" is to understate considerably. When comprehensible they are wildly embarrassing, at least to anyone who actually knows Guy and Hilda. I can't think what other people around here do when they have them to dinner or come to their door collecting for the Heart Association. Do they just blot out what they know?

Guy's most celebrated collection, the fifteen-year-old *Venus*

Accroupie, is a series of lyric descriptions of his wife's private parts. He uses her name. He uses her body. Abby and I went swimming with her once. She really does have a small egg-plant birthmark high up on the inside of her right thigh, an arrow, like a tattoo, pointing straight at her crotch. She is not, nor has she ever been, or pretended to be, an attractive woman. The arrow, Abigail says, is just as compelling as the arrow on a Band-Aid wrapper, the whole viewed prospect just as appetizing as a Band-Aid.

Guy describes her, literally warts and all, in what is for my money one of the most nauseating literary performances of all time. In one of the poems, "Werewolf," he describes her menstrual cycle as it is manifested in changing odor. The poem is divided into twenty-eight stanzas, each one evoking, with great art, a particular smell. Such is his genius—and I don't deny him this—that you hallucinate olfactorily. You actually reach for your handkerchief, or your gas mask.

He has graduated now from Hilda to Women Everywhere. His poems are more sexual than ever, more personal, if that is possible. Having exposed his wife to Art, he now fearlessly exposes himself. After one brief unwise glance at "Transfiguration," I, who have seen, in my life, only one naked man, only one, could pick Guy DeVilbiss's penis out of a police lineup.

He truly loves women, say the book jackets and the critical studies, he "literally" worships them, but not in the bad old chauvinistic way. "The Woman, to Guy DeVilbiss, is not the mysterious, unknowable 'Other.' [Although she is, apparently, The Woman.] 'She is the perfect knowable,' says DeVilbiss." This is the rock foundation of his faith, the first and only commandment of his church. "There is no Other."

He is the most ardent of feminists. He makes Kate Millet look like Barbara Cartland. Women with young children bore him visibly, but all other women fall into one of three categories: splendid, superb, and magnificent. "He expects so much of us," says his adoring wife, and this is true. If Robert Lowell and Robert Graves had cross-pollinated, Guy De-Vilbiss would have been the orchidaceous result.

Abigail is of course "magnificent." (I am merely splendid.) She met Hilda first, while making her postal rounds. Guy got lots of registered mail, for which Hilda would have to sign—galley proofs, I suppose—and Hilda would engage Abigail in conversation. Abigail has never been chummy with women. She's not catty. She just doesn't see the point of other women.

"I think she's hot for my body," she told me, in the early days of the DeVilbiss courtship. This was the only explanation she could come up with for Hilda's interest. As things turned out, it wasn't too far off.

"What's he like?" I asked, one evening over dinner. I'd seen pictures, of course, and read the puff pieces in the *Journal-Bulletin*. And I despised his poetry, while admitting his gift. You'd be an idiot not to admit his gift. But despite my contempt for his public persona and his art I could not resist a fan's fascination with the private life of anyone who stocked my shelves. Books are holy objects to me. I can't destroy even the awfulest of them.

In my basement, stacked in large appliance cartons, themselves stacked to the ceiling all around the boiler, a fire hazard at the very least, are all the books we couldn't sell at discard prices—not for fifty cents, not for a quarter, not for a bag of books for a dollar. Unredeemable trash. Volume three of the outdated Rhode Island General Laws. Portuguese paperbacks, oddly sized, with brittle shiny covers depicting dark-haired women in fifties makeup, their mouths in a fifties O to signify love and lust, and with titles which translate as *Painful Honeymoon* and *She Loved Her Doctor*. The *Book of Knowledge* from 1928. Useless texts on physics, chemistry. *Phrenology: Fact or Fancy?* An autobiography of Jack Paar. Ripped bodice-rippers, Gothics with fractured spines, Young Adult novels mutilated by young adults. *Forever Amber*.

"I haven't seen the husband yet," Abigail said. "She guards him like that dog."

"Lassie?"

"Greek dog."

"Cerberus."

"And resembles it in a way."

"Does she actually have three heads, or just a canine appearance?"

"She just resembles it. . . ." Abigail went blank then and sighed, with that bone-weary expression that always overtakes her when she is confronted by the need to articulate a complex thought. Abigail *has* complex thoughts; she just can't be bothered setting them in order.

"Spiritually," I said.

"Yeah. Actually she resembles a sheep. She's got woolly hair, dirty gray, or ash, and lots of it, close to her head."

"Does she have a shiny black nose?"

"She smiles all the time. I'll hand her the return receipt to sign and she'll give me this big smile, like she's just won the Publishers Clearing House. She always wears these heavy, dark dresses, like the old Italian women. She smells dusty. She can't be more than ten years older than us."

"Dowdy," I said. "Faculty wife."

"This one makes faculty wives look like . . ." Abigail shrugged and waited for me to tell her. I don't even believe in ESP and I've been doing her thinking for her all her life.

"Coco Chanel." Abigail pouted and shook her head. She

actually makes me anxious to please her at times like this. I did her math homework for four years. "Elizabeth Taylor. Twiggy. Jesus, I don't know."

"European," said petulant Abigail. "Old . . ."

"-Fashioned? -World? Old World dowdy? You mean, striving for some phony cultural effect?" Abby shrugged. "Striving for a certain timelessness. Is that it? No, that's not it."

"She's dusty, musty. Like a book."

This did the trick. "Striving for a historical quality . . . she could be Tolstoy's mother, Dickens's wife . . ."

"Yeah."

"She is woman. She stays in the murk, in the shadows, with the great artist in the foreground, and when he needs a *woman*, in the abstract, she shoots out into the footlights like a funhouse gorilla." How do I do that? Exhausted, I poured myself a drink.

"I wonder what he does," she said, "when he wants a woman in the concrete." Abigail is never impressed when I read her mind, never grateful for the brute work of it. At such times I exist merely to straighten out her thoughts, like the President's speechwriter. "Anyway, she always gives me this lightbulb smile and draws me out. Everything I say is delightful, don't you know. She drips. And the thing is, she's really fascinated with me, you can tell. All the time she draws me out you can see her *learning*. She makes me feel . . ."

Sigh. "Exotic. Endangered, like a dodo. Self-conscious? Surely not that!"

"Prepped," said Abigail.

"Prepped?"

"Yeah. What nurses do to you before an operation." She saw my ignorance and grinned, yawning. She loves to twit me; as we age, this is harder for her to do. I grow entropically, unwillingly, corrupt. "They shave you, Dorcas," she said, wiggling her eyebrows. "Down there. Bald as the capital dome."

"She makes you feel like *that*?"

"She makes me feel like that," said my sister, who is just lazy and a slob. Who is nobody's fool.

So we were both betting that Hilda was a lesbian. But then came the day that she reached out, smiling loonily, and took my sister's hand, gently, with a magical hush, as though finally getting up the nerve to pet a wild deer ("I almost popped her one") and led her to her husband's study. "I'm sorry," Hilda kept saying, "I'm so bad at these things, but *Guy has been aching to meet you*." Abigail wrenched away. "So that's it!" she said, and stalked out the door, leaving her mail sack in the hallway. God knows my sister is no stranger to perversion and orgiastic pursuit, but she was genuinely shocked by this. "I wonder why," she said, that night.

I set to work. "Because you had her down as a lesbian and she turned into a pimp. You're shocked at your own lack of perspicacity."

"Nah."

"Because . . . you were being treated like a thing."

"I like being treated like a thing."

"Nothing degrades you, does it?"

"Yes! *She* degraded me." For a second she looked almost upset. "The thing about being treated like a thing is . . ."

I snorted at her and folded my arms. There are limits.

She brightened then. "She treated me like an *idea*! That's it. She treated me like an idea. Can you imagine the nerve?"

My sister outraged was a fabulous sight. If my camera had been handy I would have caught it for posterity. "Why, Abigail, I do believe you've got scruples."

"Nah. I always sit like this," she said absently, not attending to her own joke. With her heels side by side and her toes turned out, her plump ankles stretched and loose, her plumper knees hanging wide. She really does always sit like that. I asked her why once. Taking the air, she said.

When she went back to the DeVilbisses' the next morning to retrieve her mail sack, they both opened the door before she could ring the bell, and went into what she later described to me as a vaudeville routine.

"We're sorry," cried Hilda.

"I'm sorry," said the great man, in what Abigail described as a cognac voice, whatever that means. "We've behaved abysmally."

"God knows what you must think of us."

"Please don't blame my wife."

"Please don't blame my husband."

"Gimme my mail sack," said Abigail.

"I only last night realized," said Hilda, a hideous purple blush climbing up her neck, "what you must have imagined we wanted from you."

"She vomited," offered the great man. He spoke with such genuine pride that Abigail was taken aback, wondering whether what he so admired was his wife's sensitivity or "her actual puke."

"Let's have it, people. What exactly *did* you want from me?" Abigail was already beginning to be mollified. She has always been unable to hold on to a bad temper. She lives in a hospitable world. And Guy fascinated her right off, because she couldn't categorize him, or, to be more accurate, his perversion. He's some brand-new kind of pervert, she thought.

"Do come in," he said, "and let us fix you tea."

He had the saddest, most limpid, liquid eyes, fixed on Abigail and her alone of all the objects in the world. His body was hairless, white, defenseless. She thought his skin would have no temperature to the touch, like a corpse in a heated room. If human beings really were evolving constantly, further and further from their animal origins, then Guy was the latest prototype. He looked fetal. There was, she told me, correctly, something sketchy about his physical presence, something merely humanoid, as though he had been incarnated at the last minute, out of grudging necessity. Only his mouth gave away his kinship with the rest of us. If she stared at that self-indulgent bee-stung mouth she could imagine him "shitting and pissing and *almost* fucking. I can see him," she told me that night, "sitting in a chair in a corner of someone's bedroom, staring. Not touching. Never touching. He's disgusting," she said, "but sort of wonderful, too. He takes you in with that stare. He makes you feel like anything you did would be wonderful, as long as he could watch."

"And write about it later," I said. Abigail smiled.

DeVilbiss led Abigail inside, one plump weightless hand on her shoulder, guiding her into his study, with Hilda trailing behind. There he made a great show of debating with Hilda about which of them would fix the tea. His wife won, arguing that it would make her feel so much better to do something for Abigail, to atone. Guy shook his head at his wife's retreating black back and said, when she had closed the door behind herself, "She still cannot quite break herself of the old oppressed ways. She takes comfort in brute servitude." Abigail could see he was really put out with his wife for making the tea. "I got the feeling," she said, "that there would be hell to pay for it later."

The study was lined with books and decorated with the torsos of naked women. The largest of the three-dimensional torsos stood on a pedestal beside what Abigail realized must be his desk, since there was no other workstation in evidence. It was a high school desk-chair combination, the old kind with an inkwell, which contained a jar of ink. The torso, of pink marble, dwarfed the desk-chair, and would surely loom over the writer seated there. If it were to tip it would crush his shoulder, possibly his skull. If he were to look up at it, amid his creative throes, he would be confronted with vast flat buttocks, massive truncated thighs. If he were to reach up he could just caress the cold childish breasts, inverted marble nipples; he could just trace the puckered appendectomy scar on the loose abdomen.

Abigail knew with intuitive certainty that this was Hilda's torso. Half the statues and paintings in the study resembled it, to the scar. The rest depicted other sorts of women's bodies, and children's too. Butterballs. High-waisted torsos with long breasts and slim hips. Lanky adolescent slabs. The bodies of very young girls, prepubescent, pot-bellied, waistless; the most purposeful looking bodies of all, with their lack of animal fur. Looking at one such, a larger-than-life sculpture of bleached cherry wood, Abigail was overcome, and determined to start shaving herself. Prepping herself, I reminded her, but she told me to mind my own business. "I can handle those two," she said.

"I understand," Abigail said, smiling evilly, "that you were aching to meet me." She sat in a huge wicker throne, looking down upon him at his child's desk.

Guy brightened, unteased. It is impossible for most people to tease Guy, to catch him entertaining the notion that he might not be taken seriously. "Hilda gave me her impressions of you. This is how I meet people, you know." He nodded, as if he really expected her to know this. "She screens people for me, just as she reads newspapers for me, and tells me what she thinks I ought to know, if, in her opinion, I can bear hearing it. Hilda is my filter, and my buffer, and of course my muse."

"You give her a lot of power," said Abigail, thinking aloud. Hilda had never struck her as a powerful woman.

"Yes," said Guy. He spread his plump arms wide, an awkward, creaky gesture, referring to the whole room, the torsos. "I revere powerful women," he said, "as my work proves."

Abigail told him she'd never read his "work."

"Of course you haven't," he said, delighted. "And you shouldn't."

Abigail drew herself up. "I can read, you know."

"Yes," he said, oblivious, "but why should you? Why read, why write, when you can . . . occupy space!"

"Go to hell!" said my sister, just as Hilda came in with the tea. They both turned identical smiles on Abigail.

"Magnificent," said Guy. "All that vitality, and wit, too."

This threw Abigail off stride, since, reasonably, she didn't consider "go to hell" a particularly witty riposte.

"What Guy means—"

"I understand English. What Guy means is, *It thinks! Stop the presses!*"

"Look at the anger," said Hilda to Guy.

"Visceral rage," said Guy. "Magnificent."

"So long, folks," said Abigail.

Guy rose up to speak. His knees caught under the kiddie desk, so that he addressed her from a half-crouch, looking up at her, as she was already on her feet. Still he spoke with great authority, which impressed Abigail, under the circumstances. "You think I patronized you. You are right. This is inexcusable. But the point I was trying to make is that my art—my poems, my sculpture—is so poor alongside your reality, alongside the truth of powerful women, that all of it amounts, alas, to condescension. You are art itself. This is what I was trying to say. Forgive me."

Abigail sat and chewed her lip. She liked the "art itself"

part but something still bothered her. "You're talking about my looks?" Abigail has never been vain or deluded. "I'm a blowsy broad" was how she had summed herself up since her mid twenties, after the baby was born and she had obtained a permanent belly, to go along with her breasts and all the rest of it.

Guy cleared his throat. "I'm going to be frank with you. As I said, Hilda brings me . . . news of the world, and this includes the local world. News of Frome. In short, gossip. Gossip she thinks might be pertinent to my work."

"Ah ha."

"Your reputation precedes you," said Hilda, blushing again. She had, thought Abigail, the ugliest blush in the world, with no pleasure to it, only shame.

"Exactly how does it precede me?" The blush darkened to a bruise. "Who? Name names. Who shot off his mouth? Lucier? That little weasel next door?"

"We're not at liberty to disclose—"

"George mamma's-boy Lucier! I only grabbed him because he was always sneaking around, answering the door in his bathrobe, asking me stupid questions about priority mail and zip codes. Lucier's a slimy little weasel, the kind of guy who looks and looks and then runs away and plays with himself. I hate that," said Abigail, who genuinely does. "I despise a sneak. So I reached into his little silk bathrobe one day, to straighten him out, if you know what I mean, and he screams and backs away, if he had a cross he would have held it up, and you know what he says to me? *I'm at risk! I have a type A personality!* I told him he had a type F personality. And now I suppose he's bragging to the little woman here about his exploits—"

Guy laughed out loud, a sexy, smoky laugh, Abigail said, and after an alarmed glance at her husband, Hilda joined him, laughing instantly, as if she genuinely thought something was hilarious. Since she was no actress, Abigail marveled at this phenomenon. "Wonderful," said Guy, wiping his eyes. "You're so right. George's version was somewhat different." He began to laugh again.

Hilda leaned toward him, smiling admiringly. "You guessed it, remember? That he wasn't being truthful." She turned to Abigail. "He's uncanny," she said.

"You've been canvassing the neighborhood about me? How do you do it? Questionnaires? 'Has Abby Mather jumped you, and if so, how often?' "

Hilda rose—she had been kneeling beside her husband—and knelt down before Abigail, grabbing her arm with evangelistic zeal. The whole abrupt performance was so unnerving that Abigail closed her mouth and listened to her with that wariness we show to maniacs on a train. "You're thinking, 'How degrading,' " Hilda said, "and 'How can she lower herself?' and 'Where's her pride?' " (Abigail was thinking: They must do it from behind. Otherwise he'd have to look at her face. She pictured Hilda on hands and knees, patient, mottled, swaybacked from all the pointless weight—for Hilda, according to the torsos, had the most unfecund, powerless fat body Abigail had ever seen—and felt a rare pity for her which matched, for a moment, her contempt, and a flash of inarguable insight. *This one should have been a nun. She's shaped for worship; she was born with mortified flesh.* And she got the tantalizing beginnings of an idea about just what sort of brand-new kind of pervert Guy DeVilbiss was.) "And I must tell you," said Hilda, with her crazy smile, "that art is more important than dignity, reputation, morality. There is nothing, literally nothing, I would not do in furtherance of Guy's art. The work is all."

By that point Abigail was, by her own account, greatly excited, which surprised her, since, as she often put it, "Threesomes give me the creeps, when the other two are married.

They gang up on you. They know the rules already and they won't tell you what they are. They turn you into a beanbag."

This couple was different. In the first place, if they really had a sex life—Hilda on hands and knees was a dolorous, anesthetic vision—clearly they were too delicate, too metaphorical ("academic," Abigail said), too mannered, to drag in third parties. Their brains, Abigail said, are simply too large. They do it all with their giant brains. She stared at Guy's bald head and pictured his brain, fragile and mushroom-colored, bulbous, pulsing in a sexual tattoo.

The only excuse she could later come up with for her physical arousal was the smoky, masculine voice and laugh of the Great Man, his odd, surprising authority. He intrigued her. She didn't want him, and she felt absolutely confident that he didn't want her. (Abigail is never wrong about these things.) He made her feel like a sexual field worker. "He's like a different species," she told me. "He makes you feel like Jane what's-her-face, in the jungle."

"He reminds you of Tarzan?" I asked, amazed.

Abigail laughed and laughed. "No, my God! No. *Jane*. You know. "Born free . . ." She began to sing.

"The woman with the lions?"

"No, no, no. Monkeys, apes, whatever. Chimpanzees."

"Jane Goodall?" I shook my head. "He reminds you of an ape?"

Abigail laughed and laughed. This was a pretty typical conversation. "Dorcas, you never saw anyone further from an ape in your whole life. If anything, he looks like . . ." She looked at me expectantly.

"Abigail, is this thought actually worth pursuing?"

". . . a reptile. A newt. But what I meant was, *we're* the apes, and he's the human. That's it. Bomba the Jungle Chimp comes to the New World, you know, to live among the humans in their native habitat and study their ways."

"And you're Bomba the Jungle Chimp."

"Right."

"That's idiotic. Besides, what does it have to do with . . ."

"Getting turned on? Easy. You think old Jane Goodall doesn't have funny thoughts out there, in the jungle night? You ever hear her on TV going on and on about 'dominant males' and 'the posture of submission'? Hubba-hubba!"

"Look, folks," Abigail said to the adoring humanoids, one kneeling at her feet, one crouching on miniature furniture, both transfixed, "do you need a model? Do you want me to sit or something, while you write a poem?" The DeVilbisses whooped with delight. "I know better than that," said Abigail, getting angry again. "I was making a joke."

"Of course!" cried Guy. "And what a magnificent joke it was."

"Well, what *do* you want?"

The DeVilbisses looked breathlessly at each other, and after a solemn moment, turned identically solemn faces toward her. "We want you to be our friend," said Hilda.

"We want you in our lives," said Guy.

"You see," said Hilda, "we have very few friends."

"By choice," added Guy.

That's what you think, thought Abigail.

"Most people bore Guy."

"Boredom is my greatest torment."

"And yet . . . he hungers for human companionship." Hilda shook her head at the wonder of it. "Just like any ordinary man."

Abigail thought about it. "Friends usually sit around and talk, don't they?" Abigail doesn't have any friends, so she wasn't clear on this. "Well, what are we going to talk about? I'm not too big on talk. I'm not very abstract."

Guy grinned hugely. "You're not abstract at all. That's what's so magnificent—"

"If you want to talk," Abigail said, "you'd be better off with my sister, Dorcas."

"The librarian," said Guy's interpreter, out of the corner of her mouth.

"My twin," said Abigail.

"You mean," said Guy, looking less than delighted, "there's another one just like you?"

Now it was my sister's turn to whoop.

And this is how we became part of the DeVilbiss circle, a group so small that we could all hold hands around their round oak dining table, and did on one occasion, the day a collection of Guy's finally won the National Book Award. Abigail and I were the only nonartists in the group. The rest were all couples, gay and straight, at least one of whom had been published, or shown in Manhattan, or performed at the Marlboro Festival.

Even the nonprofessional spouses did "something with art." There were two potters and a dance teacher and one man, the composer's husband, who claimed he was "keeping a journal." His name was, and is, Tim Paine, and he was my favorite. Whenever we got together Guy would ask him, *mano a mano,* how his journal was coming, his "work." Tim would say something like, "I think I may have made a break-through" or "I'm blocked," and the rest would rejoice or commiserate. Tim was a bright, slobby drunk, a Pooh-faced failure with a contagious laugh, and carloads of charm he was born into, the way some people are born into money.

His wife was an anorexic Spaniard whose English was

poor, even after fifteen years in this country. What little she said was indecipherable. No one paid any attention to her except when she sat at the piano, where she was eloquent, so long as she was playing Chopin or Brahms. (Her own compositions were thin, angular, painful to hear, very much like herself.) Whenever the conversation turned to Tim's journal— Guy was scrupulous in his attentions, especially to the lowliest and least talented of his dear friends—Pilar would mourn, "Tim never show me to it. It is secret." And Guy would admonish her, smiling, that her husband must never show his journal to anyone; that exposure would amount to violation. And I would wearily, dryly protest the idea of inviolate art, keeping my arguments as abstract as possible. And whenever words like "inviolate" were used, my sister would snort and help herself to more of Guy's excellent white wine.

Throughout, Tim, the ostensible focus of the debate, would hang his head and smirk, occasionally throwing in an "I should say *not*," or "I should say *so*." I was positive that he held the DeVilbisses in total contempt, that he and I were soul mates, but no matter how carefully I watched for signs I could never either confirm or deny my reading of him. For all I know he really does keep a journal.

Guy condescended to everyone in the circle except Abigail and me, the two without pretensions. Us he respected, for insulting reasons—because we simply *were*. He was wary of me. He listened carefully to me, no matter how trivial my remarks, giving me a depth of attention that always made me feel silly, but he did not, I think, put me on in doing so. I was some sort of threat to Guy from the beginning, and I thought it was simply my relation to Abigail, my obvious amusement at his adoration of her. Abigail thought it had nothing to do with that. "You scare him," she said once, "because you've rejected sex."

I was driving at the time, late at night, home from the

DeVilbisses'. I clenched my teeth in the dark. "How does he know sex didn't reject me? I don't see what's intimidating about a dried-up middle-aged—"

"They always know," said Abigail. "You don't give men credit for much. Even he knows. You're above it all. You're like an aristocrat."

"You're bombed."

"Which means that his work has no power over you. This is very threatening to him. He thinks you're smart. Smarter than him."

"Even."

"Yeah."

"He's a jerk."

"Worse," she said. "Did you see what he was doing to Hilda? The woman obviously doesn't want to do anything but care for him and wash his feet, and he keeps bullying her about doing something creative. He practically had her in tears tonight. Do you know what she told me? He's threatened, more than once, to divorce her if she doesn't fulfill herself in some way! The poor woman's been—"

"Oh, come off it. You loathe Hilda."

"Well, but still. She's actually going through with the doctoral thesis and everything, just to please him. She couldn't care less about Socrates."

"Sophocles."

"So now he's got it in his head that she's a poet and he's browbeating her all the time, like tonight, about her 'work.' She just hangs her head like a sheep. *Baaaaaa.* Jesus."

"So why," I finally asked her, "do we keep going over there?"

Abigail was quiet for a while. I pulled into the driveway and shut off the engine. "He's dedicating the new collection to me," she said. "To Abigail Mather. The Ultimate Knowable."

I cracked up. "Well, no one's going to quarrel with *that*. Hoo, boy!"

"Yeah, well," Abigail said with some asperity, "I tried to explain that to him, how some people would snicker, and he just said, 'Some people are wicked,' and shuddered. The way he does, you know. Mr. Sensitivity."

Sooey Generous and the Dominant Male

Chapter 8

The Meeting

. . . most capricious of ironies that Abigail should meet Conrad Lowe at the home of an ardent feminist. Guy DeVilbiss has always been a feminist *sui generis*. Lowe was his old college roommate, and an artist of some small talent himself. . . .

———————

. . . And presto! My sister becomes a murderess, spends half a year at the ACI, achieves an international reputation as an avenging feminist, and writes the scurrilous piece of ordure on my desk. Some registrar's secretary threw Lowe and DeVilbiss together, and here we are.

Physically they were opposites, Guy and Conrad. Conrad was tall, whippet-thin, predatory. His brown eyes were feminine, long-lashed, moist. They stared out at you from the wrong face. "He's got Jewish eyes," Abigail whispered the night she first met him. And though I made fun of her and asked her what this could possibly mean (she kept saying she didn't know), she was right. He had a Jew's eyes and a Nazi face.

The eyes were the bait. They said to women, Ignore the brutal wit of my hard smiling mouth, my jackal posture, ignore especially that warning bell in your head that is never wrong, that animal alertness at the scent of danger, and look in here, sweetmeat. See how sensitive, misunderstood, peaceloving I am. I may talk mean, I may leave you feeling bruised for days after just five minutes of cocktail flirtation, but this is just a pathetic diversion on my part. I can be had. Trust me.

He had a large sharp nose that preceded him everywhere. He walked canted forward, with his narrow shoulders hunched, as though heading into a bracing wind. He wore whatever he wanted to. Salvation Army raincoats, cashmere mufflers, ratty English tweeds, tennis shoes. I saw him once on Westminster Street in the city on a cold January morning wearing a pair of child's earmuffs. His finely molded skull was small enough, just, for that. One of his front teeth, the right-hand tooth as you faced him, was nicotine-stained and crooked, swiveled slightly away from center, like a door stuck ajar.

Women rushed at him like lemmings. Wondering, even as they unhooked their own bras, folded their skirts and laid them over the backs of chairs, wondering, Why am I doing this? What's in it for me? Who's in charge here?

He was just there one night, at Guy and Hilda's, when Abigail and I came by for drinks. There was another couple, too, but I don't remember who they were. Not the Zamora-Paines. Guy introduced me first, as "our splendid librarian."

"Conrad and I," he told me, in an oddly simpering voice, "go all the way back to Harvard, if you can imagine such a thing."

"I don't think she's going to have too much trouble," said Conrad Lowe, his eyes on me.

"What? Eh?"

"Imagining such a thing. It's not so astounding, Guy, that we were both young once, and from there it's a short imaginative leap to the idea that we were young in the same place. Miss Mather looks capable enough."

"I should say," said Guy, squirming, reddening. "I only meant—"

"He was always like this," said Conrad Lowe, to me. "Picture him with actual hair, all gussied up in his knickers and his Buster Browns . . ."

"Oh, you're so awful!" said Hilda, giggling.

". . . and the only guy in the dorm, the entire class of 1960, who brought a full-sized steamer trunk full of crap from home, you never saw anything like it. First editions, fuck books—you always laugh, Hildy, but it's true—his official Communist Party Membership application blank, his father's false teeth, his mother's sanitary belt, and his seminude pinup of Gale Sondergaard—one of the most sobering sights of my young life. This was in 1956, Miss Mather, Dorcas, when it was *literally worth your life,* on an Ivy League campus, to be a *fellow traveler. . . .*"

"We're the same age, Mr. Lowe," I said.

"My God, you certainly don't look it."

"I most certainly do."

"Good for you! So you do! Good for you. So, here was this fearless young politico with a trunkful of false teeth, and he starts unpacking reams, and I mean reams, of paper, bound in pink ribbon, and I said—I was just some dumbass from Hollywood, you know, the only book I'd ever read was *Gone With the Wind,* and here was this simple, pudgy, weird young man, already showing me worlds I'd never dreamed existed, and I said, 'Are you in the stationery business?' and he said, I'll never forget this, he said, 'My name is Guy DeVilbiss, and this is my work.'

"I said, 'You mean, unloading all this paper, and then, what? Loading it all back in again? Are you practicing to be a stevedore?' I was already impressed as hell, and then he came right back, in no more than half an hour, with the stunning riposte, 'Well, you may laugh if you wish, but I am going to be the greatest American poet of the Atomic Age, and this—he pointed at the mounds of paper on his bed—'is my juvenalia.' "

Throughout this merciless basting both DeVilbisses laughed uncontrollably, Hilda covering her mouth, with her eyes popping, obviously, at some deep level, enjoying herself immensely, and why the hell not; Guy red-faced, clutching his stomach, eyes squeezed shut, wallowing on the sofa like one of those penguin toys for budgies. Guy was absolutely humiliated, absolutely hilarious, absolutely impotent. This was, as Conrad Lowe would say, a sobering sight, but I was soon to grow used to it.

Guy's old roommate was clearly ascendant, his hero, the dominant male, and Guy assumed one of two postures, always, in his company. This was the first, that of the honoree at a "roast," whose duty it is to endure vicious public abuse with visible good nature, to laugh loudest when the jokes are cruelest. His laughter now had just this quality, at once real and desperate, pitiable, and I actually felt sorry for Guy. Especially since he so richly deserved it. The other posture was even more striking, more ludicrous, and would shortly be on display.

Lowe had been speaking to me, and directly to me. He had not even glanced a second time at my sister. This was, to say the least, unusual. I divined he was doing it on purpose, to put her in her place. The man was obviously a sadist, a manipulator. I despised him instantly. He inspired in me an absurd crusading zeal.

It was the oddest, most unhinging thing. I hated him, gladly. It was as though I had waited all my life to do battle with this terrible man, and the unhinging aspect of my emotion was the gratitude, the bridal joy. He scared me to death. For one thing, despite all my efforts, I had laughed at the end of Lowe's story, and the laughter had been forced upon me from the outside, I was sure, for the story was not funny, to me, and the general hilarity anything but contagious, and yet I had laughed, a short loud bark, and covered my mouth like girlish Hilda. I hadn't turned to look at Abigail, or heard a sound from her. I didn't know what she was doing, though surely she was as aware as I of his intentional snub.

Guy was helplessly shaking his head and telling us that yes, indeed, he had really been that young once, that pretentious, he cringed to think about it now.

"We were all that young once," I said, to Lowe. "We all took ourselves seriously. We had to. It was our job."

"Yes," said Hilda. "We all do silly things."

Lowe smiled. "Did you, Dorcas? Do silly things? When you were young?"

"You don't know me well enough to ask me that," I said.

Lowe spilled a little of his whiskey, which he had been putting away professionally. It dribbled down the side of his chin. "Excuse me," he said, "Miss Mather."

"I don't care what you call me. I meant only that your question was too personal."

"Conrad's from southern California," said Guy. Though he said it in unthinking defense of his buddy, without demeaning intent, the accidental wit of his remark delighted everybody but Conrad Lowe. Even Guy, with evident trepidation, laughed at his own unintended joke.

"You must be what they call a Yankee," said Conrad

Lowe, and I let it stand, wrapping all that bogus symbolism around me like armor. "You've got noble lines, like Kate Hepburn. You come from sturdy stock. Sure, we know about Yankees out in California."

"You know about stereotypes, then," said I, giddy with success.

"Well, of course," he said, "being illiterate, sun-ravaged vulgarians, we are capable of grasping only stereotypes. Our attention spans are so short."

"You're right, of course, we were all laughing just now at a stereotype of Cal—"

"You got me good," he said, and didn't need to add *you bitch*. "That's the beauty of the Hepburn maneuver. There's never any point in the dialogue where you can't turn around and say, 'You don't know me that well.' "

"It wasn't any kind of maneuver," I said. "You do me disservice, or credit, I don't know which. It was an honest response."

"Well, as long as it was *honest*."

"I'm explaining, not excusing. It's just that, well, intimacy cannot be enforced."

"Intimacy cannot be *enFOWahssed*," he mocked, in a Hepburn drawl, his mouth widening, his lower jaw thrust out. This was a distinctly feminine jibe, yet it did not diminish him. It was perfectly clear that he would use any weapon available to win, that there was in this man no sense of proportion, that all challenges to his power were alike and insupportable. He could not bear to lose. If there had been an axe there on the coffee table I would have feared for my life.

He looked me over now. Stared at my bosom, stared down at my lap, my locked knees, so that it took all my will not to shield myself with my hands, and his expression was confident, insolent, and here it came, the sexual insult. It had been so long since I'd had to take one of these. *Hey, Dork, where are ya tits? What's long and thin and comes by itself?* "You have beautiful legs," he said. "You have legs like Kate Hepburn."

"Nonsense," I said, blushing hotly.

"No, Dorcas. I'm not backing down on this. You do look your age, whatever that is, and you do have beautiful legs."

Guy cleared his throat. "My old friend," he said to me, "is an unreconstructed chauvinist."

I had never known Guy to remark on any woman's physical aspect. With Guy there was always the pretense that we were pure spirit, pure intellect and "sexuality," and our bodies were incidental, negligible, beside the point. This was part, Abigail said, of his weird original perversion. "He doesn't stare in an ordinary way," she told me. "He doesn't sneak peeks. He looks right at your tits, but wide-eyed, like a child, which isn't quite it, but he looks right at them, like *nothing up my sleeve!* He looks at your tits and you can watch him turning them into words on a page. He turns your tits into ideas. It's disgusting, in an interesting way."

"Are you saying she doesn't have beautiful legs?" asked Conrad, leaning toward his tormentee, who sat on the couch beside him, his face inches away.

Guy cleared his throat. "I'm just saying," he said, "that it's demeaning to a woman when you—"

"Look," said Conrad. "Look at them."

"*No.*"

Conrad smiled, his first full smile in front of us, and it was dazzling and full of charm. The swiveled front tooth, fully exposed, somehow rendered him harmless, trustworthy. It was an imperfection upon which you could focus and think, look, he's just an ordinary fellow, nothing menacing here, he was a child once, he had parents who didn't give him braces, he didn't spring full-grown out of someone's, everyone's, my, neurotic needs. "Remember Betty Alice Bascomb?" he asked Guy in a stage whisper.

Guy, who had been trying to be manful, was startled into a look of baby surprise by the name of Betty Alice Bascomb. His bee-stung mouth contracted into a little O, and he snorted, like an infant eructation.

"Well, this one makes Betty Alice Bascomb look like a Clydesdale."

Guy began to giggle, and this was alarming enough, but then his giggle lowered into a masculine range, and the transformation was suddenly complete. He laughed full-throated, a coarse, locker room laugh, an elbow in the ribs in the men's corner of the cocktail party laugh, while Conrad expatiated on the charms of Betty Alice Bascomb, the length, shape, proportion of my calves, and speculated about the length, shape, and proportion of my hidden thighs. And all the while Guy snickered and slapped his own plump thigh, and threw me, from time to time, a panicky, trapped look, like *Help me, can't you see this isn't me, I'm not like this, make him stop!* They were sitting so close together that, if Conrad Lowe had simply pressed his right hand into the small of Guy's back, the illusion of ventriloquist and dummy would have been unmissable.

This, of course, was Guy's alternate posture with his old roommate, and when he assumed it for a long period of time, which on this night he did not, he accepted the role fully, or at least appeared to, and the panicky look would disappear, and it would become possible to believe that he had been a more or less ordinary young man, who snickered and told dirty stories with the rest of them. He would relax into his old incarnation, and take some delight in it, I think. He would look younger, and not disingenuous, but really ingenuous.

His language would become genuinely offensive, even to a woman like me, who hates to take knee-jerk offense.

They would talk about women, about oneself, as though women were nothing but ambulatory body parts, the container for the thing contained, the part for the whole. They would tell repugnant jokes with horrid imagery, comparing us to carnivorous plants, dead carp, snails. At such times Conrad Lowe would eventually extract from Guy some explicit hateful remark, some punchline of his own, and then he would abandon Guy, slip out from under him like a retracted gangplank. Lowe's face would transmogrify, the contagiously filthy-minded young man would disappear, and in its place would be this bemused adult with an ironic face, staring at his old chum in mild wonder. And there would be poor Guy, the focus of shocked attention, and the echo of his own obscenity ringing in everyone's ears like cookware spilling from a closet. It was impossible to look at him at such times, or to enjoy his horror, and we would all spend the rest of the evening pretending that nothing had happened, while Guy sat paralyzed in our midst, or sometimes just rose up and left the room and went upstairs to bed.

As for the rest of us, we did nothing. Nothing to stop it, or even slow it down. Even Hilda did not protect her husband, but simply watched, as we did, fascinated, wondering how it would all come out: how Conrad would dispose of Guy. We all accepted his ascendancy from the beginning. He was the dominant male. The wickedness of the man, the wickedness of his behavior, of his corrupting influence upon us, of our submission to him, all this was beside the point. He was the dominant male. Everything else was just talk.

It took all my strength to sit still, back straight, as he attacked me, to keep my legs crossed and still, to keep my complexion pale, to keep my stare fixed upon him and his giggling dummy, to keep my expression stern. To be judged desirable, to have any part of my body found desirable, was insupportable to me. Somehow he had known immediately what course of action would be the most vicious. What he did to me that night, and many times thereafter, amounted, if such a thing were possible, to psychological rape. And this was surely his intent. Ever since, my legs, about which I had had no particular attitude—why should I?—have felt heavy and cumbersome. I drag them around beneath me. They give off a sickly public glow. I have dreams in which they are diseased, life-threatening, and I beg to have them cut off.

I saw myself for the first time as a thing, a thing in someone else's mind. Of course I had always acknowledged my body, the fact of my visibility, but I had not been a thing, really, because I had been of no *use*. A pebble is a thing, a blade of grass a thing, the broken thread in an old binding. But no one holds these things in mind, they exist in solitude. In privacy. I had known myself to be a perceptible object, a serviceable body, unlovely, unugly, unremarkable. Plain and capable, I moved through the perceptible world, and people nodded and asked questions and sometimes shook my hand, but no one, no one shrank me, remembered me, kept my image prisoner, arranged my body in poses, put words in my mouth, imagined me, used me, *used me,* like a spread-legged thing in a magazine, like a *thing.* I had not known until this moment, really, I had not believed that anyone had this power.

And this despite my sister, whom I have never been without, who loved being treated as a thing, who derived power from *that*, and I had not looked over at her once since meeting him and could not look at her now, or away from him. But I wondered at the power she derived from *this* and did not doubt it, or doubt her power now, even in silence, even in his denial of attention to her.

And for the first time in my life I called out to her, silently, for help, like an overwhelmed child, and she was my older sister, who knew the ropes, who was bigger and stronger, who could beat the shit out of this son of a bitch, who would feed upon his weapons, catch his bullets in her teeth and chew them like bubble gum. My great Amazon bawd of a twin. And thinking of her, taking comfort from her unseen presence beside me, I smiled, still afraid, but excited by the carnage to come, at Conrad Lowe.

Who caught my thought. He abandoned Guy in mid-leer, dismissed my leg-things with a regretful parting glance, and regarded my sister for the first time. "Who's your friend?" he asked me.

"She's not my friend. She's my sister."

"You're kidding."

"She's my twin sister."

He let his jaw drop down and stared at me with deliberate amazement, and then back at my sister's body. I watched his eyes rake her up and down, and focus ironically, comically, upon her big pink legs. He was going to say something disgusting about her body, and that was awful, but he underestimated her. He assumed she was stupid and vain and vulnerable. He thought she didn't know she was fat. He thought she was a deluded fool. "Does she have a name?" he asked.

"Her name is Abigail."

"Does she talk?"

She talks and walks. She eats little salamanders like you for breakfast. I clapped my hands over my mouth to keep from yelling, *Sic 'im, Abigail!*

"What's happening here?" asked Guy. in a dopey, querulous way, like a traveler waking up from a nap to a hijacked plane. "Let's all eat something."

"Guy, Dorcas is upset," said Hilda.

"I can see that, dear."

Conrad Lowe was staring at my sister's face, I could tell by the level of his gaze, and he was looking at her without appraisal, not as a stranger, but as if her face, her being, were long known to him and comfortably familiar. As if they were old enemies; as if she were an old defeated enemy. As if seeing her again brought old and pleasant memories. As if he had the right to stare and stare until he grew bored and looked away, and she had no rights at all. "And what do *you* do?" he asked her now, with a patronizing smile. Abigail, unseen, said nothing, but I could feel her shift on the couch. I could hear it squeak. I imagined her face, matching his expression exactly, going it one better: the confident, arrogant face of the blooded sexual warrior. She was getting her balance, there on the couch, she was biding her time.

"What *does* she do?" he asked Guy, without looking away from her. This was a favorite trick, I was to learn: looking at one person, addressing someone else, demeaning two people at once.

"I told you about her this afternoon. Abigail is that magnificent woman—"

"Whoa! *This* is the town pump?"

"Really," Guy roared, he really roared, but then sputtered and blustered and petered out into a whine. "I never said . . . unthinkable . . . you go too far . . . that was evil and you know it . . . why do you *do* these things to me?"

"The postman cometh!" crowed the delighted Conrad Lowe. "Neither snow or rain, eh, toots? Or heat or gloom of fucking night?" There was more subterranean upholstery shifting. "Abigail! Abigail. Abby-baby." His voice descended to a practiced whisper. He was making obscene public love to her. He winked. "Abby," he said.

"Yes," said Abigail.

Of course I had to look then, and of course she was sitting

there defenseless as a baby, harmless as a milk cow, with the eyes of a lovesick milk cow, and her knees apart not by design or habit but as though pried apart, and her skin was tight and pink, and a terrible musk rose from her, *They'll have to clean the couch,* and she was having trouble breathing.

My sister was in love. When he spoke her name she was transformed with joy, like a mentioned dog.

"Abby," he said again.

"Yes," she said again.

Oh, Doctor, You Struck a Nerve

Chapter 9

The Angel's Son

G uy and I elected, on principle, not to bring children into our violence-pocked postnuclear world. And though we have never regretted our decision, I here confess that if we had ever had a son, we would have named him Conrad, would have striven to raise him with all the love and respect denied his namesake. For we loved Conrad Lowe. We could not help but see, beneath the cruel wit, the icy misogynist rage, even the outright brutality of his final years with Abigail, the haunted, tortured eyes of his inner child. For the boy Conrad was ill-used indeed ...

C onsidering what holy objects books are, how mysterious the metamorphosis from thought to print, and considering how tiny and bleak our community here—we have the highest illiteracy rate north of the Mason-Dixon line—considering all this I am often struck by the number of people in Frome alone actively or formerly involved in the book biz.

There's Guy, of course. And there are Hilda and Abigail now, collaborateurs. And Gloria Gomes, one of Guy and Hilda's foundlings, a legal secretary who writes vegetarian feminist fables and gets them published locally in hand-bound stacks of two hundred fifty by a press endowed by the United States government. There's even a best-selling paperback novelist living in Frome, Dante Minuto, whom none of us has ever seen, who writes Ludlumesque thrillers with Ludlumesque titles, like *The Marchpane Cicatrix* and *The Wiesenheimer Punctilio*. One of my steadiest patrons, a Southern transplant named Shirley Joe Birdwell, writes ghastly poetry and publishes it through a vanity press. And this is in Frome alone. Twenty-seven miles to the east, in the great metropolis of Prov, writers, most of them Not From Around Here, are caroming off one another like billiard balls.

It wasn't always like this. There was a long quiet time, before the sixties, when our only writer of note was a sports columnist for the *PJB*. I don't know what happened. I used to assume it was happening everywhere, this geometrical progression of writers, multiplying asexually, without antecedents; that it was just part of the overall American demise. But *New York* magazine did a long piece on Rhode Island, and it turns out that we are atypically prolific here and no one knows why, not even *New York* magazine. The solitude, they speculate. And "the striking lack of competitiveness. Rhode Island," they claim, "is an evolutionary cul-de-sac, a Darwinian twilight zone, where anything is possible because nothing matters. To put it crudely, the would-be writer has nothing to lose." Also, regionally, this is virgin forest. Although "eventually, of course," they predict with unseemly enthusiasm, "this little plot of land will be overworked and lose its nutrients. Its migrant workers will pack up, then, and move on to fresh territory." Leaving the rest of us to the dust bowl.

Whatever the reason, Conrad Lowe, slithering into our

midst in the summer of 1975, when Abigail and I were thirty-seven years old, was himself a writer. Although Guy rarely mentioned it. Lowe's books were so dishonorable, so vulgar, so deeply trashy that Hilda protected her husband from them. Even Conrad Lowe could not bully Guy when it came to the importance, the necessity, of art; the evil contingency of trash.

Conrad Lowe had written, by the time we encountered him, three best-sellers: a tell-all biography of his parents, a Hollywood roman à clef, and a horror novel. After he came to Frome he finished two more immensely successful horror novels, and when he died he was working on a screenplay.

But really he wrote only one book, his first: *The Violet Angel,* a "no holds barred" story of his beautiful movie star mother and his physician father. Everything else he wrote was a thinly disguised reworking of this primal story. His appetite for revenge upon his mother was gargantuan, bulimic, and the public appetite no less so.

If any of these books can be said to be well written, it would be the first, the straight-out telling. Conrad Lowe's mother was Celeste Garrett, a star of the 1930s, immensely popular at the time, then falling for thirty years into obscurity, finally resurrected and resuscitated by her son, who breathed life into her reputation like a pervert blowing up a sex doll.

She was a beautiful blonde, silver from head to toe in the old black and white movies. They billed her as "The Girl with the Angel Eyes." She was the ingenue in dozens of mediocre historical pictures and contemporary soap operas and drawing room mysteries. She had the body of Jean Harlow and the luminous, breathtaking, witless face of Loretta Young.

She was terrible at comedy and sex farce. The only comedy she ever made, *The Grass Widow,* always makes those "fifty worst" lists. She came across on screen as so helpless, innocent, and unworldly (she was dubbed "The Elegant Waif") that the film's many slapstick scenes are excruciating to watch. She looks like a novice nun being manhandled by slavering thugs. The public forgave her this misstep, and she was immensely popular during her heyday, which ended in the early forties, when her beauty began quickly to fade.

So strong was the Hollywood star system during the thirties that her fans believed her to be as sweet and delicate offscreen as on, and not until after death in 1957 did anything else get hinted. And of course when her son spilled the beans in the sixties there was a terrific resurgence of interest in her old films, which people scrutinized for evidence of her depravity and sexual incontinence.

She appears to have been an evil, soulless woman who took real pleasure in the infliction of pain both physical and emotional. She took Conrad's father, an eminent Boston physician, away from his wife and children and lured him to Hollywood, where he married her, gave her a son whom she tried twice to abort, and endured her private and public abuse for ten years until it finally killed him. He died, according to his son, of a heart attack while being forced to witness his wife cavorting naked with three men in cassocks and a pin-headed whore.

Conrad hints in *The Violet Angel* that on many occasions, even before his father's death, he was forced to take part in his mother's orgies. In two of his novels he does more than hint at this. The facts of his mother's character and life are so outlandish that one would dismiss them as the ravings of a madman, except that after the book came out dozens of old Hollywood hands stepped forward to support it and elaborate further.

Conrad became a doctor, like his father. Unlike his father, he specialized in gynecology. And then, as soon as his residency was complete, he gave it up, and moved on to the mom-exposé business.

This was a story he loved to tell, how he "gave up" gynecology. "I went into it for the steady money. It's not just babies, you know. Women fall apart like they're made in Taiwan. The whole female works is a model for planned obsolescence. They get lumps, rashes, discharges, gross smells. They bleed. Or they don't bleed. Whichever, they worry about it. Their insides fall out, like the udder on a cow.

"So I had steady work. No problem there. And it was interesting too, at first. Learning all the things that could go wrong."

At this point in the telling, the person being told—always female—would ask, What went wrong? Would ask something foolish like this, with a strong sense of dread, as if something indefinably important rode on his answer. For when he told the story he was always at his most charming—boyish, ingratiating, comradely. He would light the woman's cigarette as he spoke, or freshen her drink, or wink at her, and in every way indicate that he liked her, wouldn't at that moment wish to be anywhere but where he was. A man who liked women, a man comfortable with women. A man who paid attention to women.

The woman who had his full attention at the moment would ask, What went wrong? Why did you give up your practice? Just as she had been led to do.

He would look down at his lap, blink rapidly like an anxious girl (like his mother), sigh, appear to make up his mind about something, look up at his companion with kind, honest eyes. "I could make up a long involved answer to that, but it would just be so much bullshit. The truth is . . . I came into the office late one morning, late from hospital rounds, but it was an ordinary workday, and I went in to see my first patient, an ordinary patient, in for an ordinary checkup, an ordinary smear. And she was a normal looking woman in good health, and pleasant and quite intelligent even. Good sense of humor. Nice lady. And she had on the little paper tent, and I got her to scoot down and spread her knees, and I got on the gloves and got out the speculum, just like always, and we were chatting all the while, interesting stuff about her work—she was a lawyer—and she smelled nice, I remember, the way career gals tend to do, they use an expensive talcum, a nice considerate scent. And everything was, you know, ordinary. And then I inserted the speculum." Here he would pause. "And I really looked at it. It was like it was the first time, you know? All I can tell you is, I had this flash. Zap! And I suddenly *knew*."

Knew what? asks the patsy.

He would smile then, sadly, and shrug, and hold out his hands to her in supplication, for moral support, often getting her nodding agreement before he opened his mouth. "I just *knew*. That it really is never too late. That I could change my life. That money isn't everything. The whole megillah, you know?"

I don't understand . . .

He would stutter a little, as though frustrated, and his voice would rise with evangelistic zeal. "That I could just get out! That I could walk away from it! Start fresh! That I didn't have to live like that! *That no one has to live like that!*"

And the woman would shut up, try to smile, continue nodding, mechanically, as though indeed agreeing that *no one has to live like that,* and often she would hug her stomach reflexively, as though holding in her repulsive "female works" with her hands alone.

The most chilling thing about the whole performance being, of course, that the performance, the assault, was obviously the reason he became a gynecologist in the first place. Abigail never did believe this. "You're crazy," she said. "I'm the one who knows men, remember? I'm never wrong, and I'm always right, and you just don't like him and you won't admit it." Well, she had always been right until now, but this was a man I knew and understood, from the beginning, to my sorrow, and she was wrong now, and I knew without a doubt, as well as I know my own name, that this creature so despised and feared his mother, and all women, that he applied to medical school, studied for six years, interned for two, worked for three more, built up a small beginning practice, attended medical conventions, bought malpractice insurance, all of it, just so he could entice women at parties to sit still and listen to him tell how he gave it all up because *no one has to live like that.*

"That's insane," Abigail said. "He'd have to be some kind of monster."

"He is," I said.

She studied me. "You want him too," she said. "My God, it's finally happened. It's *you.* Well, Dorcas . . ." She looked away from me for a long time and held herself still. "You can't have him," she said. "I know it isn't fair. But this one is different for me too. And you can't have him."

"He's already made you crazy," I said. I left the room, then, the house. I was shaking. I wasn't sure of anything, except that he *was* some kind of a monster.

The only motel in Frome is the Howard Johns. It used to be a Howard Johnson's, and when they lost the franchise they sold it, in pretty decrepit condition, to Sippy Siniscalchi (who saved my sister's behind in 1953). Sippy just painted the tile roof turquoise and whacked three letters off the neon sign, and *voilà!*

No one ever understood why Howard Johnson's chose Frome in the first place, or why it survived as long as it did. Frome lies smack in the middle of the Providence-Willimantic route, which is to say, nowhere. We have an interstate highway in Rhode Island, and we are a microscopically small state, and yet a great deal of Rhode Island is practically inaccessible. Like Frome.

At any rate, the survival of the Howard *Johns* is no mystery at all. All you have to do is drive by on any Saturday or Sunday morning, and you'll notice the parking lot choked with cars bearing R.I. license plates. This can mean only One Thing, as it is literally impossible to be so far from home in Rhode Island that you have to put up somewhere for the night. You can't drive for an hour in any direction without crossing into Connecticut or Massachusetts, or driving into the Bay.

The night of our apocalyptic meeting, Conrad Lowe was staying with the DeVilbisses. The next day he took a room at the Howard Johns motel.

In short order a young female *Journal-Bulletin* reporter came around to interview the famous author of *The Violet Angel, Corinna Gabriel,* and *The Mantis.* I clipped the interview and kept it on file here, in my secret desk drawer. I thought I was gathering evidence about the man. I had no idea what I was going to do with it, but it seemed at the time a worthy task. In the end, when Abigail became notorious, it was joined by masses of clippings from newspapers all over the country. Slobby Hilda, uninterested in mere facts, makes no reference to the interview; doubtless she was too busy sharing my sister's feelings to look it up.

The reporter, a doughty young woman named Sheila O'Bannion, starts out by asking how long Conrad is planning to stay in Frome. "At least," he says, "until I finish my current novel." Sheila dutifully elicits the information that his new book has the working title *Night of the Gorgon,* and is going to be "a chiller in the *Mantis* tradition."

"Is that, more or less, the Stephen King tradition?" she asks pertly.

"No," he responds, *impatiently brushing back a forelock, which seems to have a life of its own,* "it is *exactly* in the Stephen King tradition."

At this point Sheila begins to lose control over the interview:

And how do you think your work compares with King's?

It's even worse.

How did you happen to choose our state?

I was kicked out of New York City.

[Sheila might have gotten testy at this point, because she has "his hazel eyes twinkling" as he says this, and, a line later those same eyes "dancing merrily," punishing him with clichés. Either that or she was on drugs. His eyes were moist enough, I'm sure, and alert and lively, in the sense that fire is lively, and he certainly had a penetrating stare. But he was no more capable of twinkling than a Komodo dragon.]

I am *persona non grata* in New York City. My publishers love me, but I am unwelcome at parties.

Why?

I make myself obnoxious.

On purpose?

[At this point he was quiet "for a long moment, as though making up his mind about something." This is the same pause he always used just before dropping his stink-bomb on the "female works."]

It's the women, really, I can't stomach New York women.

Oh, come on. You're talking about five million people.

I'm talking fifty, five hundred people, tops. I don't know five million people. Do you? New York women are idiots. They're pushy, trend-happy, promiscuous, and pathetic. They live in depressing apartments and spend all their money on terrible clothes. They wear too much makeup. They have cigarette breath. They are shrill. They're all Jewish.

[Eeeeek!] You can't say that!

I just did. What you mean is, you can't print that.

[At this point we get a dialogue-free interlude, in which his nicotine-stained fingers play with various items and his amazing autonomous hair does some more tricks.]

Do you plan to be obnoxious here, Mr. Lowe?

[His eyes twinkle to beat the band.] **I don't like to make too many plans. Spontaneity is my middle name.**

You seem to be implying that Rhode Island is no more than a dumping ground, where you end up when you get kicked out of the majors. [Atta girl!]

Is that a question?

Well, no, but surely the question is implicit.

Really? What is it?

Well, do you really want to say that coming here is a step down for you?

What do you mean, "do I want to say it"? What are you asking for? Truth or consequences?

Well, I guess I'm asking for the truth.

You guess?

Mr. Lowe, are you a misogynist?

I beg your pardon?

You have that reputation.

I do?

Of being a misogynist.

In New York City.

Well, yes.

Well, no wonder! In New York City I *am* a misogynist! There's your answer.

What about Rhode Island women?

Now you're talking!

Well, do you plan to, do you think, what do you think of Rhode Island women?

I've only met a handful so far. You're nice.

[At this point the reporter "succumbed to his boyish charm and burst into gales of laughter." This is so hard to comprehend that one wonders if, while thus deranged, she succumbed in some other way.]

Seriously, Sheila, [he finally says, laying his finger aside of his nose] **I came here to your lovely state, and to this gentle, pastoral place, for the peace and quiet I require for my work. I very much look forward to making this place my home, and meeting as many people as I can, women and men. I intend that our relationship be amicable, fruitful, and long-lived.**

[Whereupon he ushered Sheila to the motel door with "easy gallantry" and paused with her at her car, looking up at the sky, squinting and shading his eyes.]

Storm's coming. How are the storms here?

Pretty good, actually.

Great. I love bad weather.

And Sheila drove off with his tagline ringing in her ears and the strong conviction that "whatever happens, Frome will never be quite the same again."

CHAPTER TEN

Abigail Gets What's Coming to Her

Hilda titles this chapter "Abby in Love," and is for once right about something. Conrad Lowe was Abigail's first true love.

The mature Abigail, that is. When she was sixteen, Abigail thought she was in love with Everett Esser. They kept steady company for a month or so, long enough for her to get pregnant, anyway. He was a sandy-haired boy with glasses and a dimpled chin, a bright kid with a weak character. A romantic. He used to call her his "woman," and Abigail told me he had forgiven her her past indiscretions.

I watched them together once, in a crowd of kids at Scarborough Beach, and she was unpacking the sandwiches and he was pouring the punch; and they were encapsulated in that aura of intimacy and exclusivity that young couples cast about themselves like a toreador's flashy cape. She was playing wife, he was playing husband, and they were both full of shit. Had Everett lived he would have clung to his illusions for, perhaps, a couple of years. I'll give him credit for that. He was very young. But Abigail, she was just trying the whole thing on for size. When she got the news of his ridiculous death there was a moment of genuine pity, but that was it. What followed at the funeral was of course theatrics. Her farewell performance. Love, for Abigail at sixteen, was a big hog wallow, and when he died—and not a moment too soon— she went to the showers.

She had a sentimental streak, especially when drunk, and she's always been good-natured. So most of her relationships have been amiable, many lastingly affectionate. She loved it when one of them fell in love with *her*, which happened often. She never lost interest in the drama of *that*. At such times our house would fill with flowers (which I had to put in water), the telephone would ring off the hook, and the big ham would shuffle around wearing a faraway expression. "Poor X," she would sigh. "He's got it bad." As she aged, X tended to get younger. She was the first big romance for an awful lot of young men. But sometimes an older one would fall, and more than once a marriage disintegrated while Abigail sighed and shook her head in fond exasperation at the crazy devotion, the total loss of perspective, of X.

She would try to dissuade these kamikazes. I think her efforts were genuine. I heard her once on the telephone, talking down some poor sap with four kids, and I remember her saying, "No, Jack. You go out that door now and I'll never open mine to you again." Of course, she had allowed Jack to get to this point: to frighten his children, to wound his wife. She hadn't lowered the boom until he stood there in his foyer with his hat on and his suitcase all packed, with shirtcuffs and pieces of sock sticking out of it, and his hysterical family clinging to his knees.

The worst case was Big Bob Flynn, who used to be our

tax assessor. He was twenty years older than Abigail, with children grown up and a grandchild on the way. A big man with a ruddy face, who told the world's best jokes and knew half of the citizens of Frome by their first names. We got along terrifically well. Like me, he thought most people were horses' patoots, but he liked them anyway, a lot better than I did.

Anyway, he fell for Abigail, the old dope. It hurt me to see them together. He would come by to pick her up and always look sheepishly at me, because of his family, because he knew I didn't approve. They never slept together here, in the house, and I think this was at his insistence. He used to send her singing telegrams, though, and balloon-o-grams. They started off funny. I got a song once by mistake, when I answered to "Miss Mather" without thinking to qualify. A nervous, tuneless young man sang three stanzas of "Let's Do It" before I plugged him with a tip. Big Bob sent her helium balloons with silly faces on them, a Swissy Mouse balloon, a Harpo Marx balloon, a balloon that said BALLOON.

But he fell, eventually, hardest of all. He did leave his wife and disgrace himself, for good, with his children. Abigail tried to stop him, but he was older and more stubborn than the others and, I think, more desperate for happiness. In the end he left Frome, financially broken, drinking too much, a ruin.

I won't say Abigail was unmoved, or that she never grieved for him, or even that she was incapable of feeling guilt. All I know is that one of the last balloons she got from Bob Flynn remained aloft through some fluke for over three months, growing imperceptibly smaller every day, gathering dust, in the dark northeast corner of the living room. It said I LOVE YOU. I could have pulled it down and disposed of it, but it wasn't my job. And she knew it was there. One night when we were sitting in the living room and had just turned off Johnny Carson, I broke down and demanded, "Doesn't that depress you?" pointing at the little puckered dull-skinned balloon, and "Why don't you get rid of it, for God's sake." And she said, "Yeah, it's sad." And chewed her lip. "I just wanted to see how long it would stay up."

Before Conrad Lowe, sentiment played second fiddle even to the transient spirit of scientific inquiry.

But that was B.C. A.C. was a brand-new day.

Abigail went off her feed immediately. Starting the day after their meeting at the DeVilbisses', she jumped whenever the phone rang, and mooned around the house like a teenager who's two weeks late. Her appetite dwindled and I caught her more than once staring at herself in the full-length bathroom mirror as though looking at some pathetic stranger, some down-and-out dame glimpsed on a bus, whose history you try to determine from visible clues.

"You're too old for this," I told her.

"I know it."

At this point she still had too much pride to pump Guy and Hilda for information about his whereabouts. But, she admitted to me, every time she approached their house with the mail she got so excited she could hardly breathe, knowing it was just possible that He could open the door.

Then she read the newspaper interview, and took to driving by the Howard Johns in the early evening, afraid to stop and stake out the place, afraid that he would catch her out.

One evening, when Anna was staying overnight at a friend's house, I sat Abigail down for a talk. She was beginning to worry me. "Look at me," I said to her. "That man is the most objectionable person I have ever met. He's a sadist. He's a manipulator. He likes to hurt people, and he especially likes to hurt women."

Abigail nodded like a cow, her eyes luminous and large. Just talking about him made her bovine.

"He may even be a psychopath. He made the little hairs on the back of my neck stand on end and quiver."

"I know."

"You know? Abigail, what I'm saying here is dead serious. The only thing confining him to merely emotional destruction is self-preservation. If he thought he could get away with it he'd kill people." I heard myself and this sounded a bit much. "I don't mean that. I just got carried away."

"No," Abigail said. "I think you may be right."

"Jesus Christ, what's the matter with you all of a sudden? You're no masochist! You're no martyr! Why, the very idea—"

"I know," she said. "It's going to be horrible." She doubled up in some kind of pain and bowled over on her side of the divan, clutching her middle, her face screwed up and unrecognizable. "Oh, Dorcas," she said, shamelessly crying.

"What's the matter now?"

"I've got to have him! I can't stand it! I want him so bad!" The precise nature of her want would have been obvious to a Martian. She was jacknifed and keening in a rhythmic, hopeless way.

"Abigail, stop it. Stop it this instant." She keened louder. I lost control then, so awful was this spectacle, and degrading, to both of us. Especially to me. If she had smeared herself with wolf dung and sacrificed some helpless creature to a gibbous moon I would not have been more dismayed. She had always had pride. Pride alone, I could see now, had kept her from this bestial state. She was mindless now and desperate with need, where once her sexual confidence had been, and the sight was more than ugly and degrading. It was frightening, and in a way I have never been able to explain.

All I know is that watching her so out of control, so frustrated, so *empty,* made me feel that something was terribly wrong, on a scale which dwarfed us both. The spectacle was *unnatural.* It made me mindless, too, it made me panic, and I couldn't shake the conviction that this was *wrong,* that my sister must not be denied, that her present unnatural state was a piece of cosmic bad news; and I became frantic, and for a crystalline moment I considered how best to satisfy her, I imagined going to Conrad Lowe as a supplicant, begging him to come, or in a threatening posture, kidnapping him, bringing him here, trussed and in prime condition, to my sister, *pimping for my sister.* In just the way that the screams of a newborn in pain will bring strangers running, covering their ears, ready to sacrifice anything to save it, so the sight and sound of my needful sister aroused in me the subhuman instincts of a pimp.

I drew back, at the brink of what I don't know, and slapped my sister across the face for the first time in our adult lives. This had no effect on her, nor did the second slap, nor the great shake I gave her so that her body wobbled bonelessly like a thawed carcass. And in the end I went to the kitchen and filled my biggest pot, my old pressure cooker, with cold water, and threw it on her as if she were a tantrumming child or a dog in the street; and this slowed her down some, but did not stop her, so that I had to refill the pan again and again, and by the time I had won, the divan was sodden and wrecked and there was water standing halfway across the living room rug. At which point we both came to, and stared at each other, and the telephone rang, and I picked it up. "Surprise!" said Conrad Lowe.

Wordlessly I handed the telephone to dripping Abigail, who listened for a second and handed it back to me. She whispered, "It's you he wants."

I brought the receiver to my ear. ". . . wrong foot," he was saying, "and I was wondering if I could take you someplace for dinner tonight. The restaurant of your choice?" His voice was distorted. It sounded as if he were applying a toothpick between some late molars. It sounded as if he were flat on his back in bed with the receiver cradled between ear and pillow. It sounded as if his bed were unmade. ". . . surf and turf? What is that? Boiled kelp?"

I couldn't speak. I was staring at Abigail, and my mouth was dry. I wanted to speak up: to let him know I could see his game. He was trying to play us off each other, just for the hell of it, the way certain little girls enjoy breaking up friendships. Conrad Lowe had a feminine appetite for social mischief. He was calculating in just the sort of way a particular sort of amoral female is calculating. I thought of this, while he spoke, and wondered how to use it as a weapon against him, and saw that I could not. That this female side of his nature made him even more formidable.

"Come on, Dorcas," he was saying now. "I'm going nuts in this burg. Just give me one evening. A few hours of your time. If you still don't want anything to do with me, you could point me in the direction of some interesting people. What say?"

"No, thank you."

Abigail snatched the receiver from my hand and buried the mouthpiece in a sodden cushion. She hissed, inches from my face, "It's going to kill me. But if you don't go I'll never forgive you."

"But I don't want—"

"Don't you dare feel sorry for me!"

"This has nothing to do with you. I just don't *want*—"

"Tell him! Tell him you'll go!" She thrust the receiver into my face with such force that she almost chipped a tooth. She had never in all our lives used her superior size and strength against me. I had never before been physically afraid of her. She was not in her right mind.

"Mr. Lowe?"

"Yes?"

"I'll see you. But just this—"

"I'll come by at seven."

"No! No, I'll meet you."

"Where?"

We settled in the end on Lobsterama, a South County bayside place. I insisted on meeting him there, even though this would mean identical twenty-five-minute drives for each of us. We'd probably chase each other down the highway. He didn't argue. He was laughing when he hung up.

So it came to pass that I had the first "date" of my entire life, with Conrad Lowe, a man I feared and despised, and at the insistence of my deranged, lovesick sister.

When I was halfway out the door—I have a real thing about being late, and it was already six thirty—she shouted at me. "Where do you think you're going, looking like *that*?" I was wearing my best suit, my only suit, and I had shined my shoes. She said I looked terrible. I said I had always looked terrible, if by "terrible" she meant "sexually unappealing." She said something could still be done about that. Grimly, over my weak protests, she did something with my short thin hair to give it "body" and rouged my cheekbones so roughly that even after I wiped them off they remained pink and glowing, from the abrasion.

First he had turned me into a pimp, and now he was doing the same for my sister. "Take off that hideous suit," she ordered. "I've got a dress that might fit you, if I can find that wide belt," and she started to wrench the jacket back off my shoulders, whereupon I did finally, like the old hand which I by now was, give her a smart clop in the chops. This was all it took. She started sobbing and collapsed into a chair.

I lectured her for five minutes before leaving. I said she was to pull herself together, stop being disgusting, show some respect for herself, try self-discipline for a change. I said I was ashamed to have her in the family. I promised to do my best to steer Conrad Lowe in her direction.

Declaration of Moral Bankruptcy

Hilda apparently didn't know about my date with Conrad Lowe, for which I give Abigail grudging credit. Her chapter eleven, of course entitled "Herstory," explores the "psychosexual histories" of her two sexual psychos. Hilda expatiates upon our parents' shortcomings, Mother's "feyness," Father's insecurities and consequent "failure to validate"; and when she finishes slandering them, she starts in on Dr. and Mrs. Lowe, who are by now, I guess, fair game. The centerpiece of this dreary pseudo-scholastic chapter is a pull-out chart in which two Circles of Abuse (which look like those weather cycles you see in high school science books, where OCEANS & LAKES & STREAMS, CLOUDS, and RAINFALL chase one another around with little curved arrows) overlap each other with perfect symmetry.

My chapter eleven is not so theoretical.

. . .

I was early, of course. Or he was late. I was seated by a window looking down over a little marina. The waiter, "LARRY," asked me if I wanted to face the window or sit with my back to it. I didn't know which I was supposed to want. I elected to face the large brightly lit room, so I could see him coming. I ordered a sherry, Fino.

This was not, I was pleased to note, a place for dating couples. It was way too noisy and roomy. It was the kind of place you brought your extended family to, and all around the barnlike room babies in high chairs littered the floor with crushed oyster crackers, and clattered their plates, and screamed with frustration and fatigue.

I saw him before he saw me. He stood at the entrance beside the hostess's lectern. She was scanning a list and say-ing something. He cut her off with a familiar hand on her back, dipping quickly toward her for an instant of charm, and then quickly away, for he had spotted me. He moved toward me through the crowded room with absolute ease. There was no trace of self-consciousness, even though he had to stop three times for waitresses to glide by with heavy trays, and was forced more than once to squeeze sideways between the chairs of obese diners. He brushed past obstacles, human and otherwise, with indifferent grace, never acknowledging for an instant the possibility that he could stumble, or trip someone, or get stuck somewhere in the maze and have to backtrack and reroute. He cut through the crowd like a shark through choppy waters, and he never took his eyes off me.

He smiled and sat down opposite me, without saying a word, the early evening light, the last rays of sunset, full on his face. He told Larry, without looking up at him, that he wanted a double bourbon on the rocks with a dash of bitters. When Larry left he leaned forward on his elbows and widened his smile at me, and continued to say nothing.

He was absolutely familiar with me. The easy way he smiled, as if he had the right to say nothing, the right to a companionable silence, made me wonder, crazily, if we had done this before, many times, in some other life. I could have been, on the evidence of his smile alone, the depth of his apparent pleasure in my company, the only woman in his life. It just about made me sick.

When Larry brought his drink and the big wooden menu, Conrad Lowe put the board facedown on the table without looking at it, and drank his drink, still looking at me. This was too much.

"Aren't you going to read the menu?" I asked.

"Oh, is this a menu? I thought it was a fraternity paddle." He actually winked at me.

"Are you going to read it?"

"You decide. You pick something out for me."

"No! Don't be ridiculous. I do not know you. I have no idea what your tastes are."

He laughed. "You're perfect. You're totally consistent."

"You are totally objectionable." This time I thought deliberately of Katharine Hepburn. "Food is an intimate subject, and intimacy cannot be enforced, Mr. Lowe."

Now he was not stung, but pleased. "Sure it can," he said. "Take rape. That's enforced intimacy."

"What I meant, of course, was that it *should* not be enforced."

"But you didn't actually say that."

"With some people I would not *have* to say that."

"Because some people," said Conrad Lowe, "actually feel the force of the categorical imperative. The buddy-buddy between *should not* and *cannot*, between *ought* and *is*. Because some people are moral agents." He finished his drink. "And some are not."

I nodded, unable to speak. It had not occurred to me that he could know himself so well. I could not use the truth against him. He had already appropriated it.

Conrad Lowe procured another drink and continued. "They call these people psychopaths. They often say, of these people, 'They are not like us.' They are born without consciences, they say, like babies born blind."

"I never called you a psychopath," I said, silently adding *to your face,* crossing my fingers under the table, to preserve for my soul's sake the letter of the moral law.

"A lot of women have. But they're wrong. Do you want to know how I know this?"

No, I thought, because I already know how important it is for you to believe yourself complete. No one wants to be a monster.

"Because my earliest memory is of the experience of moral outrage. How many children can say that? Now, my father . . . My father was a walking advertisement for the categorical imperative. My mother, breathing air, laughing, happy in work and play, was a living illustration of injustice. These were the first facts I knew." He regarded me in dead earnest. "I was raised by a nurse, a succession of them actually, but the first was Concetta. She lasted for four years, and then they canned her, but I saw her again about ten years ago. She wrote to me when *Violet Angel* came out, and we met for lunch. She wanted to talk over old times. To fill me in on stuff I didn't remember. To help me, she said, in case I ever wanted to do a sequel. Well, she was hustling, but that's okay. That's inevitable. Anyway, do you know what she told me? My first words. Can you guess what my first words were?"

I had no idea.

"Bad Mommy," he said. "Bad Mommy."

There was on his face a slack and tortured look. He seemed utterly vulnerable. The sight so confused me that I looked away and off to the side, where a child of perhaps eighteen months, a wide-mouthed little girl with a purple bow on her wispy topknot, was handling her scoop of ice cream as though it were a lump of clay, and I was the only adult to see her look around, spot the large sacklike leather pocketbook of a stout woman seated at the adjoining table, and deposit the dripping blob inside with a bull's-eye drop from the height of her baby chair. Her attention remained fixed on the interior of the pocketbook for about three seconds, at which point she forgot what she was doing and looked up at her parents with a sweet, loving expression, which *was* seen, and instantly rewarded.

The idea of this or any other small child saying "Bad Mommy" or bad anything was all too ludicrous, and I laughed freely with derision and, I must admit, relief. Every child born, monster and human alike, recognizes injustice when it is visited upon *him*. Conrad Lowe never universalized the experience. Now he comforted himself with the memory of outrage. Whereas the only persuasive evidence for his humanity would be a memory of remorse; an experience which I very much doubted he ever had.

Knowing all this about him, seeing his weakness at last, relaxed me as the sherry had not. I leaned back and placed my forearms on the table. I said, "What do you want from me? What are you up to?"

He was still distracted, his eyes fixed on some inner vision. The two rapidly consumed drinks (he was to put away one more before dinner) had effected a change in his manner, in his appearance. Drinking was bad for him. It robbed him of total control. I was very surprised that he drank at all. He thought about my question now, slowly closing one eye, staring idly with the other at his empty glass, his slender fingertips. Just then he reminded me of something, but I couldn't get exactly what it was. "What do I want from you, Dorcas? Companionship. Fellow feeling. Entertainment." Each word rolled out without inflection, or conviction. He was trying these ideas on for size. He looked shrewdly up at me then, one eye still shut, the fine dark lashes delicate upon his cheek. "Maybe I want a challenge," he said. "Maybe I plan to seduce you."

"And why would you do that?"

"Because I could."

"Just to prove that you could?"

"I don't need to prove anything. That would mean I was unsure of myself. Which I'm not."

"Of course."

"You don't believe me."

"I believe that you're sure of yourself, yes."

"You don't understand," he said. "You're my type."

"That's too bad, because you're not mine. I don't have a type. Any fool could see that."

He smiled, in a lazy, profoundly unpleasant way.

"I'm an old maid, Mr. Lowe. I was born to it. When I was twelve I took a long, slow look around and said, 'Nope. Not for me.' "

"With your sister there, you didn't have to look far."

"With my sister there, I didn't have to do anything."

"You must have resented her."

"I was never jealous. She had nothing I wanted." Was this true? "Abigail and I divided up the world. Sacred and profane. Spiritual and physical. Mind and body." It couldn't have been the sherry. Something was getting to me, though, making me reckless.

"Male and female?"

"No. Certainly not."

"Girl and woman? Artemis and Aphrodite?"

Polyphemus, I thought, confronting his one-eyed stare. Like the cyclops, he should not have drunk so much. Polyphemus was not civilized, and neither was my sister, and neither, despite his disguise, was this man. Sitting there across from him, and thinking these things through calmly, made me happy in a way I had rarely experienced. "Abigail and I," I told him, "were both born naked. We each came into the world with longings and needs. I am not some mutant. Mine is not some third sex. I could tell you things. . . ." I smiled, despite myself, thinking of Abigail and me at twelve, and the games she made everybody play, boys and girls, the delicate operations under the gazebo, with the afternoon sun slipping through the latticework in orange diamonds, and the spiders and shovels and rakes and mousetraps.

"What things, Dorcas?" he whispered.

I laughed at him. "Do you think that nuns and spinsters are all hormone cases? Can't you imagine for a moment that at least some of us know what we're missing? Exactly what we're giving up? And that we sign on the dotted line fully informed of our rights, and sign happily, and consider that we got the best of the bargain?"

"How? Tell me."

"You see, I know what an appetite is. I know what it feels like. I know, as well as Abigail, as well as you, what it feels like to want. To experience desire."

"Yes."

"Yes, but because I lived with Abigail, I also knew what it *looks* like."

"Ugly? Disgusting? Ruttish?"

"Ridiculous! That's all. Ridiculous."

"Silly?"

"Exactly. My sister has great power, but no dignity."

"Ah."

We were both quiet for a while, listening to my reverberating pronouncement. Seafood platters were placed before us, upon which we each ravenously fell. Conrad Lowe with, I suppose, that indiscriminate, senseless hunger that comes from too many drinks, and I from what? I don't know.

The food was terrible, the breading orange and tasteless and soaked with old grease, the scallops distinguishable from the shrimp only in shape. I ate everything—fried food, cole slaw, tartar sauce, corn bread; chomping and breathing to the accompaniment of *power* and *dignity*: the sounds. Eventually, when my plate was clean, I could no longer avoid the thought I had been pushing away. That these two were just words, just alphabet pieces and noise. This was a foolish thought, but I couldn't shake it, or shake off their echo.

Conrad Lowe put down his fork and leaned back. "Name something with power *and* dignity." He said this in a companionable way, as though we were playing "Botticelli." Logy with bad food, I had the awful bloated thought that he could read my mind, hear with my inner ear. "Okay, name something with dignity and no power." He picked up the fork and played with his fried fish. He shoveled a big piece into his mouth. Grease ran down the middle of his chin. "A hurricane, say, or the sea. Do they have dignity and power? Or—"

"Only people can have dignity," I said, trying to clean my fingers with a red cloth napkin that would not absorb anything. They make napkins now out of shiny, handsome material that won't even pick up water.

"My mother," he said, chewing his fish, "now she had

power. No dignity, though. Except on screen. My *father*. No power, no dignity, no nothing. This is interesting." He looked up at me and pointed at my nose. "Now, you. Now, *you* have tons of dignity! But no—"

"Go to hell."

"When I was a kid we had this Great Dane. Cromwell, his name was. Big as a pony. He was Mom's pet, really, and I'll spare you the grisly details, but you know I'm pretty sure Cromwell had power and dignity, both." He put down his napkin. "When Father died I took Cromwell out behind the stables and blew his brains out."

"I don't believe you."

"You don't believe what? That I could kill a dog?" Conrad Lowe threw back his head and laughed, suddenly sober, suddenly happy. "That's the twentieth century for you. It's significant now when a man kills a dog. It means something about his character. I mean, not just *anybody* can kill a *dog*."

I have always had a strong stomach, and this is the only thing that kept me from bolting across the room with my hand over my mouth, like a squeamish child in frog-dissecting class.

"Look, honey. Power, dignity, bullshit. You looked at your sister and saw an amoral, rotten, monstrous ball of fat. You knew evil when you saw it. You are a mutant, Dorcas. You're a woman with a conscience. I'd like to believe you're a hint of things to come, an evolutionary feeler, so to speak, but I'm afraid you're just one of nature's oddballs. You have a sense of *honor*. Shame on you. No real woman knows the meaning of the word."

"You're insane." I started fumbling with my purse, trying to fish out ten dollars and change.

"You're so honorable that you're going to pay for your

half of this grotesque meal. Not for boring feminist reasons, either. Not to prove anything. Just because it's the right thing to do."

"You're very good," I said, standing. "You study people and think about them and make clever inferences, and you're very, very good. You're a gifted psychologist. But the fact that you do it for *fun*..." I was shaking so badly that I couldn't continue.

"Yes?"

"Ought to scare you to death. It certainly does me. Mr. Lowe, you are a bad man." Conrad Lowe blinked at that, actually blinked, and paled. "Stay away from us." Carefully I turned from him and made my way across the bustling room, every movement slow and deliberate, for I was light-headed and my heartbeat was shallow and if I did anything too quickly I would lose my balance, stumble, fall. I didn't look around until I was in the parking lot and opening my car door.

He had not followed me. I was safe.

When I let myself into the house Abigail was asleep, passed out on the wet couch, her face still swollen in misery. I hated to leave her like that, all damp, but it seemed a worse cruelty to wake her, and I went straight to bed, exhausted myself, without bathing.

Sometime later I had a nightmare, the only part of which I ever remembered being a great wooden door exploding in-ward into lethal splinters, the explosion being the occasion for my sudden waking, and when I came to, which I did all of a sudden, disoriented, I was staring at my own closed bedroom door. I lay for a few minutes, frightened, listening, wondering, but there were no noises in the real world. And I was too tired to ponder the mysteries. Dreams are always banal anyway. I went back to sleep and slept straight until morning.

When I rose to use the toilet I could see, from the light in the hall, that the door to Abigail's room was open, but I was just shuffling, still waking, my eyes on the floor, and did not pause to wonder or look in. I started coffee and picked up the living room. I was going to have to take the couch outside on this sunny day and dry it out. There was a man's herringbone jacket folded over the rocker. I saw it and did not take it in. There was an alarming scent in the air, half horribly familiar, like the smell of rotting roses, half horribly unfamiliar, like the lather of a mutant horse, and I smelled this and took note of it and set it aside for later. There was a strange old car out front, parked badly, its right front wheel up over the curb and dug into the grass, and I stared out the window at it, interested but not really curious. I was handling myself like an invalid on her first day up. I was emphasizing the positive. How delicious, I thought, sipping my coffee; and, What a beautiful day.

(While in the next room my other selves, the rest of me, the part that notices and the part that analyzes and the part that takes care, conferred in anxious whispers. "Should we let her know?" "No, no, no!" "Look, she's going to find out sooner or later. Why not now?" "Too soon! Let her wake up first! Let her get her strength!")

I padded back down the sun-drenched hall to my room to get dressed and from this angle could not miss looking into Abigail's room on the way. I made my bed and got myself into jeans and sweatshirt. I drew the curtains. I leaned against the glass. I closed my eyes then and only then and saw what I had just seen, when I passed my sister's open door. That morning it was as though I could not see anything directly. In high school biology they always compare the eye to a camera, and now the analogy was exact. My eyes had functioned independent of my brain. I had not been able to register anything until the picture developed. And then I could see, from every angle

my sister naked, pink and enormous, inert, unconscious and perhaps dead, perhaps sleeping, cast up on her own rumpled bed like some sea creature on an alien beach, a sight at once hypnotic and deeply frightening, because you're so afraid you'll see something awful, a human resemblance, a human being, a dead human being, deformed forever by the appetites of cold-blooded predators, and scuttling, clicking spiders of the deep. And behind her, just visible beyond the rolling pink hills, the narrow head of Conrad Lowe, eyes open, mouth grinning wide, nodding good morning to me.

I ran out of the house that morning as though it were on fire, pausing only to scrawl a note to Abigail. "GET OUT OF HEAR," it said. That's how distraught I was. I didn't even catch the mistake. And "NOT ONE MORE NIGHT UNDER MY ROOF." I taped it to the bathroom mirror and fled.

When I returned very late that night they were gone, and her closets cleaned out, except for cobwebs and enough dust cotton to make a human being and a couple of filthy cardigans abandoned in the far corner. She took no furniture, although half of it was hers. She left most of her toiletries behind: dusty bottles of drug store cologne, puffs of matching talcum. I don't know why she bothered to take her clothes. She left everything else, including her scent, which filled the abandoned bedroom like a mournful and corpulent ghost. Her bedding was left on the dusty floor, tightly wadded and tied into a perfectly circular hassock shape, the two sheet corners sticking out like rabbit ears. This was not Abigail's style, and it had not been her doing.

My note remained on the bathroom mirror, with Abigail's additions, printed like my own. Our handwriting had always been similar.

GET OUT OF HEAR

SORRY ABOUT THE SHEETS

BE HAPPY FOR ME

NOT ONE MORE NIGHT UNDER MY ROOF

The Gift of Health

Chapter 12

Her Daemon Lover

The time has come, the walrus said...
Abby gnaws her fingertips. She will not look at me.
...to talk of many things...
"No," whispers Abby, eyes downcast.
"Abby," I say to my old friend, as gently as I can, "the time really has come."
"I can't do it. Please don't ask me. I'm so ashamed."
"Let it go. You must. The time has come."
She sobs and sobs as if her great heart would break. As if one unbroken shard, until now miraculously intact, has finally shattered. At last, she nods.
And so, yes, the time *has* come, as that terrible old walrus said, to talk of how this sadist caught her, held her in thrall, bound her without chains, silenced her cries, unmanned—unwomanned—this powerful, lusty Wife of Bath—Wife of Frome! What was his weapon? *[Gosh.]* What was her window of vulnerability? *[And did she clean it with vinegar or ammonia?]*
The time has come. To talk. Of sex.

Oh, let's not. Let's talk about Abigail's bridal shower.

Everybody was there, or rather here, in the reference roomette. The whole damn town crammed in with the *Encyclopedia Judaica* and *Famous Crimes A–Z*. T. R. Corrow, Heimlich maneuver enthusiast and police horse stompee, whose brilliant idea this had been, festooned the stacks with burgundy velvet ribbons. Abigail's coworkers at the post office contributed a dot matrix banner wondering HOW LOWE CAN YOU GO? which was funny despite itself, owing to the clucking embarrassment of Guy's literary circle, who had for months pretended that Abigail was one of them and were now squarely confronted with the working-class truth.

Guy handled it by zeroing in on Ob Minurka, the most rough-hewn of the lot, and a dwarf to boot, and engaging him in political debate, to show off his egalitarian principles. He pantomimed a blue collar stiff, planting his legs wide apart, pushing up his sleeves, clamping his chubby hands on his hips. Ob played him beautifully, deliberately making increasingly Neanderthal statements about the death penalty and the fuckin' A-rabs, but he couldn't shake off Guy's camaraderie. With Guy, who'd bring out the bully in Mother Teresa, the school playground is never far away.

I nudged Abigail, to get her to check out Guy. I said he looked like an amateur-night Petruchio from *Kiss Me Kate*. She looked up from unwrapping her booty, gave him one shrewd glance, shook her head. "Mary Martin," she said, "as Whozit, in green tights. What the hell am I going to do with a DustBuster?"

She was surrounded by bridal plunder and crumpled wrapping paper and kneeling women from all walks of life. Hilda kept the list of who gave what, Anna passed gifts around for inspection, Gloria Gomes, my children's librarian, stuffed trash into plastic leaf bags, and some motormouth from the post office took down every single remark Abigail made, so that she could later read aloud the list of exclamations as "What Abigail Said to Conrad on Their Wedding Night." Is this a strictly Rhode Island custom? I hope so.

"Bust dust," I said. "For that matter, what are you going to do with a Hot Dogger? Never mind, spare me."

She was paying me no attention. Her eyes scanned the crowd in a worried way.

"You don't really expect him to come, do you?" I asked.

"He said he'd try to make it."

"Ha. He said he'd rather chew off his legs."

"He was joking."

"He said, and I quote, 'My dumpling, I would rather chew off my right leg than go to one of those goddamn pussy-klatsches.' And so would your sister, he added, accurately, thus forcing me to announce that I wouldn't miss it for the world. "He advised you to, and I quote again, 'shut your hole' on the subject of the shower."

"Thank you," said Abigail, "for reminding me."

Anna set a square silver-wrapped box on her mother's lap. "This one's from Rudy and Sylvia Fusco," she whispered. Rudy and Sylvia were DeVilbiss people.

Abigail tore viciously at the black satin ribbon, muttering at me under her breath. "You could at least *pretend*, you bitch, you could at least be happy for me. You could at the very least lay the fuck *off*."

"Rudy and Sylvia Fusco, everybody," said Anna.

Abigail ripped the corrugated box apart like a strongman's telephone book. A large delicate cranberry glass sphere popped up and arced over the heads of well-wishers, smashing out of sight against the window seat.

"It was a vase," said Sylvia Fusco.

"It was lovely," I said, for Abigail, who obviously didn't give a shit.

"Cranberry glass, wasn't it?" asked dutiful Hilda, scribbling away.

"Dorcas made me do it," said Abigail. "It's Dorcas's fault."

In then came the Walrus, with a blast of Arctic air, twirling his waxed mustachios.

"There's our man," said hearty Guy, and a wan cheer went up for the groom, who advanced toward us with a heavy oblong package under his arm, wrapped in kiddie paper potato-stamped with pastel balloons and cartwheeling elephants.

"I told you!" shouted Abigail, jumping up to embrace him. He sat her back down with the elephant box.

"For my lady," said Conrad Lowe. Amid appreciative groans he knelt at her feet. He smiled tenderly, right at her. His eyes were guileless. "Open it, sweetmeat."

I couldn't bear to watch. I tiptoed backward, then made a dash for the cellar broom closet. I was going to clean up the broken glass, and I was going to take my sweet time about it.

Which I did, but even in the cellar, directly underneath them, I could hear the long, awful silence, broken by uncertain titters and the scraping of chairs, and more silence. And more.

What had the bastard given her? A vibrator? A cow flop? Why didn't somebody kill him? Why was I lurking in the bowels of my own library, like some sullen child on the lam?

"It's a really good one," I heard my sister say, in a small muffled voice, as I trudged upstairs with the broom.

"The best," Hilda said, "according to *Consumer Reports*."

"It's in the Hammacher-Schlemmer catalogue, too," said Guy.

"I wouldn't mind having one myself," said Gloria Gomes.

Ob Minurka stepped forward and stared down at Conrad's gift. "If I gave my old lady one of these she'd ream me out with a snowblower."

Conrad had given his fiancée a Health O Meter Professional Dial Bathroom Scale, doctor-quality, with a precision heavy-duty rack and pinion mechanism. Ob showed Conrad his bad, gappy teeth. "You know, pal, pardon my French, Abigail, you're a real sack of shit. Pardon me all to hell."

"Shut up, Ob," said Abigail, giving the little man a hug and a kiss on the cheek. Her eyes swam in tears.

Conrad Lowe glided up to me, proffering a cup of punch.

"I have a mess to clean up," I said, turning away without meeting his eyes. I was so angry I was afraid I would cry too.

He followed me over to the exploded cranberry vase. "So do I," he said.

"What's that supposed to mean?" I began to sweep the glass onto a sheet of cardboard, chucking it bit by bit into a metal wastebasket. "Do you think you can just apologize? Make it all right with a few hypocritical phrases?"

"Apologize for what?" He drained my punch glass and made an incredulous face. "What the fuck is this? Rum and clam juice?"

I dumped the last pile in the basket, crumpling up the cardboard, stabbing myself in the palm with a stray cranberry blade. "You said, you implied, that you had a mess to clean up. I assumed you were talking about one of your own messes."

"I was talking about your sister. I don't intend to have a fat freak wife."

"You're despicable."

"Thin is in. Besides, I worry about her health. Don't you?"

"She's as healthy as a horse."

"She's a porker. Not my type. As I mentioned before."

"Then why? Why? Why?" I screamed at him in a whisper, my face inches from his. We were unnoticed because the rest of the crowd was gathered around Abigail and her new bathroom scale, taking turns weighing themselves.

"Because she's the next best thing."

"To what?"

"You, Dorcas."

"Horseshit."

"You're probably right." Suddenly bored, he handed me the two empty punch cups. "See ya' in jail, sis," he said, and started for the door.

A hush rose up from the crowd as Abigail ascended the scale. She held her head high. She looked like some sort of fertility goddess. "Read it out, Ob," she said.

"One-ninety-eight," said Ob.

"One-ninety-eight," said Abigail, regarding her husband-to-be. Her expression was unfathomable, neither defiant nor submissive. Whatever it meant, Conrad didn't like it. He flashed her an all-too-fathomable look, then swept out the door like Snidely Whiplash.

I remember thinking that she looked heroic, standing there on the scale, facing him. What struck me was the lack of shame, the lack of fear. *You have not hurt me. You cannot hurt me.* But now I'm remembering too what Frank Calef said, about the way she looked on the ice, naked and undiminished. *She just handed it to you, the responsibility for her life, for her character, her future, her past, she just handed it over.*

. . .

For the record, here's

WHAT ABIGAIL SAID TO CONRAD
ON THEIR WEDDING NIGHT

"Hey, that looks handy."
"Sterling, isn't it?"
"Great, now I have two."
"This will last forever."
"Mauve! My favorite color."
"Oh, dear, you really, really, really shouldn't have."
"Jeez, this weighs a ton."
"Where are you supposed to put this? Does anybody know where this goes?"
"Great, now I have three."
"These will look beautiful on my chiffarobe."
"I can't read the inscription. Where are my reading glasses?"
"Is this some kind of a joke?"
"Wow! Look at this!"
"Oh, oh, oh, that's gorgeous, that's absolutely incredible."
"I just love this."
"Thank you, oh, thank you, so much. Thank you."
"I don't know what to say."
"Dorcas made me do it. It's Dorcas's fault."

Homage to King Philip

Chapter 13

Spring Bride

The bride was truly radiant, the groom dignified and handsome, the occasion festive. All of us who loved them both rejoiced upon their formal union. Even my husband, who ordinarily shuns what he calls "ceremonial goose-stepping," joined the rest of us in pelting the laughing couple with rose petals and sunflower seeds. The sun shone brightly on the newlyweds and their loving circle of friends. But even on this day of bright beginnings, ugliness was just around the corner. . . .

Isn't that a song title? This is really hilarious. Also, it turns out there was half a bottle of Jim Beam in the window seat compartment in my reference roomette. The sky is turning Deep Purple, and the day is shaping up. Whoopee!

Well, Hilda's memory is a mite addled, natch. To start with, I forget whose bright idea it was not to throw rice—it was a minitrend of the times, a trendette, a trendoid; people with nothing better to do worried about rice kernels bursting the stomachs of house finches—but I do distinctly recall that

Abigail wasn't "laughing" as she was showered with birdseed. She was pissed as hell, and spent fifteen minutes shaking out her hair and picking black husks out of her cleavage.

I don't know why Conrad Lowe insisted upon a church wedding, but since Guy was his best man they had to pick a church which Guy ("I won't goose-step; don't ask me"), a conscientious agnostic, could enter without disgracing himself. Before whom? Before himself, I guess; before the Great Void. Which meant they needed a Unitarian church; which meant trundling all the way to Providence.

The ceremony took place during Lent. The marquee on the church lawn read

EASTER FOR NON-BELIEVERS
WEDNESDAY NITES UNISEX AEROBICS

The minister, or facilitator, whatever, was a youngish man with haunted eyes, ginger-haired and flabby. Behind his professional nuptial smile he radiated despair to such a degree that I couldn't keep my eyes off him. He looked like a man in hell.

Guy stood up for Conrad Lowe. I should like to say that I stood up for my sister. But if anyone had stood up for Abigail that day I wouldn't be sitting here now, drunk and disgraced, and Abigail's book would never have been written.

We all saw the sunset-colored bruise on her right lower jaw, under heavy orange powder, carelessly applied. Abigail was never artful with makeup, but I had the feeling that she wanted us—me—to see the bruise.

We all saw that she had lost at least ten pounds. Which wasn't much, but there was enough difference in dimension to make me uneasy. Abigail had never dieted in her life. She was an utter sensualist and took pride in all her appetites. She was foolish about many things, but never about fashion. She had lost it all, I think, around the hips, so that there was something oddly scrawny about them, though, to the objective eye, she sailed down the aisle like a great white barge and her husband, had he stepped ahead of her, would have disappeared completely from view.

We all saw that Conrad Lowe had started off his wedding day with a drink. He was steady on his feet but his coloring was high, and you could smell it, the juniper smell. His drunkenness, however controlled, introduced into the already oppressive air inside that dead church the charged atmosphere of violence, in a way that Abigail's bruise, stark evidence, did not. The violence was like Mother's ozone, instantly recognizable though encountered for the first time: a new and horrible sensation of the nose.

We all saw how happy each was, and how different in happiness. Abigail shining-eyed, foolish. Conrad Lowe glittering, triumphant.

And I think we all saw how appallingly sexless the ceremony was, the occasion. Which was maybe the worst part.

There is more erotic promise, more bawdy anticipation, in even a typical Congregational wedding (the function of which would confound a Samoan anthropologist) than there was in my sister's wedding, and the wrongness of this was deeply oppressive to me. She was desexed here, and unaware of it. The sad minister pronounced them man and wife, and Conrad Lowe kissed his bride and grabbed the flesh of her midriff and squeezed it in his long hand, on the side facing us, so that we could see what he was doing; and the chunk he held seemed unimportant, merely matter, no more significant than a fistful of batting.

The minister went with us to the "intimate reception," which was held at the Rational Tap, an old haunt of Abigail's. Conrad Lowe had insisted upon the venue.

The Rational Tap was built and named by an immigrant who made good named Manny something. It's been here, on the western fringe of Frome, since I can remember. Manny himself is long gone, taking with him whatever explanation he could have offered for his choice of name. It's pretty clear, though, that he meant something like "cheap watering hole." He just wasn't too sharp on English nuances. Until about ten years ago the Rational Tap was just a fixture of the town, a neighborhood bar, grungy and welcoming, unremarkable, familiar. I even went there once in a blue moon. Frome is a small town, with only one other tavern, the Blue Moon, an unsavory dive.

Then some clown from Brown University discovered the Rational Tap, and in no time the place was inundated with day trippers who came to tipple and giggle. The first time I caught one snapping a picture of the sign over the front door I wanted to feed the woman her Minolta. I could imagine the term "Rational Tap" working its way into students' letters home, faculty lunches. That Rhode Island had a Rational Tap would be one of the first things a Brown newcomer would learn. It was, overnight, a legend in its own time.

At first Joe Enos, Manny's nephew, who owned the bar, was understandably pleased about his burgeoning profits. But as the regulars got crowded out by the day trippers, or stopped coming in on principle, Joe, in a stunning combination of conscience, brilliance, and greed, hit on the idea of buying out the moribund Happy Hour on the other side of town, right off Route 10, which he could afford to do with his soaring business, and naming the new place the Original Rational Tap. The ploy worked.

The new bar was much more convenient for the academics, plus they went nuts over the "Original" part. Nobody From Around Here goes to the Original Rational Tap, and at night under the flashing neon, parked in orderly rows, are Japanese and German cars, every one of them legible, by which I mean decorated with messages. They all have Ivy League parking stickers and bumper stickers that say

YOU CAN'T HUG CHILDREN WITH NUCLEAR ARMS

BABY ON BOARD

REPEAL THE SECOND LAW OF THERMODYNAMICS

JOE ENOS' ORIGINAL RATIONAL TAP

The Mather-Lowe wedding party trickled into the truly original Rational Tap on a bright Saturday afternoon, when the sun was only halfway down the sky and Joe's venetian blinds could not keep it out. There is nothing more depressing to me than to be in a dark room on a sunny day, with the shades pulled against the light, and the false electric lights trying to assert themselves. I remember as a child loving to get into dark small places, like under card tables draped with blankets, and hide from the sunlight. I loved rainy days too. Children have this luxury. Children can spurn the sun.

And of course it seemed fitting that we come to this place, hiding from the all-revealing rays, etc., skulking in the gathering gloom. Considering what we were up to. Considering what we had witnessed and allowed to happen unchecked.

We were the only ones there at first, except for two teens playing Pac-Man. We sat in a corner booth and ordered a pitcher of Narragansett. Conrad Lowe fed quarters into the jukebox and made at least ten selections. We all watched him in silence. (The tunes included Sinatra, Peggy Lee, and some awful maudlin pop thing about a boy whose father always ignored him. He repeated that one twice.) Abigail's dress glowed in the murk. The minister got himself a glass of red wine at the bar and brought it over. His name was Stanley. He didn't say anything either.

Guy was probably the least uncomfortable of the lot of us. Guy is by nature a melancholic anyway, and I don't think that this depressing occasion was any sort of watershed for him. He was comfortable in his misery, you could tell. He looked as though he had been here before. His weary, tragic sighs gave me a weird kind of comfort. Looking at him I could believe, for seconds at a time, that this was an ordinary occasion, and not the beginning of the end of the world.

Guy finally spoke. "I hate ceremonies. I abominate ceremonies. Ceremonies allow us to do the cruelest, most unspeakable things. The most elaborate ceremony I ever witnessed was a Kenyan rite of female circumcision. Ceremonies make wars possible. I shall never participate in another ceremony."

"I agree with you," said Stanley.

Conrad Lowe blew smoke in his old roommate's face. "When were you ever in Kenya?"

"He saw it," said Hilda, "on channel two. I made him turn it off."

"What do you mean, you agree?" I asked Stanley. I despise namby-pamby religions. Give me a Charismatic Catholic any day. "I don't believe in anything myself, but at least I have the guts to follow through."

"Yes," said Stanley.

"You performed the ceremony yourself, for God's sake. You do this for a living."

"You're absolutely right," said Stanley.

"You guys kill me," I said. "You're so goddamn *agreeable.*"

"I know exactly what you mean," said Stanley.

"So what?" I was being unconscionably rude, but I couldn't resist the distraction argument offered. "What's the good of all your agreeing and understanding, if it doesn't inform your behavior? What good are you? What good is your church?"

"Dorcas, cut it out," said Abigail.

Stanley burst into tears, sobbing hoarsely, pinching the bridge of his nose between two fingers. Everyone looked at me. I was instantly beyond guilt and embarrassment, teleported to Golgotha, far from the sight of righteous men. I fumbled in my purse for a Kleenex and handed it to him, feeling as though I were forcing a Band-Aid on someone whose arm I had just lopped off.

"My wife is dying," Stanley said, and this is when he told us about her terminal cancer, his loss of faith (which, he avowed, had once been strong, even though he was a Unitarian); and he told us in detail about her suffering, and his, and the cruel irony of his profession, and what torture it was for him to ascend the altar, and so on. He said, "I feel like God's mortician."

This was my sister's wedding reception.

Stanley talked for what seemed like hours, and when he finally wound down, the Tap was filled with Saturday evening regulars, many of whom I knew, all of them known to Abigail. They saw our bedraggled little party, the pathetic white satin costume, the sobbing cleric, the rest of us inclined toward him with terrible impersonal solicitude, as though we were an encounter group. They took it all in and looked away and went on with their business.

That's one fine thing about Rhode Island, and most of New England, and New York, too. No, not New York. New Yorkers genuinely have no curiosity. They don't want to know. New Englanders do, but they'll be damned if they'll ask.

One time Father and Mother and Abigail and I went bass fishing on Tucker's Pond. The rowboat turned over and we all fell in. Father had to dive repeatedly to the muddy bottom to recover his tackle and car keys. When we got back to the car we were covered with mud and slime from head to foot. We had nothing with which to wipe ourselves off. Father wanted some cigarettes, so we stopped at a country market on the way home, and we all got out and sloshed in. Father squelched to the counter and asked the man for a pack of Luckies. The man handed him a pack of Luckies. Father reached into his pants pocket and pulled out a palmful of mud from which a minnow leaped, flip-flopping on the wooden floor. He had to poke through the mud for the right change. He paid the man and we left. No one ever asked what happened. They stared, but they didn't wink or smile, and they didn't ask.

Because (a) it was none of their business; and (b) they didn't want to give us the satisfaction.

And now, if we had all joined hands around the Formica table and swayed, chanting, no one would have said a word.

We tried to get Stanley to stop crying.

"Stop it," I told him. "You'll remember this tomorrow, and cringe."

"No I won't," he said, sobbing afresh. "Tomorrow will be no different from today."

"You must stop," said Hilda. "Be kind to yourself." This was the first time I had seen her show concern for anyone beside Guy, and it bothered me until I realized she was just pretending. She was really protecting Guy, who was visibly upset by Stanley and his horrible problems.

"I despise cancer," said Guy, looking angrily at his clenched white fingers.

"You must stop," said Abigail, gripping Stanley's arm, pouring beer into his wineglass.

"Why?"

"Because you're ruining my wedding day."

"I'm sorry," said Stanley, blinking, and stopped.

We ordered another pitcher. Conrad Lowe ordered a double bourbon with a dash of bitters. He was drunker than I had ever seen him. He kept staring, in an unfriendly way, at his new wife, and at Stanley, back and forth between them, as though he were adding them up over and over again. He had, of course, not said a word while the rest of us were trying to console Stanley. At last he cleared his throat and asked, "What kind of cancer?" He would.

Stanley wordlessly placed one hand over his heart and squeezed, tenderly, a delicate imaginary mass. All three of us women hunched over a little then, instinctively, and kept our hands from shielding our own breasts.

Conrad Lowe smiled. "See that? Nothing scares 'em like breast cancer." He took a long drink. "I diagnosed a number of cases myself, when I was in practice."

"I bet you did," I said.

"I might surprise you."

"I doubt that."

"Could we please talk about something else?" asked Hilda.

"Once," said Conrad Lowe, "when I was in residency, I

took a long weekend at Lake George. I was going to stay at a lodge, but there was a nudist colony close by, a real posh place with new pine cabins and a decent chef and tennis courts. Not volleyball–grass tennis courts. And young clientele. And, let's face it, naked broads. So I thought–we thought–I had an intern friend with me–we thought, what the hell.

"Well, it turned out to be pretty boring. Within a couple of hours I was used to it. This was such a predictable response that I was kind of disappointed in myself. It turns out to be true, though, what they say about clothes, and perversity.

"Anyway, I'll never forget, they threw this cocktail party on Sunday, and this well-preserved gal in her forties, real looker, great figure, ash blond hair, that colorless hair, great tan, and smart too, you could tell, well, she and some guy, I'm sure it was her husband, stood around for a while talking to me. Didn't know I was a doctor or anything. Talking about Vietnam, mostly. He was phony, but she was really upset about the whole thing, sincerely. A nice woman, beautiful, and standing there naked, with dignity. Not much power, though, now that I think of it." He flashed a grin at me. "She wasn't sucking her stomach in or anything. Not that she needed to." He flashed a grin at Abigail. "She just wore her skin, and worried about Vietnam.

"Only all the time she was talking I couldn't take my eyes off her right zoob. I mean, I *could* take my eyes off it, I made myself do it, but I had to keep sneaking glances. She had an inverted nipple. Doesn't necessarily mean anything, but . . . This one meant something. Not just the shape of the breast, but the whole picture, the nice woman, beautiful body, bad news. The whole thing fit together. A presto diagnosis."

"What did you say to her?" asked Abigail.

"Well, that's just it, isn't it? I mean, she didn't know I was a doctor. She hadn't come to me for consultation. What was I supposed to do?"

"You didn't tell her, did you?" I said. Of course he didn't.

"Did you ever see that movie *Death Takes a Holiday?* Well, I was on vacation, for Christ's sake. They never made *Death Takes a Busman's Holiday,* did they? Hell of a downer that'd be."

Stanley began to chortle. "No rest for the wicked," he said. "Busman's holiday. Hee hee hee."

"Is that how you think of yourself," I asked. "As Death?"

Conrad made a droll face at me, a *moue* they used to call it in the old Nancy Drews. "Dorcas baby, in a case like that, the messenger becomes the message. The fact is indistinguishable from the telling. You'll see. I'll see myself, someday. You're immortal until some jerk in a white coat gives you three months to live."

"You should have told her."

"Kill the messenger!" cried Stanley.

"I am become Death," Guy intoned. "Destroyer of worlds . . ." Guy often quoted J. Robert Oppenheimer quoting the Bhavagad Gita when he'd had too much to drink.

"Stop it," said Hilda, quite harshly, to Conrad Lowe. "You're upsetting him."

Abigail, who had been ruminating through all of this, put her arm around Guy and hugged him against herself. "It's okay," she said. "Everything's okay."

"We're doomed," he said.

Abigail clapped her hands on Guy's ears and wrenched him around to face her. His chin was buried in her right breast, and he had to look up at her face from the angle of a nursing infant. She handled him as easily as if he were a homemade doll with a loosely stuffed neck. This was the closest he would ever come to Abigail's actual body. "Look at me," she said to Guy, "and say that again."

"*Ooooomed,*" said Guy, but we could all see the pink creeping up the back of his neck to the base of his baby-bald skull.

"What? What was that?"

Guy made some noises with his lips and then immediately relaxed, like a lobster rubbed on its stomach, and then his head lolled against her breast and he was still. Hilda looked at Abigail with shining eyes. "How can I thank you?"

"Look, this is my wedding day, *if* you don't mind. I'm not going to listen to your husband whining about the bomb on my wedding day."

Stanley was convulsing. He gasped something that I couldn't catch. Apparently this was the first time in months he had loosened up. I think that Stanley was the only person in our party who actually profited from this horrendous occasion. "Rude," he finally got out. He cackled hysterically. "Impolite to mention . . . holocaust . . . at a reception . . ."

"Well," I said, gathering up my sweater and purse, "this has been fun."

"So soon?" asked Conrad Lowe, an ugly smile on his face.

"Come on, Stanley." I grasped the man's arm. "I'll take you back to Providence."

"Announcement!" Conrad Lowe suddenly stood, bumping the table hard with his thighs, so that everyone's beer sloshed over onto the tabletop. He spread his arms out like a revivalist. "Announcement!" he said again, in a louder voice that commanded the entire bar.

Stanley rose to his feet. I thought he was rising to join me, but he stepped in front of Conrad Lowe, literally upstaging him, and addressed the bar. "God is dead!" he said, then burst out laughing again, sagging back against the wall, spilling more beer.

He had everyone's attention all right. No one at the bar liked Stanley's announcement.

"Siddown and shuddup!"

"Have some respect!"

"And you, a priest!"

"I'm no priest," said Stanley. "I'm a Unitarian."

"That's worse!"

Conrad Lowe leaned forward and whispered something vicious into Stanley's ear. Stanley pivoted and sat, hard, as though a spring had been retracted beneath him.

"Drinks on the house for every man here," said Conrad Lowe.

There was a smattering of grudging applause.

"And doubles for every man who ever fucked my wife."

It struck me afterwards, when I reached out then and smashed him across the face with my bag, that there was a stylized, decadent quality to the act. I was already sick of it before the bag made contact. There was none of the "I can't believe this" quality that's supposed to accompany sudden violence. I didn't hit him in slow motion. I had known this moment was coming all afternoon. My sister's face crumpled, and the tears that rolled down her face seemed to have been ready and waiting to spill. Guy stirred, blinked at the scene, Hilda blushed horribly, Stanley sagged back into hopeless despair.

But the men at the bar! Stout fellows all! There must have been twenty, all ages, and I would estimate that at least fifteen had been intimate with Abigail. They all shut their mouths and regarded Conrad Lowe with identical, twenty-fold contempt, and turned, in a practiced, solemn way, away from the spectacle of our group, and back toward the bar.

. . .

Then I took Stanley with me, and I threw up in the parking lot, and we went to the Blue Moon, and then to another place off Route 10, and I threw up in front of a statue of King Philip of the Wampanoags, and somehow we ended up back at the First Unitarian Church, and Stanley punched out a stained-glass window.

Time Out

My Library

Squanto Library is a brick building the size and shape of a single-family dwelling set down on two acres of land on the Miracle Mile, otherwise known as the Massasoit Trail. Right across the street you've got your Frome Plaza, with your Star, Frome Job Lot, Bastinado's, Zeno Discount, and Tile World. To our left, facing the Plaza, are Mr. Meat and the Ottoman Empire; to our right Sippy's Pizza (the only nonfranchise holdout on the Mile) and Mr. Clam, and a little farther east, rising big as Atlantis in an asphalt sea, the mammoth Food Land, a bag-it-yourself, rip-open-your-own-carton-of-black-olives kind of place, with a produce section twice the size of the Star and thirty-foot ceilings. Everyone in Rhode Island, everyone actually From Around Here, shops at Food Land once a month, many at three in the morning. (Not a few academics shop here too, for the "interesting ethnic vegetables.")

Squanto Library sits on two acres, then, of solid gold, for which we could receive, from teeth-gnashing Italianate developers, enough money to pay for a building three times this size, not to mention quintupling our volume count. But on the board are no fewer than three Yankees, two false, one almost real, all of whom claim to remember when the Massasoit Trail was a horse pasture or some damn thing, which is horse poop because the oldest member has only ten years on me, and the Trail looked like hell in 1948. There weren't franchises then, of course, but aesthetically there's not a whole lot to choose between your Atomic Cleansers and your Mr. Clam.

But according to the Yankees the Mafia ruined the Trail. (They always call it "the Trail," in tones which encourage you to imagine, if you will, sure-footed Narragansetts, fleet Wampanoags, gliding soundlessly down the overgrown forest path with their maize and bags of wampum.) And even though they admit that the ruin is permanent, they keep us here out of spite, and every other year or so they plant another row of those goddamn ornamental cherries, just to "get" those "Italian bastards." In late spring you can't even see the library building for the rioting pink and white blossoms. Sometimes people drive in thinking we're a nursery, or a festival.

Squanto himself, the noble Indian for whom the library is named, was a wonderful man who greeted the *Mayflower* colonists in their own tongue and saved their necks that first deadly winter. He'd been abducted by an English sea captain as a boy and sold into slavery in North Africa. Somehow he'd escaped and made it to Europe, worked as a servant in a number of households and monasteries, and finally was brought back to the New World and jumped ship at Narragansett, only to find that his whole tribe had been wiped out by chicken pox.

Squanto was a visionary, a natural man who recognized the wave of the future when it broke over his head and sucked his feet out from under him. The Pilgrims may not have looked like much, and they weren't bright enough to come in out of the cold and feed themselves properly, but Squanto (*my* Squanto, my own well-imagined Indian) had seen St. Peter's Basilica, the operas of Monteverdi, the magnificent London slums. Squanto knew what these clowns could do and Squanto wanted a piece of that.

He was the best and truest friend the first settlers had, in exchange for which he got their trust, their vague promises of his ultimate acceptance into the white man's heaven, and a small fortune in protection beads from neighboring tribes of Narragansetts, who paid to keep Squanto from siccing the white men on them. Squanto was America's first racketeer.

I pointed this out once to the board, but the irony escaped all but the Irishman and the Jew. Show me a false Yankee and I'll show you a horse's patoot. I ought to know. I'm of good false Yankee stock myself.

These same idiots, who wring their hands over the Trail, can't say enough in praise of that excrescence, that monument to moral bankruptcy at the other end of town, the Wampum Factory Mall. The mall is a converted jewelry factory, which was turning out costume pieces as late as 1964, a place where half the middle-aged women in Frome worked when they were young, and fully a quarter of them lost fingertips in their rush to meet the quotas. These women do their shopping today on the Miracle Mile, but the mall salutes them with The Sweat Shoppe, The Clothes Shop, The Piece Works, The Assembly Line, and the Machiner's Local 182 Pub.

It's just as well the women can't afford to shop there, since they would hardly know what to do with designer dresses from Drop Dead, Victorian lingerie (What the Butler Saw), and Edwardian frocks (where the hell do you wear those things?). There's a vegetarian pizza stand. There are little booths that sell shoe trees, gift boxes, ascots, live goldfish in Lucite paperweights. There's a pedicure parlor called Foote Fetishe.

The mall is just the kind of thing that made Pompeians, those Italian bastards, glance up at Vesuvius occasionally at twilight with bleak longing in their lustrous oval eyes.

They were lucky. They had something to glance up at. Rhode Island has the third lowest mean altitude of the fifty states. After Florida, after Louisiana, comes our state, flattening out above sea level at a staggering two hundred feet. You could look it up in any good reference department. I certainly have.

Our only chance, then, is a tidal wave. And so, on days like today, we look to the east. We watch Narragansett Bay roil up. We pretend to be afraid. In 1954, during Carol, people drove down to the South County beaches to see the big wave come in. It came, they saw, and some of them left with it. We always assume, in polite conversation, that they were careless thrill-seekers out for a morning's free entertainment. Perhaps, like Squanto, they were noble gamblers.

We've got two rooms for fiction now, one for biography and history, one for reference and periodicals and magazines, and one for everything else, and the long corridor to the back stairwell is lined on both sides with mysteries. None of us can see into the hallway, which ends in a back door kept unlocked during business hours, because of the fire laws. Naturally, this makes mysteries the easiest books to steal. Which is a perfect setup, my idea, actually, thank you very much, since mystery aficionados are our most law-abiding patrons. Mysteries rarely disappear, and are even more rarely van-

dalized. Mystery readers are shocked by the mere idea of real-
life crime.

When I first came to work here I was young and as im-
passioned as I would ever be. This was 1964, and best-sellers
were big fat quasi-historicals about the bubonic plague or the
War of the Roses, and quasi-biblicals, about Salome and
Sodom; and generally the sort of thing that had been understood, during the previous decade, to be pompous smut, but
now seemed staid and safe. People left them out on their
coffee tables, as their cultural bona fides. For by then the pop
alternative was the smarmy exposé, which was in its heyday.
Every American institution, from the urban high school to
the bucolic New England village, was shown to be a snake
pit of perverted lust.

Of course, these books look wistfully innocent today. But
this is America in the waning days of the second millennium,
and therefore (Mather's Law) Everything Looks Good in Ret-
rospect.

In those early days, when regular patrons would come in
and demand the latest Douglas C. Harbinger or Mitchell
Lloyd Caldwell, or come to the checkout desk and present
me, in wordless, blushing defiance, with an upside-down battered copy of *Hormone County* or *High School After Dark*—when
these misguided souls, all of whom, I was convinced, were
basically decent, and parched for beauty and truth, would
hand me a pile of trash to date-stamp, I would let a sad smile
play across my features (God knows what that must have
looked like) and sigh and in general assume the worldly,
tragic air of a young priest in the confessional. And if, within
the pile of trash, or more likely on top of the pile, the person
were also checking out a classic, or some new thing praised
by the *New York Times,* I would favor him (usually her, actually) with a smile intended to be warm and congratulatory,

and murmur something awful like, "You're in for a real treat!" or "We always come back to the classics, don't we?"

People were patient with me, the way they are apt to be with young idiots. My patronizing intentions must have been apparent to all but the most obtuse. None of these kind people told me to mind my own business. It took Miss Marotte, the head librarian, to take me aside and explain to me what bad manners it was even to notice what a patron was reading. "It's one thing," she said, "to chat with them when they want you to, but you must let the patron start it. If she asks, for instance, 'Do you know if this is any good?' then you may speak. Tactfully." I said that my only response in most cases would be negative. "If you don't care for the book yourself, then tell her what you've heard about it. They're really not interested in your critical assessments, dear. What they're really after is the opinion of the book-reading community." I thought about this for a minute. I said, "That's terrible," and Miss Marotte said that it wasn't as terrible as censorship, which was what my inhibiting them amounted to. This shut me up, "censorship" being the dirtiest word in a librarian's vocabulary.

I repented, and throughout the sixties and early seventies dedicated myself to selfless service, and became familiar with the particular tastes of individual patrons, so that I could make discreet recommendations. This was easy, because most of the patrons are regulars, some coming in once a week, most every three. Even the casual patron can be categorized without too much overt information. I don't know what it is, exactly, but fiction types somehow carry themselves differently from biography people, and romance-lovers wear their hair differently, or use a heavier perfume or something. And of course severe intelligence, like severe stupidity, is unmistakable.

I actually kept written records, set down in code, of the

books my regulars checked out. In no time I could predict which new books would please them. I never put this in a threatening way: I was extremely circumspect. I would never, for instance, hold up some garish piece of garbage and announce, "This would be just perfect for *you*." I'd let the person ask me, "Would I like this?" Or I'd say, "Everyone likes this. I haven't actually read it, myself."

I was so caught up in the challenge, the game, that I was unaware of exactly what I had in those coded records until ten years ago. Of course, I knew that, technically, I shouldn't be keeping them. But I had always excused myself because my motives were pure. Which they were. I would never have shared the information with marketing companies, no matter how great the bribe, or government agents, even under torture. The privacy of my patrons' reading history was, is, sacred to me. But I wanted to do the best job I could. I looked at the records with only one perspective: how best to please my customers.

One day—this was about the time Abigail took up with Conrad Lowe—I looked down at one of my secret index cards, and this is what I saw:

```
Colosanto, Mildred, n. 1931
1966: Hw Gr M Vy, A T Grws in B, etc., hrtwrmg sprwlg
fam. saga [later abbreviated to hsfs]; affirm home
truths!/old vals
myst—AC [Agatha Christie], EQ
1967: O'Hara XXX, Christy, GmesPplPl, Human Sex
Response!!!
Myst—AC
ColdBlood? R's Baby
1972: Grp, Pplce, etc.—sens expose seamy underb Am
life
also—Bio—MQ of Scot, J Arc, Plath
myst—hb [hard-bitten]
```

And so on. In the mid seventies Mildred entered into a brief Rod McKuen period, but then it was back to the downward spiral of smut, dysphemism, and despair about the future of American life. So much for home truths and old vals! Once, in 1975, she checked out a pleasant memoir about Yorkshire veterinary life, but this was just a blip. Something had happened to our Mildred, and it wasn't pretty.

It turns out that my index cards are real time-capsule material, concise historical records of a peculiar sort, outlining the spiritual and intellectual course of a citizen's adult life. If a sociologist got ahold of them, of course over my dead body, he could probably eke out some sort of trend, even a town portrait. It is possible, for instance, to scan these three-by-fives and learn who's being seduced by L. Ron Hubbard, who's given up astrology for God, who's given up on traditional storytelling altogether. This one had a pregnancy scare in 1969. This one's developing into a serious hypochondriac. This one's about to cheat on her husband, who is reading everything he can get his hands on on the subject of bass fishing.

I don't know what to do with this stuff. Have it burned up along with me, when the time comes, I guess. Anyway, I won't feed it into the computer. I'm sticking with the home truths and the old vals.

We have two classes of vandal at Squanto: the building defacer and the book defacer.

The building defacers are children, who, if they get past me, have a good chance to grow up to be responsible adults. People who write on walls are simply naughty, and though I would happily punish them, I bear them no real ill will.

Pork The Dork

In a way they belong here. They are writers. The walls are their pages, chalk and marker their instruments.

Free Abigail

They turn my library into a large brick book. Their writing is not much more ephemeral than the published stuff. How well do you remember that, say, six-year-old six-hundred-pager the *Times* assured you was destined to become a classic? You know. The "monumental work of fiction" that you were supposed to run, not walk, to the nearest bookstore to purchase, the book that was going to change your life, that you must read this year if you read nothing else . . . Winner of the National Book Award. You remember. *Handleman's Jest. Parameters & Palimpsests. The Holocaust Imbroglio.* We sell these babies for fifty cents apiece, or try to, seven years after they come out. We sell them because no one has checked them out for four years.

David Nunes is a ASS wipe
I Love [Illegible]
One Nuclear war Could Ruin you're whole Day
So Couldn't My Dick

They write knowing it won't last, knowing they can count on me, as on nothing else in this fickle world, to come around in a day or two with my Janitor in a Drum and my sponge, and scrub their pages clean.

> **Sanctify Devils**
> **David Nunes is Full of Shit**
> **Eat Me**
> **That's Not Nice Denise**
> **David Nunes & S. P.**

They write on all the outside walls and on the walls of the single toilet in the basement.

> **Read Pippi Longstocking**
> **yea isn't it Neat?**
> **Read Pee-Pee Longstocking Gets Aids**
> **That's Not Nice Denise**

We here in Frome, R.I., are right on the cutting edge of the new illiteracy. So that when I see a grammatically irreproachable sentence without misspellings

> **Have a Nice Day until Some Idiot**
> **Screws It up**

I am absurdly heartened, and want to glue gold stars beside the passage. And then the opposite happens

Niğer Go Home

and I want to correct the spelling or the syntax and then erase it and wash the kid's face in the dirty water

Free The Dork

and make him drink his words.

The other class of vandal is the book defacer. These people are serious menaces, and these I would kill. They are almost always adults. I know who some of them are. Because of my index cards.

I didn't have to be Sherlock Holmes to figure out that Old Lady Whistler, or Old Man Whistler, two false Yankees, pretenders to the Miles Minden class, was deleting the words *Jew* and *Jewish* and *Judaism* and *Judaic* from every book they checked out, bearing down so hard with a soft, blunt pencil that each shiny perfect rectangle stood out in relief on the backside of the page, and a thick sheaf of pages beneath it was indented. In a couple of places so much pressure was applied that the pencil went through the page, and these holes were painstakingly repaired with tiny squares of Scotch tape. This conscientious detail never fails to give me the willies. These are *law-abiding people*.

They stopped after I confronted them. It was a classic

WASP brouhaha. Mrs. Whistler returned the book, a Bellow, and I quickly thumbed through it before she had a chance to move away. "Look at that," I said, showing her a black mark, inviting her to share my consternation, which she did. "Yes," she said, "imagine. I was just sick when I saw it." I told her to be sure to let me know if she ever came across any more of those, and she promised me she would, and that was the end of it. We never made eye contact, and it was perfectly clear to her that I knew who was responsible. We still exchange pleasantries when she comes in, and shake our heads over the declining American attention span, the entropic regress of the best-seller.

I still come across the Whistlers' old dirty work from time to time. It takes me, on average, fifteen minutes to erase each mark, for I must bear down very carefully on the outraged, distended paper, and the carbon is so thickly applied that I must remove it in layers, using the eraser tip like a sponge, scrubbing it clean. And even then the word, *Jew, Jewish, Judaic,* is faint and blotched and suspect, pariah, like any cripple in a healthy crowd.

This is a whole subclass of book vandals, the Deleters, and they are to me the most horrific. Often they delete the sex words, often neatly, with razor blades. Sometimes they razor out whole pages, whole chapters—page whatever-it-was of *The Group*; half of *Myra Breckinridge*. Sometimes they grind a smaller axe, and so we get the single-book offender. Someone went through a biography of John Barrymore and obliterated all reference to his first wife. Someone took out every reference to John and Robert Kennedy in a book on Marilyn Monroe. (And every reference to Monroe in a recent study of the Kennedys. I think of him—surely it's a male—as The Keeper of the Flame.)

There is even a sub-subclass of Deleters, the picture thieves. Instead of stealing the whole book (which would not be quite as objectionable) they steal their favorite section, which is always, given their intellectual capacities, nonverbal. They delete not to censor but to appropriate, and so they are not, in my view, quite as contemptible as the rest. These people I would merely draw and quarter. Coffee-table books, especially books about the movies, are vulnerable to their depredations; and we have been unable to keep intact a single picture book about Princess Di.

And in the far corner, we have the Expanders, the margin-writers. Some write for posterity, some, apparently, just as a mnemonic device. The latter use my books as their own notebooks, producing incidental poetry, so that we get, in an overview of Keynesian economics, at the end of a difficult chapter, in the pure white lower half of the page, in green ink:

Germans Export Steak

French Export Knockwurst

French Produce More Knockwurst

Germans Produce More Steak

I like this one. It's like a hornpipe for silverfish. I hear fiddles and clapping hands, the rowdy laughter of pirates' molls.

And in a collection of Flannery O'Connor stories, evidently borrowed for a high school course, we get

Can You Really Blame Mother For Society Taboo's?

Q Can People Live Together
A No
If your Not a Religious Phanatic Forget It

These people are solipsists, not communicators.

Other expanders imagine themselves wise, or cute, or both. They underline or circle passages which they find egregious, and give us a big exclamation mark in the margin, or

But See p. 96. Quel Airhead!

And among their number is Moriarty, who has been operating since 1979, whose MO never changes, whom I pursue through shelves and files and secret codes. His judgment is impeccable, his style ruthless and minimalist. With a blue ballpoint pen he prints just one word, in small lowercase, each letter formed around an imaginary O, as plump as a pumpkin. The word is always

wrong

He writes it on the title page.

I'm OK, You're OK **wrong**
Are You Running with Me, Jesus? **wrong**
Death Shall Have No Dominion **wrong**

He writes it under photograph captions.

Here's Bunny looking wise beyond his years **wrong**
Mums, Dada, Bampa and my beloved Pookie **wrong**

He writes it to single out passages in books he apparently otherwise tolerates.

For the first hour Leila read as the half-empty train racketed **wrong**

Racism isn't a black problem. It's a white problem.
wrong

You can say what you like about him, but Steinbrenner is a business genius **wrong**

He gives the raspberry to gothic novelists, children's how-to books, sociological studies, books on psychology and the history of music. He almost never defaces a classic, but then we don't have many of them, due to our four-year discard rule. And he lays off the reference section, though clearly the encyclopedias must afford him ample opportunity for comment. I picture him as a borderline-deranged bibliophile, a bibliomaniac, a man or woman of refined taste and insatiable outrage, pushed over the edge by the general mediocrity. He doesn't enjoy doing what he does; it gets harder and harder for him. And he's not an exhibitionist either, except, perhaps, when he writes in best-sellers. I picture him as a Bartleby type and his study, where he pores over my books with burning

eyes, looking for mendacity, moral ignorance, further proof
of cultural rot, as a kind of dead letter office, where he must
labor against his will. I don't think he imagines that anyone
reads his work.

But I do. I read, remember, think. Argue points with him.
I don't always agree—he is a harsher critic than I, and a social-
ist, which makes him vulnerable, fallible. Not his particular
choice of political belief, but the espousal of any orthodoxy.
He's a feminist too, and a bit predictable on that score. I don't
know where he finds the energy to take on the bodice-rippers
and the hard-boiled PIs. Surely there's no pleasure in it. I picture him as middle-aged. He still pays dues to the ACLU but
he does not read their newsletter anymore. He does not read
for pleasure, or for information. Reading has become a painful chore for him, and most of what he reads is

wrong

At the beginning when I came upon a Moriarty-defaced
book, I would refer to my files on that book, and match that
list up with other lists, of other books he had touched, looking, of course, for a common denominator. This was brute
work, involving hundreds of names, the sort of thing that
constitutes modern metropolitan police procedure. And in
the end it proved mostly unhelpful, for often he would write
in a brand-new book that had not even been checked out
once. Obviously he did some of his work here, or pilfered
the book and then returned it, and so his name wasn't noted
anywhere. That is, I knew his name must appear on the lists,
too, but this fact, the fact of pilferage, threw everything into
doubt.

Now we have a computer. This changes the odds. I'll bet

I could discover him now in one afternoon. This afternoon.
What used to take me hours and cause my vision to blur,
and in the end be so unreliable and confusing that I couldn't
profit from it, would take seconds on the machine. Sooner or
later there would be one common denominator, and I would
have him.

Then what?

He is my henchman, really. He does my dirty work for
me and absolves me of the moral responsibility. I don't tell
him to do these things. I can't be held accountable. He is my
thug. I worry about his health. What will I do when he is
gone?

And what will he do with *this* book? I will place it lovingly
on the New Book shelves, like a plate of cookies on the
Christmas hearth. I will tremble for his opinion.

In the Driver's Seat **wrong**

For Dorcas who knows and won't tell **wrong**

Up the Flagpole

Chapter 14

A Marriage Made in Hell

Imagine this: A honeymoon hotel by the New England sea. Feather mattress four-poster, milk glass globe lamp hand-painted with lavender thistle. Dormer window with lace curtains, overlooking a rocky beach. Deep brick fireplace generously supplied with sugar maple logs. Ten days here, in this peaceful place, with nothing to do but talk, sleep, walk in the sand, make love in front of a blazing fire.

Now, imagine:

Four handcuffs, attached to the four spiral-cut cherrywood bedposts . . .

Three brand-new dresses hanging in a small mahogany armoire, a bridal trousseau, crisp and clean and never worn . . .

One antique porcelain chamber pot, furnished purely for decoration, for ambiance, now reekingly functional, filled almost to overflowing, standing beneath the unkempt bed . . .

. . . **a**nd a par-*tri*-hidge in a pear tree.

What Hilda is telling us, with reekingly functional coyness, is that he took her to Block Island, chained her to the bed, and starved her for a week.

Here, in the middle of the book, are the Doomed Couple photographs. Snapshots of both must have been taken by strangers. Abigail, unchained, on the Block Island ferry. Conrad and Abigail, uncuffed, on the veranda of the Seawitch Boarding House. Conrad in his ratty tweed jacket, chinos, and dirty U.S. Keds, looking annoyed on a pebbly beach, the sunlight glinting off his tooth. Still life: a hideous red, white, and blue afghan, somehow constructed of interconnected wagon-wheel shapes, arranged like a dropped mink on the canopied hotel bed.

She tried to fob the afghan off on me. She showed up at the house the day after they got back from their honeymoon. She looked so frail I assumed she'd been down with the flu, and she didn't disabuse me. "Sick as a dog the entire week," she said. "So I made this. You want it?" She extracted the afghan from a brown paper Food Land bag. We stared at it together.

"You *made* this?" Abigail had never made anything on purpose in her life. The blanket, though ghastly, had been constructed according to some plan, with orderly repeating patterns. "For *me?*"

Abigail slumped into her old La-Z-Boy. She seemed depressed. "If you don't want it I'll give it to Anna."

"You've lost more weight." She must have lost twenty pounds at least since taking up with Conrad. She was starting to look deflated and old, and anything but healthy. I thought of cancer. Conrad the busman-on-holiday had somehow given it to her. "When was your last checkup?"

"Just before the wedding." Abigail looked down at her thighs. "I'm perfectly all right. I'm just on a diet."

"When did hell freeze over? Hey, look at me."

"Doctor's orders, as a matter of fact." Abigail gave me a glancing, unfocused look when she said this. She didn't expect to be believed.

"Since when do you take orders from the Stooge?" Our doctor was Fred Dick, Frome's only ob-gyn, younger than us by fifteen years. He was a born-again Christian, outspokenly opposed to nonmarital sex and abortion, which effectively relegated him to backwater town practice. Abigail loved to scandalize him with her various exotic infections and fungi. He was a small man with delicate, fine-boned hands. He had a cowlick. Abigail called him Dockery Dick, the Stooge for Christ. Once he suggested that she'd do better to spend her nights with a good husband. "I'd settle," she said, "for just one night without this terrible itching."

"You know damn well who wants me to lose weight." Her defiance was pointless. This was me she was talking to. "Anyway, it *is* healthier to be thin."

"I've never in our life been any healthier than you." I hated the way she looked at me, pleading, tired, begging me to drop the whole thing and accept what was happening to her. Where was her pride? Where was my twin, the Warrior Bawd? She was dying away, and against all reason I feared she would take me with her.

For the first time, and not the last, I thought of her old conquests with nostalgia. What she had done to Big Bob Flynn was wrong, but not evil. Conrad Lowe was killing her. She was helping him.

Abigail tried for an airy smile. "You've got to admit I'm looking pretty good these days."

"You look like an old balloon," I said.

"Fuck you."

"I'm sorry." I was.

"You certainly are!" she said, her voice breaking, and she

was out the door before I could stand. "You're a sorry excuse
for a woman. You'll never understand me, and it's your loss,
you, you dried-up old sonofabitch," she said, and slammed
the heavy door so it bounced.

In a blind rage I ran out onto the lawn after her with the
afghan in my hand. I was going to stuff it down her pants or
strangle her with it or wrap it around and around her body
and jump up and down on it but she drove off and left me
standing there waving the stupid thing like a flag, which it
somewhat resembled.

John Bucci, soaping his station wagon, waved and yelled
something about giving me a hand and running it up a pole.
I think I had a tiny psychotic break right then, a mad moment
in which good neighbor John Bucci cheerily shouted lewd
gibberish at me while the sun shone and Mrs. Ouimette
passed between us walking her old Doberman. I fairly ran
inside, still clutching the afghan flag, and shut myself away
for the rest of the day.

It was that name she called me, *sonofabitch,* and of course it
was the sexual insult, the awful power of it, coming from her,
but I didn't admit that for weeks. All I could see at the time
was a great slur upon our mother. How Baroque is the sub-
conscious. Mine, anyway.

The Great Swamp Fight

Chapter 15

Intervention

The patient reader must bear in mind that none of us realized what Conrad had done to Abby on Block Island. She may have been slightly thinner when they came back, but none of us remarked on it at the time. Guy and I thought she looked her splendid, *zaftig* self. So when Conrad approached us, alone, soon after their return, to enlist our aid, we were credulous, indeed eager to do as he asked, convinced as we were of the sincerity of his concern.

Had we but known! *Of all sad words of tongue or pen, the saddest are these . . .*

"YOU'RE DANGEROUSLY OVERWEIGHT."

What Conrad enlisted the DeVilbisses' aid in doing was an early form of what was just then coming to be legitimized, in psychopop circles, as an "intervention": luring an unsuspecting citizen into the company of those very humans he has every right to trust in order to confront him with his most obvious frailties. Those who consider this kind of thing acceptable are able, somehow, to distinguish it in their own

minds from "sandbagging," "ambushing," and "being unfor-
givably rude," and it's gotten so popular even in the exurbs
that the prudent alcoholic avoids friendly gatherings of more
than two, and even then leaves his motor running.

I wasn't prepared for Abigail's Intervention, and this was
no accident. Guy and Hilda knew better than to attempt to enlist my services for their little surprise party. In fact they knew
better than to do such a stupid thing in the first place. But they
did. They allowed Conrad to convince them that he was

WORRIED ABOUT HER HEALTH.

So it was that on a clambake-steamy August morning the
Friends of Abigail and Conrad massed like blackbirds at the
entrance to the Great Swamp Nature Trail in West Kingston.

Anna and I had come bird-watching here countless times:
it was for me, until this particular Sunday, a place of great
peace and beauty. Here is where I taught four-year-old Anna
how to talk to chickadees, and get them to talk back to you.
Here we saw our first osprey. Here she tasted her first wild
strawberry. Abigail never came along with us, as the walk,
though not arduous, is over five miles long, and Abigail always hated what she called pointless exercise. In order for
anything natural to acquire a "point" for Abigail it has to be
flashy and vulgar: Niagara Falls. The Grand Canyon.

Abigail was as surprised as I, then, when, after I mentioned the trail at a recent DeVilbiss gathering, Conrad, Guy,
and Hilda, as one, suddenly voiced an irresistible urge to go
there. I should have smelled a rat, especially when Guy, who
had spent his whole life insulated from firsthand experience,
insisted that he pay his respects to the noble Massasoits, at
the spot where they made their last stand against the impe-

rialist English colonists. I should have smelled the Giant Rat of Sumatra, but I was too eager to set him straight—it was the *Narragansetts,* you dolt, Massasoit was a *Wampanoag* chieftain—and, I must confess, all too eager to show off the swamp itself. Instead of sniffing the strange air while the rest twittered about picnic baskets and insect repellent and who was going to drive, I was already planning our route, and wondering if there were enough binoculars to go around.

So I went for a walk, and on that walk I brought an Audubon bird guide, my Bushnells, a small flask of Courvoisier, a duck call. . . . Not a duck call, actually, but an ingenious device that makes squeaky chittering sounds which fool an odd variety of songbirds into briefly coming out of hiding, searching for baby birds in trouble, before they get a grip on themselves and remember that their own babies are grown and flown. I also brought Anna, and Tim Paine, sans dolorous wife, and Tansy Wasserman, a recent addition to the DeVilbiss group. Abigail and Conrad came with the De-Vilbisses.

We must have looked a bizarre gaggle, as we milled around the gateway to the trail, divvying up provisions. This was before backpacks were popular, and we contended with straw baskets and shopping bags from the Outlet Company. Only three of us looked anything like nature-lovers: Anna and I, of course, and the dreaded Tansy, an old nature-girl, a wrinkled Ophelia who, in addition to penning whale sonnets, grows her own dyes, colors her own homespun wool, and weaves it into what Perelman called, in 1930, "horrid super-dirndls with home-cooked hems." Apparently the type existed way before the sixties, as did Tansy herself, as well as Perelman's Mibs ("usually engaged in reading a book written by two unfrocked chemists which tells women how to make their own cold cream by mixing a little potash with a dram of glycerine and a few cloves").

Guy looked paler than ever against the glorious backdrop of the dog-days swamp. He was wearing something like lederhosen, only knee-length and made of shiny corduroy, some weird European outdoor garment. He looked like an old Hitler youth who'd fallen asleep under a rock in 1942. Rip von Ribbentrop. Hilda, swathed in something like a burlap caftan, slathered Guy's exposed whiteness with Off. I don't remember what Conrad wore, but he looked jaunty and cool, especially compared to Abigail, who emerged from the DeVilbisses' Karmann Ghia as from a Turkish bath, complaining bitterly about the group's choice of venue. Conrad, parceling out the burdens, stuck her with shopping bags full of potato salad and condiments.

"Hey," she said, "these weigh a ton."

"Exactly," he said. "That's why I gave them to you. Would you rather carry the watermelon?"

My sister hung her head like a shamed child, and, as if a bell had tolled, off we started. Anna and I, lightly burdened with bread and deviled eggs, forged ahead, locating, in record time, an American redstart, a scarlet tanager, and a pair of goldfinches. The tanager was particularly exciting; they're common enough, but so shy that despite their brilliant plumage you hardly ever spot them. We announced each find to the group, but they were already preoccupied with their burgeoning discomfort and, no doubt, the mechanics of the impending "intervention." At this time of year mosquitoes hovered in the shade and deer flies in the sunlight. The flies were worse: their stings hurt, and they were spectacularly impervious to Off. Neither flies nor mosquitoes have ever bothered me, nor Anna. Abigail suffered mightily, unable to swat them away, shackled, as she was, by potato salad.

The Great Swamp is nothing like the better known swamps of the southern U.S. The trail is dry, flanked by bogs and stands of dead maple and occasional flashes of living holly. Alligators and water moccasins could never survive here. You have to walk for an hour before you reach real water. The heart of the swamp is a largish stand, more pond than swamp, perhaps three feet deep, ringed by a dike. A footbridge bisects it, running directly beneath a march of power lines, and at the top of the poles are osprey nests, to which the great birds return every year.

By the time we neared the water everyone but us was out of sorts. Anna and I had stayed far enough ahead so that their complaints did not interfere with our pleasure, but all along we could hear Abigail swearing, and Conrad needling her, and Hilda soothing her miserable husband, whose close encounter with nature was proving intolerable. I don't think he had ever been bitten before. Certainly not by Hilda. Tim and Tansy kept up with us for a while and made an effort to enthuse, but then Tansy, spotting a small field of her wild-flower namesakes, stupidly waded in for a harvest—tansies are apparently great dye plants—and emerged covered with ticks. Most ticks fall off by themselves, and the ones that remain are easily tweezed, and they were just deer ticks, for God's sake, but Tansy got hysterical and reenacted the leech scene from *The African Queen,* with poor agreeable Tim playing Katharine Hepburn, pinching the little nippers off Tansy's quivering midsection, a sight so depressing that Anna and I tiptoed off and returned to the birds.

Anna. By my reckoning she was fourteen years old then, as this must have been 1976, the year after the wedding. The bicentennial year! Yes, and we had gone, just the two of us, to the big bash on the Charles River, Fiedler's Last Stand, and the most gorgeous fireworks display I have ever seen. I don't remember why Abigail didn't go. It would have been her sort of thing.

Anna is our child, Abigail's and mine. We have always shared custody, and Anna, who looks like neither of us, has never, to my knowledge, suffered as a result. The three of us lived together until Conrad, upon whose arrival Anna chose to stay with me, with no hard feelings on anyone's part. I had never discussed Conrad with Anna. I had no idea what she thought of him.

Between us, Abigail and me, we have been a good mother. Abigail nursed and diapered, I manned the cloth books and refrigerator magnets, and we were both there to hold her, though almost from the beginning she was a cool and independent child, not a cuddler. She walked early and talked late, waiting, I think, until her vocabulary was sufficient to her needs. Even before she walked she would make me carry her around the house and yard, pointing at various objects and inquiring, with respect to each, "Iss ta?" And I would name the object, which was clearly her aim, and I would only have to say it once. *Mantel. Dahlia. Ottoman. Snapshot. Dictionary.* Afterward I could refer to any of these objects in conversation, and she would know what I meant. She was wonderfully bright and sunny.

She took us both in, Abigail and me, her eyes sharp and amused. She listened to us quarreling, and sometimes, when one of us got in a particularly good dig, she would clap hands with delight. "The kid gives me the creeps," Abigail said more than once. Which sounds harsh, but isn't. Abigail was a serene and careless mother, and she needed me to complete her, to be the prudent worrier, but with her child, as with all her men except one, she was free of sentimentality and generous with her love, and did not require reciprocity. I suppose if Anna had hated her it would have stung; but Anna liked her mother, likes her still, likes us both. We called her "I Spy with my Little Eye," and then just "The Spy."

Abigail took the post office job when Anna was three, and

from then on I took Anna with me to the library every week-day. She grew up in the library, and not just in the children's section. Her favorite spot, when she was little, was behind the check-in desk. She would position herself beside the re-turn slot and goggle at the fall of books. She seemed interested at first in the haphazard mess they made, but soon she was stacking them neatly. By the time she was four she was al-phabetizing them, and at six she had a basic understanding of the Dewey decimal system, and kept the F's separate from the B's, and all the numbers in perfect order. She even un-derstood the Mc/Mac principle. Of course she was an early, voracious reader.

I was intoxicated, in Anna's early years, by the belief that somehow she had taken after me. The belief was silly—how could she "take after" her aunt?—and the intoxication sillier still. So what if she did? She was, and is, her own creature. Then, when she hit high school, her body, which had always been slim like mine, began to take on more opulent curves, and boys started coming around, and I thought that somehow she was both of us, Abigail and I, made sensibly whole. Re-ally, I was quite romantic about Anna.

Abigail never was. "There was," she would remind me, cruelly, "another family involved, you know. She looks more like the Essers than like any of us. She's got the German coloring, the cleft chin. She's going to be tall, like Ev." I wouldn't even consider this possibility until, three years ago, Anna came back home for Thanksgiving break, her freshman year at Middlebury, and there she was at the front door, Everett Esser's daughter, of course. But still ours, our girl.

And on this day she was fourteen, and still, in my foolish eyes, my heir and soul mate. Until we reached the Great Swamp's heart, and allowed the rest to catch up with us, we enjoyed ourselves immensely. I still have the bird list from that day. We spotted fifty-six separate species, our prize the gorgeous pileated woodpecker, a discreet red-crested creature the size of a hawk. We heard him first, of course, rattling on a dead sugar maple like the crack of doom, and then Anna spotted him, and, holding her breath, pointed him out to me. And just as I got him square in my sights, Conrad Lowe burst through the bushes behind us, vanishing the marvelous bird as though at the flick of a wand. What a terrible man.

"What the hell was that?" he asked. "Some kind of mutant crow?"

"*Dryocopus pileatus,*" I said. "The pileated woodpecker, or logcock. I only saw one before in my life, and that was thirty years ago. I'll never see another. And if you hadn't come crashing through the underbrush like that—"

"Hey, everybody," Conrad yelled over his shoulder, "Dorcas just spotted a postulated wallbanger!"

Anna giggled. I couldn't blame her. He *was* funny; this was one of his worst traits.

"Or 'logcock,' " he repeated, waggling his eyebrows at me. "I'll have to tell the little woman."

"How much farther?" whined Guy, at the head of the sweaty, deeply unhappy pack of stragglers.

They were all petulant, except for Conrad; martyred, as though I had forced them to do something onerous. For God's sake, this hadn't been my idea. "Stop where you are," I said, to all of them. "Just turn around and go back. Leave one car for Anna and me. Throw away your goddamn potato salad. Beat it." They didn't deserve to be here.

Abigail set down her load and flexed both hands. From ten yards away I could see cruel shopping-bag grooves worn across each palm. She waved at Conrad, that tentative, hopeful wave she used with him, like a shy child who has no real hope of being noticed. She wasn't. "Yoo hoo!" she called, blushing. Still he ignored her, ducking by Anna and taking the lead away from us. "Honey!"

Abigail never used his name. Conrad was, in reference, *He, Him,* in address, *You,* in supplication, *Honey.* Use of his actual given name was to her an affront to their great intimacy. I never used his name either. Using it was like summoning him up, acknowledging his importance, an affront to our great enmity. He was to me, in reference, *he, him, it,* in address, *excuse me, I beg your pardon, hey you, look you. See here.* (I use his name now that he's dead, joyfully, waving it about like a war trophy, a severed ear.) "Hey!" I cried, and then, lunging forward, grabbed the back of his shirt. It was white, I remember it now, a frayed Oxford cloth shirt with buttoned-down collar, the sleeves rolled up. I grabbed it and it pulled loose of his pants. Chinos. "Hey, you!" He looked around at me, raising his eyebrows. "Your *wife,*" I said.

"Yes?" He tucked in his shirttail with exaggerated languor.

"Are you deaf? You're not deaf. Pay attention to her."

Abigail caught up with us. "Race ya," she said softly, smiling up at him, trying so very hard. My sister never lost her pride, not really. That was one of the awfulest things. He never broke her. She bent and bent and bent.

"How much farther to the famous dike?" he inquired, of me, of course.

"Not to the dike," said Abigail. "Back to the lot. Seriously, honey, I've had it. Guy's covered with welts. Wasserman's having a nervous breakdown. Even Tim isn't happy." She tugged on his wrist. "Come on."

"We're almost there, right?" Still to me.

"Your wife," I said, "would like to go home, and so would everybody else, except us."

"How about it?" He addressed everybody but me, and Abigail. "Are we giving up?"

Guy, who looked like a lacquered chicken pox victim—

Hilda had gone insane with Off—stood gazing at Conrad with what had to be simple hatred, suffering having burned away his pretensions, and said nothing, and Hilda opened her mouth, clearly about to say, "Of course we're giving up, I've got to get him home, he's in agony," and then closed it again.

"Hell, no," said Tim, without conviction, and a muted grumble of assent arose from the rest, even the DeVilbisses.

"He's right," said Anna. "We're almost there. Look!" She pointed up and over the trees to the south, where an osprey appeared, briefly, and glided out of sight. She ran ahead of Conrad, followed by everybody else, leaving Abigail and me standing dumbstruck with astonishment and chagrin.

"What the *hell*?!?" we said.

I picked up one of the shopping bags, and, together, we brought up the rear.

Anna and I walked across the footbridge to the far side of the swamp, where Conrad had suggested we have our picnic. Everyone else took the long way, the dike path, rather than chance the bridge, which, while not rickety, consisted only of two-by-ten boards laid across the water on simple posts, with a single thick wire railing. It isn't the least bit dangerous—even if you fall off, the water is only up to your hips—but they seemed determined not to risk even the slightest chance of enjoying the occasion.

There were three pairs of ospreys nesting in the poles above the bridge, and we stopped and studied all three nests, and listened to the warning cries of the males, out hunting for baby food, but not letting us out of their sight for a moment. The male osprey is much smaller than his mate. Their cries are heartbreaking, like the cries of hawks and eagles, lonely and hopeful. And like the other large predators, they do not flock together. *Luckily for us.*

We stopped and stood, wordless, and waited out a changing of the guard, the male returning to nestle, the female soaring out to hunt. We stopped long enough for the day's mischief to get underway. Anna glanced across the water. "Uh-oh," she said. "Something's up."

From our perspective the group was smaller than the osprey nest, but we could clearly see that they had formed a circle, with the largest of their number captive at its center, like children playing Little Sally Saucer. I saw a large group of domestic ducks do this once, by Johnson's Pond when Anna was little, and then another duck came into the circle, grabbed the duck that was It by the back of the neck, and proceeded, apparently, to strangle it. Anna screamed and I ran into the quacking circle, stomping and yelling "Stop it! Stop it!" And only when I got up close to the grappling pair did I realize they were mating. Wild ducks, I explained to Anna (Abigail laughing uproariously all the while), do not behave like this. Although prenuptial rituals can be quite lovely, the act itself is never gorgeous, at least not with the higher orders—Cecropia moths being another story—but the ugliness of those white ducks had, I was sure, something to do with their domestication, their centuries of familiarity with *us*.

We hurried toward the ominous circle of humans. I think now of Frank Calef and the night of the ice circle, and I wonder if even on this humiliating day she didn't, at some level, enjoy all the attention. She certainly didn't act as though she did. When we got close enough to hear snatches of conversation Abigail was cursing out Tansy Wasserman, repeatedly calling her a name that sounded weirdly like "prune-eater." "You prune-eater!" she cried, sticking her face right in Tansy's. "You ugly silly dried-up prune-eater!" This was, in fact, what she was saying. Even more strangely, Tansy, having made peace with her ticks, was not taking umbrage, was instead stroking my sister's shoulder and nodding in rhythm with Abigail's imprecations, as though in utter accord.

Across the circle from Tansy, behind Abigail's back, the DeVilbisses quivered, white with terror, having more sense than Tansy Wasserman, but still they stood fast, even as Abigail whirled to attack. "*Fuck* your concern. *Fuck* your friendship. *Fuck you!*"

"What's going on?" I asked. No one heard me.

"It's no use," said Conrad Lowe.

"We will care for you," said Tansy, "no matter what you say, no matter what you do."

Tim Paine stared at Tansy and said nothing. He seemed to be wondering how he got involved in the whole mess. He's the real thing, I think, a genuine alcoholic.

"Just hear us out," ventured Guy.

"I've heard enough," said Abigail, "you pompous asshole."

Hilda waved me over. "It's an intervention," she whispered, and when I failed to respond to her news flash, "We're confronting Abigail."

"With what?"

"Her, um, body."

Abigail was crying with rage. I gave up on Hilda and demanded a coherent explanation from her husband.

"Her weight, Dorcas," Guy said, his mouth even prissier than usual. "We're all worried about her heart. I'm sure you are too."

I stepped into the circle and stood by my sister's shaking body. I still didn't understand. Of course I tried at first to take their meaning literally, but rejected out of hand the possibility that any civilized group, even this one, was capable of such behavior. The only thing I could figure was that everyone was uncomfortable and out of sorts and spontaneously took it out on Abigail. "You are all," I said, "acting like children. Go home. There"—I pointed at the westward path—"is the way back to the lot. Take it. You don't belong here."

Tim raised his hand. "It wasn't our idea, Dorcas. It was Conrad's idea."

I could readily believe this, even without knowing what he was talking about, the atmosphere being so foul, my lovely day in shambles.

"Shut up, Tim," said Conrad.

"And what idea," I asked him, "was that?"

Tim paused. "Diabetes?"

"What?"

"Heart trouble," said Tansy.

Guy cleared his throat. "Not to mention circulatory difficulties."

"Your sister is at risk." Conrad regarded me mildly, as though we were chatting about the weather. "And I don't want to lose her. I've tried gentle persuasion, but it hasn't worked."

Your sister is at risk. This, from him, was as obviously true as the rest of his speech, whatever it was about, was obviously false. I turned to look at Abigail, and she was staring at him, her face pale and wet. She was suffering, betrayed, and her look of naked hurt blocked out the rest of us. She was alone with him, trying to understand what he wanted from her. And what he wanted, I saw then for the first time, was to destroy her utterly. She was indeed at risk.

"Jeez," said Tim, "I didn't know it was going to be this bad."

"It *seems* cruel," said Hilda, "because—"

"—because it *is*," said Tim. "We don't have any right to do this."

"We have," said Tansy, "the *duty* to do it."

"Because we love her," said Hilda.

"Well, I hope nobody ever loves me that much," Anna muttered. She seemed to understand the scene.

I was still confused. Clearly they'd all been doing something bad to Abigail—if it was Conrad's idea, it had to be bad—and yet the only thing I could imagine "confronting" her with was the awfulness of her married state. Anna stepped into the circle and attempted to comfort her mother, who paid her no attention. Abigail had stopped crying, and color was coming back to her face, but she didn't take her eyes from Conrad.

Conrad stared back, the two of them perfectly intimate, the rest of us not there. "I told you," he said. "We had a deal."

"Have," said Abigail.

"Had. I found your little stash."

Abigail caught her breath, blinked, rallied. "I don't know what you're talking about," she said.

"That makes two of us," I said. "Stash?"

"You had enough stowed away to gag Judy fucking Garland."

Abigail raised her head and attempted an imperious tone. "I see. Well, for your information, that 'little stash' was for Halloween."

Now I was truly confounded, for it seemed, from the few clues I was allowed, that my sister was supposed to be some sort of dope fiend. This made absolutely no sense. Abigail could drink any man—any woman, except me—under the table, and we were both too old for marijuana.

"Planning ahead, were you? For the kiddies?"

"Abigail! What is he talking about?" Were they selling dope to children?

"Believe what you want to. And I'll thank you to stay out of my underwear drawer. I don't fumble around in your—"

"Gotcha!" Conrad grinned evilly.

"Will someone please answer me."

"I never went near your underwear drawer, sweetmeat. I wouldn't be likely to, would I, unless I were going into the parachute business."

Abigail swore, vilely, and stamped her foot, and hung her great wretched head.

Conrad now addressed me, with his usual gross intimacy. "Stashed behind the bathroom bowl," he whispered. "Like *The Godfather*."

I gaped at the man, who had obviously gone insane, along with everyone else, me included. I don't know what upset me more, my sister at bay or myself ignored. Which is more humiliating? To twist in a baleful spotlight? To flail and wail, invisible? In despair I turned to Anna. "Please tell me what this means," I said.

But even Anna ignored me. She stepped in front of her mother and stared Conrad in the face. "Why don't you leave her alone," she said, in an even voice, with a hint of genuine curiosity in it.

Conrad blinked at the upstart, momentarily confused by her unscripted entrance. I think he had always dealt with Anna by not dealing with her, by pretending she didn't exist (which was easy, as she lived with me, and Abigail, not being any sort of worrier, probably didn't mention her much). Anna didn't fit into his schemes. Which was odd, really, given his own mythological childhood. He saw her as neither ally nor enemy. Even now she just blocked his way, like a spring sapling on a narrow path, and I watched him debate whether to go around her or cut her down. He chose prudence. Luckily for him.

He turned away from Anna and Abigail, and addressed his merry band. "Heath bars!" he proclaimed, spreading his arms like an evangelist on a roll. This was rather like his performance at the Rational Tap, except that now he wasn't drunk. "A ten-pack of Charleston Chews! Giant slabs of Cadbury's Fruit and Nut!"

The crowd gasped. Wasserman shook her head in exaggerated disbelief, her face a billboard of pity and disgust.

"Wait a minute," I said.

"Stuck on the back of the toilet tank!"

"How?" asked Tim.

"Duct tape!"

"Hold it just a minute. See here. Do you mean this whole thing is about—"

From Abigail came a low growl that threatened to rise up into a shriek, which it did. "I hope you all fuck yourselves blind and die!"

"We know you don't mean that," said Hilda.

"—food???"

Hilda looked at me as though *I* was crazy. "Of course it's about food, Dorcas. Weren't you listening?"

I took a long breath. "And he put you up to this. Didn't he?"

"It's not a question of putting up to," said the articulate Tansy. "We were all of us concerned about Abby."

"No we weren't," said Tim, softly.

"And why," I asked them all, "did you imagine you had the right to do this thing?"

"It's not a question of right," said Guy. "It's a question of duty."

"No it's not," said Tim. "I'm sorry, ladies. I'm really and truly sorry."

Conrad said nothing. He regarded me with exaggerated insouciance. Perhaps, I thought, I had him worried.

"Guy," I said, "do you know what's wrong with you?"

"Now, Dorcas," said Hilda.

"Hilda. Do *you* know what's the matter with you?"

Tansy actually reached for me, to touch me.

"Tansy! Do you know what your problem is?"

"I know," she said, "that you're having certain feelings right now."

"Would you all like to know what's wrong with each and every one of you?" Silence. "Well, answer me."

Guy cleared his throat. "Dorcas—"

"Answer my question."

"Well," he said, "I guess you could say I'm—"

"I could say a lot of things. The point is, I won't. The point is that I would never, ever, even in the shadow of the gallows, look another adult in the eye and tell him what's wrong with him." I was breathing hard now, and advancing on Guy. "This is what we do to *children*. We are not *children*. We are grown people. We are fully formed. We are each of us responsible for and to ourselves. We have a social contract. We treat one another with the respect owed to equals. We see one another's faults and *we keep our own counsel.*" Hilda put a protective arm around her terrorized husband and opened her mouth to speak. "We do not *presume*," I spat, "to *improve* our *friends*. Decent people do not take such burdens upon themselves. We are supposed to be decent people. We are all, against the evidence of this sorry day"—and now I was shouting, my voice as deep as I could make it—"*mature adults!*"

The right side of Guy's openmouthed face disappeared behind a great magical glob of what I first took to be osprey shit, so that I immediately looked up, searching for the great soaring deus ex machina, and I missed seeing the same excellent thing happen to Hilda's caftanned bosom. "Look out!" yelled Tim. I continued scanning the skies (again, everybody but me caught on immediately; it seems that on this day I was doomed to be colossally obtuse), until Hilda shrieked, "No, Abigail, no!" and I looked down just in time to see a milk-white comet streak past my shoulder, as though fired from behind, and strike Guy's face again, this time square on his open mouth.

It had of course been fired from behind, by my sister, who now yelled at me to "duck!" Amazingly, instead of stupidly seeking out pintails and mergansers, I took her meaning right away, and I dropped and turned, and there was Abigail rising up with two fistfuls of potato salad, both of which she zinged with great accuracy at Tansy Wasserman's crotch.

"All *right.*" This from Anna, who was, though not jumping up and down and clapping her hands, smiling at her mother with measured pride.

"Dorcas," Hilda pleaded now, "do something." She was troweling glop off her husband's blushing face. Intellectual Guy, the a priori king, was having quite a day for himself. He had somehow opened the wrong door and stumbled into real experience, and now, as nature, human and otherwise, howled about him he fumbled visibly for an appropriate re-action, but could do no better than social unease. He tried on a bemused smile, as though his thoughts were elsewhere, a ruse so inept that it was almost heroic. Picture Christ, cruci-fied, trying to recall whether he'd turned the oven off. Potato salad splatted on his forehead and his wife squealed, but ge-nial Guy, at that very moment, apparently remembered some-thing terrifically funny, and just had to laugh.

A lot of things happened in no particular order. Wasser-man announced that it was "good" that Abigail was dealing so honestly with her anger, and Abigail chased her down and squished the rest of the potato salad down her bodice, and Conrad, who had been extremely quiet, told everybody to calm down, she was out of ammo now, said this in a bored drawl as if half wakened from a Sunday nap, and then some-one handed her the cold roast chicken, which she ripped apart and fired, again with great accuracy, at people's heads, bloodying Wasserman's nose with a drumstick. Food flew every-where, carrot curls, pickles, strawberry cheesecake, mostly toward Wasserman and the DeVilbisses, but Tim Paine got it too, tomato slices and hot pastrami, and then there was an oval of silence, like the center of a hurricane, and Abigail stood before her husband with a Tupperware bowl of peach compote in her hand and murder in her eye.

I could see plainly, and so could he, that he had lost con-trol, that he was in the open, naked, unarmed, and she hissed at him, "I'm going to kill you, you sick son of a whore."

Slowly, slowly, with exquisite care, he raised his hand to her, index finger extended, pointing at her nose, the fingertip coming to rest an inch from her face, and holding steady. His breathing was shallow, his body taut, he focused, expression-less, upon her eyes, as if trying to hypnotize a cobra. Abigail froze. Taking heart, he began to speak to her, softly, seducing her, perhaps, or promising retaliation, promising something anyway, it was probably all the same to those two. His deep intent fascinated me: I had never seen him work hard at any-thing, and now he behaved as though everything of value hung in the balance, and for him I guess it did. He was the dominant male, status was all, and if she managed to make him look foolish—if, say, she dumped the compote over his head—he would lose his crown for all time. And just when I saw that this was true, tears sprang to my sister's eyes, wash-ing the fight right out of them, and Anna, standing next to me, sighed and slumped.

"Oh, well," Anna said.

Do it! I wanted to shout, *Let him have it! Now! Do it now!*

But I am not a screamer. I am a civilized woman, not a creature of impulse, nope, not me. I willed her to be strong, that's all, I wished it with all my heart, and so I got to watch my sister crumple up into a sodden heap. And that was that.

After this defining moment other things happened, in no

particular order and to no good end. Tim Paine, still wishing to make amends, bless his heart, lobbed a deviled egg at Conrad Lowe, which of course struck him white first and bounced away harmlessly, unacknowledged by anybody. Tansy embraced Abigail and was not disemboweled. We picked up after ourselves and trudged back to the parking lot, and on that dreary march, dear Anna, resilient as the child she still was, spotted chickadees, nuthatches, a pair of yellowthroat warblers, and an American redstart, and a swarm of yellowjackets discovered poor mayonnaised Guy, whose whimpers still echo in my brain on hot sleepless summer nights, and Conrad made Abigail apologize, formally, to everybody, one by one.

The phrase "window of opportunity," not then in currency, is all too apt, and today, with dark rain lashing the roof and storm winds punching at the north wall, I recognize that one instant, when she faced him in fury, poised to annihilate but not to kill, as a tiny blue window on a sunlit world: not paradise perhaps, but lost forever anyway. I let my sister down that day. I did hand her the cold roast chicken. Surprised hell out of myself, too, when I did it. Thought it was a big deal. It wasn't. It wasn't nearly enough.

The Grizzly Fair

Chapter 16

The Hungry Heart

Despite her great gallantry *[!!!]* during the ordeal of our ill-advised, however well-intentioned, intervention, Abigail was wounded to the quick, and soon after disappeared for months, remaining inside the Watch Hill cottage, emerging only occasionally for provender, and precious little of that. She put herself on a killing diet. As she later confided to us, she spent the first week literally fasting, subsisting on strong black tea and celery. At some point she began to experience blackouts.

You may well wonder what her husband was doing during this time. . . .

Actually Hilda's right, she was starving, figuratively and actually, and to my lasting discredit I did nothing about it. After the Great Swamp Fight I avoided seeing Abigail at all. We kept in touch by phone. Not seeing her was easy, since they had taken lodgings at Watch Hill, a solid half hour away (a half-hour drive in Rhode Island being the psychological equivalent to a full-day outing anywhere else).

About a week after the Swamp, Conrad showed up at my library, on a Friday afternoon just before closing time. I was alone behind the desk, and there were only a few patrons left, all grazing in the mystery aisle. T. R. had left early with cramps, and Anna the Spy was in the basement rummaging among the discards. I was leafing through publishers' fall catalogues when I heard someone come in. Horror novels were just hitting their stride then, spawning their own publishing houses, and I was holding in my hand, at arm's length, a black-and-white pamphlet from Torso Press, which promised "grizzly fair, not for the squeamish," and wondering how they got "squeamish" right, when I caught his scent, juniper and witch hazel, and there he was, inches away, looming over the counter with his horrible amiable smile. He said, "Gimme everything you got on gorgons."

"You might try the Grizzly Fair," I said, zinging the pamphlet at his nose, a bizarre reflex action, my body as machine, my wrist swivel-snapping just as though a spring had been activated. That's how he made me feel sometimes. Like some old mechanical toy, unearthed in an attic on a rainy day, which works like new, against all odds and for no damn good reason. "You might try the Grizzly Fair," I said. "The Medusa booth." Come to think of it, he had just that effect on everybody. Guy, Hilda, Abigail. He knew where everybody's button was.

Conrad cocked his head and regarded me quizzically, and with even more interest than usual. "Have I come at a bad time?"

"You couldn't possibly do otherwise."

I can't remember the weather that day. It must have been bad—he loved bad weather, and it loved him—yet I see him now in a shaft of dusty sunlight. It was early fall, just before the leaves turn. How bad could the weather have been? And it seems to me now that seeing him suddenly like that cleaned the air around me, made the office colors snap to, cleared my mind like a fat new broom. I was glad, wasn't I? Sure I was. Here was my nemesis—not everybody has one of those—and we were about to mix it up, and I felt that odd bridal joy again, the same as the night I first met him. There he was, and it was as though we had just finished that nauseating meal at Lobsterama and, for some obscure reason, adjourned to my library. I must have been stunned at my own reaction. Mustn't I? I must, at least, have asked him what he was doing, coming there, at closing time.

"I vant to pick your brain," he said, with a Bela Lugosi stare. "Seriously, sistah. I've come to a snag in my latest opus, and I need your, as we say, input. Thought we'd hit the Blue Moon, chew the fat."

"Let me get this straight," I said. "You're having trouble writing one of your trashy books and instantly thought of me? You imagined that I would accompany you to a notorious dive in order to render you assistance?"

"Bingo."

"Why?"

Conrad whirled in place, gesturing expansively at the book-lined walls, carrying on as if awed, as if he were in the Library of Congress, and then he hunched his shoulders slightly forward and arranged his face into a wicked cartoon of Guy DeVilbiss. "Every artist," he intoned, "needs an arena."

"As arenas go," I said, "this one's pretty puny. Plus it isn't yours. It's mine. It belongs to me."

"Exactly," beamed Conrad. "Every artist needs a muse."

I ignored this, and suggested the Providence Athenaeum, and he announced that without my presence it would be as inspiring as a public toilet, and then I suggested with some asperity that his wife could function perfectly well as his muse, and he stuck a long index finger partway down his throat and made a gagging noise, and I jumped to my feet, my face inches from him, and he snapped his fingers in front of my nose and said, "Quick, Watson, the names!"

Watson? At that moment I couldn't remember my own name. "*Whose* names?"

"The names of the nine muses. They were nine, and their names were . . . ?"

"Terpsichore," I said, "Calliope, Thalia, Melpomene, Polyhymnia, Urania, Clio. Euterpe . . ."

"That's eight."

"Terpsichore."

"*Bzzzzzzzt.*"

"I beg your pardon?"

"You said that one already."

Why was he asking me this? Why was I answering him? Who the hell was the ninth muse? I got it. "Mnemosyne," I said triumphantly. "Now would you mind—"

"Nah. Mnemosyne was the mom." His eyes momentarily lost their obscene glint. "The Mother of Memory," he said, and then, "She said you'd know."

"Your mother?"

"Your sister, sistah. She said you'd know all the muses."

When Abigail and I were ten we went on a field trip to the museum at the School of Design. All I remember to this day was the big Buddha on the second floor, and the gift shop on the first, where I bought my first book with my own money. We bought it together, actually, for we had to pool our allowance. We decided on Edith Hamilton's *Mythology,* I because I was ready to graduate from children's fairy tales to more complicated material, and Abigail because on the cover was a picture of naked Perseus, holding the head of Medusa. It wasn't the head that interested her.

"She told me about the paper dolls. She said you had a full set of Olympians."

This was a shock, the pleasant shock of sweet detail suddenly recollected. "Not just Olympians," I said. Heroes of the Iliad, heroines from Euripedes, and the whole benighted Atreus clan. I made them all myself, of course, tracing their figures from library books, transferring them with LePage's mucilage to Father's shirt cardboards. I didn't bother much with outfits—they wore mostly togas and drapes anyway—but I kept each grouping in a separate shoe box. Abigail, quickly bored with her Rhonda Flemings and Diana Lynns, sometimes rifled through the boxes, so I'd occasionally come upon Hades in pedal pushers, Medea the all-turquoise bridesmaid.

"Which doll was your favorite?"

"Cassandra."

"Natch. And your least favorite was Aphrodite."

This was puzzling, on two fronts. One, that he cared enough about this stuff to get it out of Abigail; and two, that she had cared enough about it as a child to notice.

He read my mind again. "I guessed."

Natch.

"Aphrodite," he said, "was an amoral fatso, like someone we both know. And by a spooky coincidence she fucked everything that moved, human or otherwise."

"The Olympians were flawed, like us. That's why I liked them."

"Get your purse."

I stared at him. "It's half an hour to closing time."

"Close early." He reached out and flicked the light switch, on-off-on-off, and the mystery grazers obediently flocked to my desk with their finds. Mildred Colasanto with her Florida PIs, Ob Minurka's sister Valerie with a stack of Shell Scott.

I opened my mouth to say, "It's okay, you've got thirty more minutes," but nothing came out, and I checked them through and watched them leave, and got my purse and stood up. "Not the Blue Moon," I said.

"Then the Rational Tap it is," he said.

. . .

Inside Conrad Lowe's car it was soporifically hot. We didn't speak during our short journey. I spent the time unprofitably, wondering why I was there. The last time I had been alone with him had been at Abigail's insistence. This time there was no such excuse; I couldn't even get a handle on proximate cause. The car was an ancient two-tone Plymouth, black and white, an automatic with the shift somehow miniaturized and embedded in the dashboard. An ante-seatbelt car, cavernous and ramshackle, upholstered in slippery vinyl the color of Rhode Island Red eggshell. The interior was filthy from cigarette smoke, with ancient magazines, *Look*s and *Time*s and *Harper's Bazaar*s, sloshing underfoot, and a pyramid of fast food detritus on the back seat. It looked like a college kid's first car, and it probably was. For the first time it occurred to me that Conrad Lowe, who had money to burn, was nuts.

Inside the Rational Tap, he insisted upon "our booth," which was, of course, the site of his dreadful nuptial party. He brought over a pitcher of Narragansett and poured my first glass. "So," he said.

I drained my glass in two swallows. I don't much like beer, so 'Gansett tastes as good to me as Lowenbrau, and it's a good deal cheaper. Day-trippers never touch Narragansett.

He replenished my glass. "You come here often?"

"What exactly do you need to know about Gorgons?"

"*Nada.* I want to know about you."

"Only one was mortal, Medusa. The other two sisters could not be killed. I don't remember their names, and I don't remember who fathered them. At one time I knew. It was probably Poseidon and some nymph."

"Actually it was another sea god, Phorcys."

"You've already done your research."

"I'm doing it right now."

"What do you want from me?"

"A drinking buddy? The little woman's off the sauce. Too caloric."

"You don't need me for that. Frome's full of boozers."

"Well, I guess you'd know." He squinted and glinted. "Have some Madeira, me dear."

I said nothing. Maybe this was what I'd do: say nothing until he gave up.

"Horror novels are harder than they look. *The Mantis* was a bitch."

"They're all about bitches, aren't they?"

"They're all about women. And they're all *for* women, too. My readers are women. They eat this stuff up. They love to read about their power. You can call them any filthy name, as long as you're paying attention to them. That's all they want."

"It's not what I want."

"No, it isn't, is it?"

"Tell me again why you married my sister."

"To get close to you."

"You do realize that that makes no sense."

"You thought I was horsing around with you, that speech I made on our big date, about how you are an honorable woman. You figured I was shit-faced and shooting off my mouth."

" 'An honorable woman: a contradiction in terms.' "

"Hey, you remembered! Yes, the breathing definition of an oxymoron. But it's true. You fascinate me. From the first time I saw you, sitting on the couch next to old Sadie Thompson, all upright and stern, looking right through me. I thought, There she is! The impossible woman."

"The world is full of women like me. There may once have been more of us, in the days, say, of E. M. Forster.

Civilization once gagged on *impossible women,* ladies of a certain age, every one of them upright and stern as all get out."

"Yes, but those ladies didn't have a choice. You did. You made a choice."

No kidding. Was that true?

Maybe it was the atmosphere of the place, the luxuriant murk. Whatever the reason, I decided to let myself get sloshed, something I rarely do. I was so sick of worrying about Abigail. I was even tired of hating her husband. Sitting there, watching him pour and pour, watching him order pitchers by twos, I felt, not forgiving, certainly not to any degree sympathetic, but terrifically winded. He looked winded too. It was as if he had been chasing me for hours over difficult terrain, and we had both tacitly agreed to lean against the same boulder for a few minutes and pant.

"You're an intelligent man," I found myself saying to him, "an educated man. Why do you waste your time writing crap? If I had any talent, I certainly wouldn't throw it away like that."

"You know, I always wanted to write for the movies. You'd think I'd be a natural, with my show-biz bona fides, plus I know some people. But the funny thing is my screenplays don't work. At least that's what they tell me. I get all this horseshit about keeping it simple."

I wondered what could be simpler than your basic misogynistic horror story, but, in the spirit of our time-out, refrained from saying so.

"And," he continued, "they always insisted on changing the ending. They always wanted the monster to die. Gotta kill the bitch, they told me. Not completely, of course, in case there's a *Son of;* but she's gotta die, big time."

"Who?"

"She. Corinna Gabriel. Mantis Woman. The Gorgon. Whatever. They always want to kill her off. The public isn't ready, they tell me, for the monster heroine. What do they know? Seriously, I could have sold the mantis thing, big money, real stars. Except at the climax she'd have to explode. Humongous mess, they said, entrails all over the place, a publicity tie-in with vomit bags issued at the door, which was way off, because that noise went out with Bill Castle."

He obviously expected me to have some idea what he was talking about. Vomit bags? It did sink in that, contrary to my previously unexamined expectations, he wanted his monstrous females to survive. I pondered on this. "So," I said, "maybe your Medusa will be the charm. Maybe the public is finally ready for a gorgon protagonist." The thought was intriguing. "Anna tells me they can do anything with special effects nowadays. Apparently there's this new movie, *Battle Stars—*"

"*Star Wars.*" He shrugged and gazed into his beer.

"My point is, they could probably manage the writhing snake hairdo, and the wings." Despite myself I was warming up. It wasn't the beer, I'm certain; it was the subject at hand. "There's so much you could do with her. You do know, don't you, that she was once beautiful? And that she was punished by Athena for sleeping with Poseidon, in Athena's own temple?"

"Athena," said Conrad Lowe, looking sharply at me, "being your pet Olympian." He caught my surprise, and it irritated him. "Look, I did go to Harvard, even if I was just pre-med. I know who the Olympians are. And I know you, Dorcas. You're Athena all over."

I couldn't avoid feeling complimented, even though he had surely intended an insult. "Athena was implacable, it's true, but her expectations for the human race were the highest among her entire family, including her father. She punished Medusa, not for sleeping around, but for dishonoring the temple."

"Natch."

"And did you know that Athena gave a phial of Medusa's blood to Asclepius, so that he could raise the dead? So Medusa was really the world's first blood donor."

"I'm not going to finish *Gorgon*. Not right now, anyway. I'm working on a new idea."

This brought me up short. "Then why," I asked, "did you come to me for gorgon references?"

"To get you alone." He flashed his tooth at me and filled our glasses. "I told you, Dorcas, I want to know all about you. You're all the references I need."

This was so tiresome. I had actually been, if not enjoying the afternoon, at least not minding it, which was a small miracle. I could not easily clear my mind of Medusa and her great cinematic potential. Which was ridiculous, because I had never been much of a moviegoer. When I tried to picture Medusa on the screen I could manage only Elsa Lanchester in a remote-control fright wig. The ideal Medusa movie would need to be animated, and what better artist than Steele Savage, the pen and ink genius who illustrated Edith Hamilton's book, whose gods and mortals looked etched in marble, and I grew captivated, instantly, by the very idea of these figures in motion. It's crazy, but sitting there in the yeasty gloom, buzzing with too much beer and the promise of much too much more, three feet away from a man whose very existence threatened everything I held of value, I could focus only upon "The Rape of Europa," my favorite of the Savage drawings, and I pictured the great bull flying, static yet magically in motion, arcing over scrolls of sea foam, with his lovely passenger, astonished yet unafraid, trailing clouds of wildflowers, and all of it black and white, and perfectly beautiful. God, I was pathetic.

He was saying something else about the remarkable Me and getting the amazing creature I am off alone to do with as he would, and so on. It made my head hurt, deep in the back of my eyes. I tuned him out for a while, which forced me to tune in on something else, a plangent jukebox offering currently favored by the Rational Tap regulars. *Ooh I wanna do you, ooh the way you do me, ooh do you up against the wall.* I had never, in my heart of hearts, required a lover. Never tormented myself with yearning, nope, slammed the door on that, and over time, and of course in my native humid climate, the door swelled tight against the frame and stood as fast as if dead-bolted in blue steel. I did not suffer that gaping want, I left that to my sister, I would rather have endured unanesthetized amputation than admit that breach. And this when I was *young,* when my skin was firm and I could run and run, when desire, however ignoble, would not have been ugly. Imagine actually becoming that staple of cruel farce, the *lustful spinster,* all bones and shimmering shame, a naked elongated skeleton. I did imagine this, trying it on for size, and then I imagined I could see the door itself, weathered metaphor complete with panels and brass fittings, snug against the virtual jamb, and then I imagined it bulging out ever so slightly, pulsing with the inane juke beat, *ooh.* I imagined all this. This is important. It was in my head, the thumping door. Which was awful enough, but it *was* in my head, no farther south, and it *was* so goddamn trite and drear that I would have cried, if I had been the crying sort. Our old wooden booth hummed along, *Ooh,* do you up against the *wall,* and I thought, *I had walled the monster up within the tomb.*

"What?" He was sitting back down with more pitchers, placing them with a drunk's exaggerated care, attending to me only when he was satisfied that they weren't going to run away. Our glasses were still half full. He had planned ahead. He asked, "What did you say?"

"Nothing." Had I actually spoken aloud? For the love of God, Montresor. "I said, I think we should go."

"Soon. Drink up." We did. "So," he said after a short while, or perhaps a long one. "What do you think?"

"I think I'm blotto."

"*Moi aussi,* but I'm talking about the novel."

"Look, I can't keep up with you. You said you were junking it."

Conrad Lowe slapped the sodden table and swore, thick-tongued. "Pay attention, woman! You didn't hear a goddamn word. Here I pour my heart out and what do you do?"

I leaned forward and stuck my face in his, intent, I believe, upon voicing disdain for his hemorrhaging heartlike organ, but just then remembered Mnemosyne, the goddess of memory, and that I had had trouble *remembering* her name, which, though ironic enough, certainly would not have seemed excruciatingly funny to me under sober circumstances, which these were not. We had a jolly hootfest then, initiated by me, our heads bowed together like dear friends, after which I invited him to repeat his important news.

"Gonna tear the roof off the joint." He smiled cunningly. "Gonna make Peyton Place look like Sunnybrook Farm."

"Good for you," I said, rummaging around for my car keys, having lost track of how I had gotten there. Time was speeding up by then; I remember this part of the scene in snapshots and sound bites, an antic slide show produced by one of the lesser gods, Bozo, God of Ignominy. During this period I visited the Tap's disgusting unisex lav at least three times, so that it eventually began to look homey, stopping off at the jukebox once on the way back to study the selections it offered. Somebody yelled from the bar to play "Melancholy Baby," which unfortunately was unavailable, and I slipped some quarters in and punched up four buttons at random, which turned out to be two Stevie Wonder numbers book-ended by a sappy country tune apparently entitled "My

Woman, My Woman, My Wife," as these seemed to be its only lyrics.

This struck me funny, although a cracked crown or an air raid would probably have had the same effect, and I giggled through the laborious reiteration of Conrad Lowe's brand-new book idea, which involved ripping the lid off of something and exposing it, and was going to be set down in our fair city. "Not," he said at least three times, "a woman's novel. A novel about women. It's never been done before, and I'm gonna do it."

In this slide you can see me literally under the table, on all fours, still looking for my keys, still chuckling, my nose a foot away from his U.S. Keds. "I think you may be wrong about that," I called up to him. The next slide sequence clearly shows me bumping my head hard on the way up, my pilsner glass tipping and shattering, and Conrad Lowe distractedly mopping his crotch with some discarded Sunday *Journal* funnies. "Wrong, my ass. Plus, if I do it right, my agent says I got a long shot at the National Book Award."

This was goofy. "On what planet? Besides, do you actually care about critical accolades?"

In apt response, he belched operatically. "Piss hell out of DeVilbiss," he explained.

Discreet Joe Enos reached beneath the bar and came up with a beach towel, which he tossed over to us, refraining from comment (here you see it frozen in mid-zing, stretched out between Joe and us like the Zeus-bull rampant), and we used it to blot the tabletop. It was a Block Island beach towel, with the Lowes' honeymoon hotel, the Seawitch, prominently featured in the center frame, sandwiched between a laughing gull and a tuna. We studied together its intricate design, all the while arguing about whether his book idea was all wet too. I offered in evidence *Madame Bovary* and *Anna Karenina,* and he blew them away with a beery whoosh. Tolstoy, he informed me, was "bullshit," and Flaubert, Guy DeVilbiss's idol, the Bullshit King. They were too sympathetic, Emma and Anna, and all the rest, they were men in drag is what they were, they were what their creators wanted desperately to believe: that women were human. "*Emma Bovary, c'est moi,*" sneered Conrad, with a raspberry chaser. "Not me, man. I'm the real McCoy. I," he said, leaning back in his seat, throwing his arm over the booth wall with a thump, "am the Doctor Livingstone of women."

"You presume," I said. He didn't get it. Neither, when I tried to understand him, did I. "You're an *explorer* of women? You can't explore people. Maybe you're an anthropologist." This sounded familiar. "Wait a minute," I said. Had I had this conversation before? How was that possible?

"The undiscovered country," he agreed, pouring from a new pitcher, which had somehow appeared between us. "Cuntaroon. Twatville."

"Let's keep it clean." My jollies were in danger of wearing off. This would be too bad, since I certainly wasn't sobering up. "West Vagina. Estrogenia."

He bowed to me. "There you go."

"The Cervical Canal."

"The point is—"

"And the far-flung Fallopian Archipelago."

"Shut up. The point is, I'm gonna spill the beans."

I snorted. I'm afraid that beer actually spurted from my nose. He found a dry section of beach towel and delicately blotted my mouth and chin. "Don't you think," I said, "that you might be overreaching just a tad?"

"Two women." He lowered his voice and enunciated with a bit more skill, making me wonder if he had been feigning drunkenness all along. But no, he was really drunk. Just not as drunk as I had thought. Not as drunk as I. "One the town pump. One the Oracle of East Clamcake."

"Two women." Oh dear.

"*Uno,* Miss Grabass of 1955. *Duo,* the Josephine March of Little Gasbucket."

"I don't think so." His intent was beginning to take form in front of me, like pulsating ectoplasm. "Look, I can't speak for my sister, as we all know, but my life belongs to me, thank you very much."

"Your inner life, maybe. The rest is public domain."

"What the hell are you talking about?"

"You appear nightly on the world stage, sis, along with your ever-loving twin."

"Ridiculous." I remembered the night we met, and how horrible it had been for me to see myself, for the very first time, as a perceptible, public object. I had felt on that occasion like the narrator in *War of the Worlds,* cowering in a ruined house, sniffed at by wormy Martian tentacles. That this creature even knew I had an inner life (*The Martians understood doors!*) froze me with dread. And here it came again, the tentacle of doom. But this time it didn't scare me at all.

I could have lived my entire life without ever being known, in just this sense, by anyone. Abigail knew me well, but in an entirely different way. My inner life was not her business; to Abigail I was a set of comfortably predictable behaviors and responses. I was the not-Abigail, the other half, the shell to her oyster. And I have never needed to imagine, or cared to, how the world looks from Abigail Mather's point of view. I've had enough to do just tidying up after her. And I found that now, upon Conrad Lowe's second intrusion, I was receptive. I was going to be known. I was going to be held in the bowl of someone's mind.

He wasn't just playing games with me, as I had thought.

He was up to nothing good, and I didn't trust him any more than before, but he was dead serious in his focus upon me. What an amazing thing. Someone was paying attention to me. To me.

I needed to get off by myself, to understand this, and to make sense of my own response to it. I had figured out by this time that my car was back at the library. I had to persuade him to take us back. This was not going to be easy, as he was on one of his rolls.

". . . the American reading public," he was saying, and ". . . the sexual habits of librarians," and ". . . pith her like a goddamn frog."

"That's interesting," I said. "Listen, I have to go."

"Everyone knows I'm a hack. What they don't know," he whispered, "is that I'm an *intellectual* hack."

I patted his forearm. "You'll show 'em," I said. "And now we really must go."

He took my hand and looked at me intently, without artifice. "If you promise that we'll do this again. Many, many times."

"Why? For your 'research'? Come on."

"Gotta promise."

"Look. The mere fact that we didn't kill each other this afternoon does not make us buddies. Let's not get carried away here."

"Jesus, Dorcas." Tears shimmered in his eyes, sentimental inebriate tears, but still they moved me. What a red-letter day. "You gotta promise. I get so fuckin' lonely."

"You have a wife. You have no excuse to be lonely."

He stared at me for the longest time. "Don't you know anything?"

I could believe, without effort, that he was wretched. He was a dreadful man, furious, in the modern and the mythological senses, unable to fend off his horrid mother, to protect his weak father, or at least to avenge him properly, as no matter how assiduous he was he could not, literally, destroy every woman on the planet Earth. Had he been a man's man, the sort of creature most comfortable with others of his kind, he would have at least had the comfort of company. But he wasn't, there was too much of the feminine in him, and he was too acute not to know it. He was a ladies' man who hated ladies. Except for me. Lucky lucky me.

"Tell me more," I said, "about your book."

The book was of course going to be about the three of us, pretty much just as we were, not all tarted up with supernatural powers and trunkloads of deliquescing body parts. The narrative engine would be fueled by spectacular sexual tension between the husband and the unmarried sister. He would not tell me how it ended. Which was okeydoke with me, although I affected, I think, a certain frustrated curiosity.

I remember the rest of this evening, the inaugural of our civil relationship, solely in underdeveloped color slides. This is how the profoundly drunken memory works (mine anyway): just visual snatches, glimpsed from the corner of the wary eye. No sound-memory at all. Clock faces, for some reason, register with perfect accuracy, so I can trust that he began to tell me about the book at 7:05 and pretty much wrapped it up at 10:40. Meanwhile, at 8:00, on the black-and-white TV above the bar, Mickey Rivers got chased down trying to steal home, and at 8:15 the Sox lost anyway, six to five. Apparently I didn't check the clock when Abigail's husband put his hand over mine. I didn't do anything about it, except, apparently, stare at the intriguing picture this made. *Click*.

In this shot you can see that we have been joined by T. R. Corrow's uncle-in-law, Ernest Crosby, who blew us to a pitcher of Carling and then slunk off, having been frozen out of our intimate discussion. I remember him smiling at me, just before leaving, in an unpleasant way.

Here's the bathroom again, and again, and again, out of paper and the hot water faucet rusted shut. Here—*click!*—is my long face in the bathroom mirror, slyly captioned:

LAVESE LAS MANOS

And here we finally are, having closed down the joint, scooting out of the booth, our booth, and here he is, facedown on the floor, toppled and bleeding from the nose and lower lip, and here I am, solicitously stanching his wounds with a paper napkin while Joe Enos disunites his Keds. Some prankster has apparently tied Conrad's shoelaces together. Here I am in the front seat of the swerving Plymouth, laughing myself into hiccups, having just recalled that it was me. Here is his profile at the steering wheel, limned by streetlight, hawknosed, squinting, intent. On what? On getting us home in one piece, on evading the law, on finishing his book, on destroying my sister, on me, on me, on me.

He got me to my car. He did not touch me. He did not need to. I don't remember driving home. I do remember throwing up in my own john. I do remember waking up the next morning with no hangover, feeling like a million bucks. I do remember wondering why, and then remembering, and shrugging and shaking my head with stagy rue, for the benefit of God's camera. Here we see the good sister, only human, repentant. Here we see an honorable woman. A contradiction in terms.

CHAPTER SEVENTEEN

Watch Hill

Now Hilda gives us a Watch Hill interlude, ostensibly to describe my sister's downward spiral (she uses the phrase "downward spiral") into anorexia and madness, but really to show off Agincourt Cottage, their "unpretentious little Norman farmhouse." Unpretentious little Norman must have had his head up his ass, architecturally speaking, because the Francophile DeVilbisses had overelaborated upon their modest French farmhouse knockoff (a style popular on Watch Hill between the World Wars), tic-tac-toeing its white stucco walls with black-painted timber which served no structural or aesthetic function. The house was too small for all this fuss. It looked like a tea cosy crocheted by Piet Mondrian.

The DeVilbisses were always fussing with it, collecting notions and gewgaws during biannual trips to Camembert, where Guy did most of his heavy writing, in their endless

quest to create a little Old World island for Guy's muse. They
were always prattling about daub and wattle and the inordi-
nate expense of unseasoned oak and the outrageous provin-
cialism of local zoning laws, which forbade finishing their
steeply pitched roof with genuine thick reed thatch, whatever
the hell that was. Hilda furnished the place in what she hoped
was the Bloomsbury style, artlessly artful, ostentatiously play-
ful, but any success she might have achieved was deliberately
spoiled by Conrad Lowe's mischievous additions. Her tasteful
"pearwood bread trough" kitchen counter contrasted pain-
fully with the de Sade-inspired coffee table in the next room,
a glass-topped horror supported by a naked mannequin wearing a dog collar. Conrad loved to taunt Guy with stuff like
this, backing his old roomie into an aesthetic corner, forcing
him to defend de Sade as a revolutionary feminist instead of
the crazy old pervert he clearly was.

A week after the Rational Tap truce, Abigail phoned me
at the library and invited Anna and me down for the weekend. Conrad had gone to L.A. for a series of meetings, and
Abigail claimed she would "die of boredom" without him.
Her voice was small and strained, so hard was she working
to sound airy. "Do what you like," she said at least three
times, and "only if you have nothing better to do," and so
on. I tried to talk her into visiting us, but she claimed that
would be impossible, as Conrad had left their only car at
Logan Airport. I didn't quiz her about this. Obviously Conrad had stranded her deliberately, and she had let him do it,
but I didn't give her a hard time, as I would have done before.
I told her Anna had a paper due and would stay in Frome,
and that I was on my way.

We are all sinners. So say most clerics, except Stanley, I
guess, and the other pious humanists, and I guess they're
right. But there are sins and there are sins. Before colluding
with Conrad Lowe, my sins were, in my not so humble opin-

ion, pretty mediocre, and had not tormented me much. I could face them all, known and unknown, squarely. If God chose to burn me for hurting Mike Callahan, or needling T. R., or taking some small pride in my own rectitude, well then poop on Him. But now things were different. When I tried to confront my own mendacity I found the prospect blurry, and myself easily distracted from the task.

When we were kids Abigail and I would watch scary movies together, both fearful but perfectly matched, because, while visual cues upset her and aural ones did not, I was her exact opposite, so that we could attend, say, *The Tingler* or *House on Haunted Hill* together, she with her eyes squeezed shut, I with my fingers jammed into my ears, and afterward reconstruct a seamless narrative. I saw two gloved hands reach out of a closet and strangle a woman while she was getting dressed; Abigail heard the choked scream, the piercing violins; we were both unscathed.

Now, as I drove south toward Agincourt, and tried to view my own calumny in full sobriety, I found myself, metaphorically speaking, deliberately unfocusing my eyes, clapping up my ears, and singing *la la la* in my loudest voice. It was no good. When I pulled up to Agincourt, she was squatting in a bed of withered chrysanthemums, tending to them ineptly, and in any event too late. She looked as wilted as they. She had lost enough weight by this time that her skin had begun to look like a husk. It aged her. She was now merely, ordinarily, middle-aged plump, and you could see the substance leak out of her by the minute. Her eyes, when she looked up at me, were frantic. "You're early," she said, and the smile on her face was way too hopeful. How could I possibly help her?

"I brought a picnic lunch," I said. "I thought we could take it down to the Point." She led the way inside, where it was dark and smelled like the sea. I have always hated that salt smell. "I've got Genoa salami and some halfway decent mozzarella and two loaves from Tony C's."

"I can't eat any of that," Abigail said, her back to me.

"Well, then, I've also got a pretty good take-out antipasto. Surely you can eat a salad."

"Not with all that olive oil."

"Oh, for Christ's sake."

"Not with *oil*. No pepperoni either. Use your head."

"Well, what *can* you eat?"

"Lettuce," she said, in an obscenely cheery singsong. "Carrots, tomatoes. Pepperoncini, I guess. Lots of cukes. One egg."

"Now you're talking. I've got deviled—"

"No mayo. Anyway, I had my egg this morning."

"Sorry I missed it."

"But let's go anyway." She fished around in the cabinet over the refrigerator and came up with two bottles of Nuit-St.-George. "What I do, I save up my carbs and have one of these every three days. Not bad, eh?"

No, not if you're going for the enlarged-liver-bas-relief-on-skeletal-frame look. "Are you doing this with a doctor?"

"The Stooge? Please."

"Abigail, you shouldn't be doing this on your own."

"I'm not. Conrad's helping me."

I had a wild urge to wrestle her to the ground and stuff her with Italian bread and cheese. She looked weak enough, almost. "That explains," I said, "why you look like crap."

Abigail bagged the bottles, and put a corkscrew and two goblets in my picnic basket, and we set out for Napatree Point.

Napatree Point, the southwesternmost tip of Rhode Island, can be reached only by tramping over a mile and a half of barrier beach. There was once a road of sorts; there were houses, too, but all that ended up in the drink after the unnamed hurricane of 1938, dubbed the "Long Island Express" by chauvinistic New Yorkers. The harborside waters off the remaining sandspit are sometimes referred to as "the kitchen," because of the wealth of common household items still to be found on its kelpy bottom. Napatree is a fantastic place for birding, especially in the fall, because southward migrating birds can't resist the stopoff, and so I had at least that to look forward to, as Abigail slogged on ahead of me, insistently carrying both wine and food, for exercise. She walked this beach every day now, sometimes twice, often at dawn. I couldn't recognize this new industrious creature, except, thank God, when she opened her mouth.

"The only thing that shits worse than walking on sand," she called over her shoulder, "is sitting on it. I brought this blanket." Which she whipped out midway to the Point and attempted to spread out before us in the damn wind. We each put a foot on two corners and knelt down at the same time, facing each other. For me it was more of a pitch forward than a controlled act, and while the landing wasn't too bad, I must have jarred myself, because I had a moment of real vertigo then, kneeling, my face inches from hers. Not so much loss of inner balance as bewilderment of place. I lost track for a second of where we were, and how old, and what was going on in the world. We were wordless in some ancient, private spot, and weightless too, and peaceful. She still had a baby's face, to me.

"What the hell's the matter?" she asked. She regarded me with alarm. "Are you crying?"

"Apparently," I said, sitting back and fiddling with the picnic basket. I couldn't look at her right then.

"You never do that."

"I just suddenly thought about Mother," I said. In a way this was true. After a while I heard a cork pop, and she handed me a goblet of what turned out to be pretty good red.

After a time I said, "The seashore is so beautiful in books. I keep forgetting that I don't care for it all that much. It smells bad and the surf makes such a racket."

"You'd always rather be reading."

"That's not true." I thought awhile. "I like real birds. I like a few real people."

Abigail snorted. "Name one." I opened my mouth. "Besides Anna and me." I shut it again.

"Big Bob," I said, after a long pause. "Big Bob Flynn."

"Yeah." Abigail sighed. "He was a sweetheart, wasn't he?"

"He was a good man, and he loved you."

"No, he didn't. You were always wrong about him."

"He ruined his life for you. I wasn't wrong about that."

"He ruined his life," Abigail said, "for . . . I don't know . . ."

I knocked back half a glass. "For laughs? For nothing? For a Platonic ideal? Give us a tiny clue."

Abigail scooted off the blanket and crawled a few feet to wet sand. She began to mold something. "He did ruin his life," she admitted. "But he didn't really want me at all. I would have made him miserable."

"You would have shortened his life, for sure."

"That too. His heart was bad." She was making a sand castle, a pretty good one. I couldn't remember her ever having this skill, so she must have perfected it recently, during her exile here. She had piled up a big mound of loose sand and was digging a moat on its outskirts. "We didn't have sex much, actually. I had to be very careful. It was kind of fun, to tell you the truth—"

"Spare me."

"What we had was good times. We laughed a lot. He had a great laugh."

She was building a tower, not a castle. A cylindrical structure etched by the tip of her corkscrew with rectangles of stone, narrowing gradually, with a single window at its apex. There was no doorway at its base. She tried to make a conical roof, but the sand kept crumbling. It was impressive nonetheless. A medieval prison tower, a place of durance vile. She must have built them before; her steps were so economical.

We talked about Anna for a while, about where she might go to college. We had plenty of money saved up between us, fifty-fifty. Abigail and I were both equally prudent about money. It was about all we had in common. As we talked we were briefly visited by two stilts and a killdeer, and she widened her moat to accommodate the encroaching sea.

When we pulled the cork on the second bottle, she began to talk about her husband.

"I know you think it's some kind of sicko masochistic thing," she said.

I said nothing for as long as I could stand it. "Well," I said, "that's what I can't understand. You're not a glutton for punishment. You never went in for that foolishness. Not to my knowledge, anyway." It was fantastically hard to talk about this. Abigail and I have always been close; necessarily so. And it's true that we liked to analyze things—people, events, local gossip. But we rarely got personal. Twins are hypersensitive about that sort of thing. We are intimate enough by our very natures. We don't like to push it. Most people are alone in their lifeboats, for the duration of their lives; twins share theirs, and so our lifeboats have deck plans, drawn up over time. It isn't all shared space. It couldn't be. You'd go nuts.

"He's mean to me, all right. But I don't like it. I hate it. I put up with it."

I just stared at her.

Abigail smiled.

"Look, I really don't want to hear about your goddamn sex life. Hell, Abigail. Just leave it alone."

"I've had better," she said.

"What?"

She looked right at me. "I've had better. It's not about sex."

"I'll be back," I said, rising, and hurrying away toward the Point. She didn't call after me. She was newly patient, as though she had all the time in the world.

It was autumn, and warm everywhere but here, by the damn sea. The constant wind chilled my face, whipped my hair into my eyes. Sandpipers and their cousins, the whimbrels, avocets, and whatnot were all over the place. They are my least favorite birds. I don't know why. They are delicate creatures, all with long crooked stilts for legs, and fancifully drawn bills, and they leave enchanting patterns on wet sand. But they do little for me. By the sea I prefer the common herring gull, a creature much maligned for its Dumpster-feeding and its raucous cries. They are so common that people don't notice them anymore, except to badmouth them. We don't notice, for instance, their substantial size and weight. They could do us spectacular damage, if they chose to.

I had assumed it was all about sex: that Conrad Lowe provided my sister with the Ultimate Orgasm, or some such thing. *I've had better.* What did this mean? For the first time I wondered if Abigail truly loved him, loved him in a complex, adult way that began in carnality and extended to compassion, humility, readiness to sacrifice. Loved him in the sense that our parents must have loved each other; in the sense that I have loved no one. I had always taken it for granted that Abigail was equally incapable of this emotional and spiritual feat.

And for some reason this was distressing to me. Even though the object of her love was unworthy, I should have been happy for her. So her husband was a creep. So what? Who deserves complex, adult love? Everyone or no one.

In a quarter hour I came to the tip of the Point, to Fort Mansfield, built some years after the Civil War, when politicians and generals began to worry, in a hypothetical way, about naval bombardment of the Atlantic coast. At first they were hypothesizing about English or French bombardment, which must have been fun: Picture boatloads of Fabianists and Apache dancers lobbing shells into Long Island Sound. When the Spanish American War came, Hearst whipped the country into such a paranoid frenzy that a ghostly Spanish fleet, intent on the annihilation of New London, menaced its dreams, and Fort Mansfield, along with sundry other tri-state fortifications, became a near reality, which it still is. The war ended before Mansfield could be armed, and it remains hypothetical to the present day. It's just a low, square concrete structure, festooned with graffiti. There are supposed to be tunnels underneath, running nowhere in particular. I sat down on a slab. The wind stopped, and soon I was hot, sitting there with my face exposed to the October sun. I picked up a clamshell and scratched

Dork

next to

Albert Rumford is an A hole

The calumny, if such it was, about Albert Rumford had been accomplished with cobalt blue spray paint. It's probably good that I didn't have any of that with me. I was in a confessional mood.

While in this mood I saw my one and only American oystercatcher. A jaunty black bird with a silly bright orange beak
regarded me from the battlements, and we had a long moment
of mutual inspection. Many birds, songbird and not, are performance artists: starlings, gathering in alarming numbers in
late summer on the branches of a suburban tree, sing a Wag-
nerian chorus of steadfast intent (hypocritically, since they
never actually migrate); cardinals, those great showoffs, are re-
splendent, seductive mike singers; and, in the hush of afternoon in the deep woods, the hermit thrush, whose voice is
loveliest of all, begins his ballad, like Bartell D'Arcy, only when
he's good and ready, when the party's over and the other birds
have gone home for a nap. The oystercatcher, who doesn't
sing at all, is a true vaudevillian in his aspect. This one looked
like he knew a million jokes. *Hiya, hiya, hiya! D'ya hear the one
about the librarian and her brother-in-law?* Yes. I'd heard that one.

She was lying on her back, munching on limp celery, and
there were two inches of wine left in the second bottle. "Sometimes," she said, "I'm not hungry at all. I can go for half a
day without thinking once of food, and then at night I dream
about it." She rose up on an elbow. "Last night I dreamed
about Cheerios and milk. The bathtub was full of Cheerios
and milk. And sugared blueberries."

I told her I wanted her to move back in with me. I told
her she was killing herself. She didn't deny it. "I'm stuck,"
she said, "at one thirty-five. I've hit some sort of plateau."

"Why did you get me down here? What do you want
from me?"

Abigail sighed. "I want you to be nicer to him."

I thought I saw the whole thing then, and it made me sick.
"This was his idea, right? He made you call me? I quit." I
rose unsteadily, whacking sand off my legs, trying not to cry,

again. "You're disgusting, the pair of you. You deserve each other."

"Sit down and shut up." She said this extraordinary thing softly, with her eyes closed. After some time I sat back down and waited. "He wants you," she said, "just around. He says he can talk to you. He says he's lonely." She sat up and regarded me seriously. "I don't mind. I mean, I wish I were enough for him. I wish he could talk to me." Her voice broke, but she went on. "I'd rather just talk with him than fuck a hundred other guys."

"Just what do you mean by 'around'?" I asked her. Did she know that I had already spent a drunken evening *around* her husband? I honestly couldn't imagine. Should I tell her now? I honestly didn't know. My ignorance was the only honest thing about me that day.

"I mean, just come down more often. Anna's okay on her own once in a while. Come down next time when he's here. Which is most of the time. As a matter of fact, Guy and Hilda are coming back next month, just for ten days. It would be great if you came then. Guy's going to be driving me around the bend."

"Abigail. Did he tell you . . ."

"I'll say it again. He wants you around, to talk to. You interest him. Okay? You always did. I was jealous at first, but I'm not now. Come on." She was shy with me. She had never been shy with her needs—*what's that guy's last name, take Anna for a week, gimme that cookie*—but this was a favor, and she couldn't quite meet my eye.

Which was handy for me. Had he told her about the other night? Well, did it matter? Sure it did, and still I said nothing. Until finally, in my most censorious voice, I promised to come. And I let her be grateful, too. And after a while I got back in my car, and went *la la la,* all the way home.

Paeans from the Peons

Chapter 18

The Last Golden Time

The reader will forgive the inevitable elegiac note in this chapter, for we have arrived at what *[apparently]* I can only call the last golden time of our association with Conrad and Abigail Lowe. I refer, of course, to the occasion afforded by the National Book Award which Guy earned for *Persephone's Grotto,* and our joyous celebratory reunion at Watch Hill....

This was also the occasion of the last major literary award her husband received. Even if we had all stayed in place, drawing breath and out of the slammer, the De-Vilbisses' golden days were numbered. Guy made a big pretense of nonchalance about his critics, not to mention his book sales, but really it just about killed him to be overlooked; and after 1976 he joined the ranks of the literary dust gatherers, shoved aside to make room for the Next Great Writer. Which even I will admit was unfair. But it was fun to watch, too.

The three of us met them at Logan, an absurd two-hour

drive each way, as Hilda wouldn't hear of shuttling. She claimed they were too anxious to see us, but obviously she didn't want Guy to experience any more mass transit than he had to. They were a sight, struggling down the concourse, Hilda manning the heaviest bags. "When you see him from a distance like this," Abigail said, "you remember he has legs. It's kind of a shock."

"Look at that lazy asshole," Conrad said. "If he could figure out how, he'd make her carry the fucking typewriter." He approached them, tossing his keys to Abigail. "Bring the car around," he said. "We'll be lucky if he makes it to the curb." Conrad, to my astonishment, embraced Hilda and kissed her on the mouth, and then relieved her of both suitcases, pointedly ignoring her wish that he "help Guy." She gleamed as though burnished, and I wondered as much at her reaction as I did at Conrad's generosity.

He was, now that I thought of it, unfailingly courteous, almost courtly, with Hilda. It seemed to come naturally. I don't think he liked her, and he wasn't capable of pity. If he had any designs on her, they must have involved emancipating her from the prat she was married to. "We had a terrible flight," she called to me. "There was a baby in first class, and Guy couldn't sleep a wink."

Guy gleamed with sweat, as though mere existence on the material plane were physically exhausting; which I think it was. The cabin of a commercial jet, first class or no, must be almost as real as the Great Swamp. "They should have special flights for children," he said to me. Hilda had run off to get him something. "Really. Or soundproof compartments." He looked, as always, like a big fussy baby himself.

"Welcome back, Guy," I said, relieving him of a carry-on, just to occupy my arms, in case either of them expected some sort of hug. They weren't, as Abigail said, physical people, but you can never be too cautious.

Guy beamed at me momentarily, and then at something in back of me, which apparently disappeared, or failed to materialize, curdling his smile. "Where are the others?" he wondered. "Where are Tansy and Pilar and Tim?"

"They're at work, Guy." How did he expect us to fit everybody into the Plymouth? Another real world glitch. "Where I should be, as a matter of fact—"

"There's Abigail!" Guy toddled past me toward the curb, trailed by Hilda, who had acquired and now flourished a bottle of club soda and a pack of antacids. Conrad and I followed behind, and ended up with Hilda in the back seat. He sat in the middle, with an arm stretched out behind each of our necks, and quickly dozed off.

I was by now used to this proximity. True to my word, if not to myself, I had moved in with them two days before, for an open-ended stay. Anna was home alone, and fine—I was commuting to the library every weekday, and had just popped in on her the day before. She barely looked up from her reading. Anna likes to check out the new books, and there was a two-foot-tall pile of them on her desk. "Give my love," she told me, "to the H. C."

Happy Couple.

After two days alone with the H. C. it should have been something of a relief to have the DeVilbisses around. Yet as I watched them settling in, commandeering the phones and fussing with the parlor furniture, I found myself alarmingly discommoded. Apparently I had settled already into a routine comforting enough to be jarred askew. Conrad and I (*Conrad and I!*) had been using the round oak dining table as our office, and I was genuinely annoyed when, within a half hour of our arrival, Hilda swept the table clean of our papers and ashtrays and began to massage it with linseed oil.

I had agreed to help him write his new book. Initially I pretended to think he wanted help with grammar and syntax, but of course he was after what he called *deep background*. What, you mean like "Deep Throat," I asked, and he said no, he'd leave that sort of thing to the Little Woman. Still, I agreed.

Now we had to regroup in Guy's small den, from which we were immediately chased, in case Guy were suddenly mugged by his muse, and by the end of a long day we had set up shop in what had obviously once been a children's nursery, and was used by the childless DeVilbisses as a catch-all. The whitewashed pine table and chairs were undersized, yet Conrad was not diminished in using them.

Because the chair hurt my back, I soon developed the habit of sitting on the floor, leaning against an old mahogany hope chest, my eyes closed more often than not to the sight of him on his stupid little chair, all spidery angles with his overlong arms and legs and jutting knees, jotting God knew what on his yellow legal pad. Abigail appeared from time to time, bringing coffee in the morning, tea or beer in the afternoon, Calvados (of which Guy had laid in an inexhaustible supply) late into the night.

Guy and Hilda paid no attention to our project, so immersed were they in Guy's ascendancy. Journalists from the *Journal* and the *Globe* and the *Times* traipsed in and out of Agincourt. Robert J. Lurtsema persuaded Guy to grant a live in-house sunrise interview for NPR, which the rest of us were invited to attend but didn't. It wasn't necessary to be in the room anyway, as their deep voices, especially Lurtsema's, vibrated the walls and bed frame, and if it hadn't been for Hilda's punctuating giggles and lead-foot kitchen forays you could imagine a subtle musical performance, instead of the obsequy festival it actually was. "Robert J.," Hilda reported with shining eyes, "says that Guy is the Berlioz of poetry."

"Wasn't Berlioz that *idée fixe* guy?" asked Conrad.

"Yes!" said Hilda. "That's it exactly. Sex is Guy's grand

idée fixe!" She ran off to attend to Guy, leaving Conrad shaking his head.

"Lurtsema's having fun with him," Conrad said. "Berlioz was a hack."

"Arguably," I said, "but he was an intellectual hack." See, we were sharing jokes.

It was a jolly time for all of us. Guy and Hilda, for obvious reasons, were delirious as clams, and Abigail was close to content, the closest she ever got in that marriage, because Conrad was treating her almost considerately. I even spied, on rare occasions, tiny gestures of affection; his hand resting lightly on her hip; an absent pat on her bottom as she poured us tea. Maybe he was placated by my presence there. And I think, too, that the DeVilbisses channeled whatever contempt he was still able, effortlessly, to muster. We were united as spectators and critics.

Our sleeping arrangements were odd. Conrad and Abigail moved out of the master bedroom, and of course I offered to vacate the guest room and use the convertible settee on the back porch, but Conrad insisted that Abigail move in with me. He wouldn't hear of me sleeping on a couch, even though I protested that I could sleep anywhere. "So can I," he said, and I never did figure out where he did sleep. The settee remained unrumpled, and there were no other sleepworthy surfaces in the cottage. Some nights I would come awake predawn and picture him hanging upside down from the rafters, like a giant bat.

Abigail didn't mind sleeping with me. When it came down to it, neither did I. After the light went out the decades fell away and we were kids again. I've always liked to read myself to sleep, which habit had annoyed the young Abigail, even when I moved into my own room. She had then been passionate about sleep, throwing herself into it with her customary abandon, and the depths of her slumber had been legendary in our family. She slept through squealing brakes and thunderclaps. Her eyelids never even fluttered the night Hank McAdoo threw one of Father's tomatoes at her bedroom window with undue force, so that it shattered and sprinkled little shards like fairy gems around her sprawled form. But now she was slow to doze off and slept fitfully, and seemed to welcome my reading light, the rhythmic scrape of pages.

Of course she never let me read for long, seducing me into reminiscence, and most nights we lay awake for an hour or two, rehashing the amorous adventures of her youth, which were much more interesting to me now than they had been at the time. I could not help but admit a certain heroic quality in my sister. She had been a jolly girl, wild and irresponsible, but courageous as hell. She had taken on the boys at their own game. Now I let her divulge all the details I had warded off thirty years before. Who was the worst lover (a tie between Frank Calef, no surprise, and Carmine Previte, whom everyone, even I, had called, with blundering accuracy, Carmine Perverty). Her most technically accomplished lover was Ob Minurka, the hairy dwarf.

One night, when the DeVilbisses had been home for three or four days, she asked me to explain myself. My constant celibacy. She had always deferred to me on this point. She had ridiculed me, and tried to win me over, but she had never once asked why. "Actually," she said, in the dark, "I kind of got a kick out of it. It seemed so romantic."

"Romantic?"

"Yeah. Like a nun. Romantic and mysterious, and something I could always count on. I felt like you were keeping something for me. You know. Like Catholics."

No non sequitur, but shorthand to me. She was thinking of meatless Fridays and magical beads and how comforted we Protestants are, in our irrational heart of hearts, that somebody somewhere is out on a limb, observing the invisible. My virginity was to Abigail a ritualized, idealistic thing. That she valued my choice would seem to imply that on some level she regretted her own.

"Hell, no," she said. "I just mean it was interesting. I loved it that you could live in your head."

This was exasperating. "Now I'm some exotic animal, like a winged hedgehog. Anyone can live in his head. If you were in an iron lung—"

"Yeah, but that'd be a whatsit. A deal. Begins with A."

"Accommodation. Adaptation. Appomattox."

"Adaptation. With you it's different."

Is it? Was it? "Maybe," I said, "I adapted to you."

"No, absolutely not. You were never not this way. You were always this neat little package. You had everything you wanted tucked inside."

"Now I'm an earthworm."

"Did I ever tell you about Mel Brezniak, and his amazing—"

"Good night, Abigail."

"Lord, I'm hungry. I'm so hungry."

"Eat something."

"Good night, Dorcas."

So I was Sister Dorcas of Frome, and some day my dessicated, indestructible hymen would be a holy relic, but for now I haunted the temporal plane, restless and prone to giggling fits. Conrad made me laugh before my morning coffee, sometimes just by appearing, slumped and rumpled and snide, in a doorframe. I could not sit still, except in our "office," and once found myself drying dishes with Hilda and commiserating with her over the impossibility of concocting a decent *poulet vent vert* without *estragon,* which is apparently the French word for "tarragon," but which I assumed for a hilarious quarter-hour was capitalized and Hilda's wonderfully subversive pet name for Guy, who no doubt saw himself as the Vladimir type. Existential chicken!

At Guy's prodding she was working her way through the Alice B. Toklas Cookbook. The "Murder in the Kitchen" chapter had turned into an operatic tragedy, on which topic Hilda was unusually candid. Some months before Guy had brought home two live pigeons for Hilda to smother, then rabbited, pausing in the kitchen door for a final admonition: "Memorize every detail." She couldn't bring herself to use her hands, and it turns out that you can't smother pigeons with a feather pillow; they just keep dozing off. In the end one died much harder than it had to, and the other she released into the Camembert streets. That evening, she presented Guy with the mangled, uncooked body of her victim, nestled, with Shakespearean cunning, beneath a domed tin lid. If this was a revolutionary act it was undercut by Hilda's ruminant silence. "I didn't need to say a word," she crowed, "and of course we never spoke of it again." No, she needed to ram the feathered corpse down his throat, but no matter.

At the time I was conscious only of my own strangeness; I was at ease not just with my brother-in-law, but with a small houseful of people, two of whom were idiots. This was not like me. I should have longed for solitude. I kept one bag packed against just this eventuality, and I never even opened it. Looking back, I can see it was like summer camp, except that I was buoyed, not by rustic novelty, but by the bracing unpredictability of my own moral character. Who knew what was going to come out of my mouth next, or whom I'd see in the bathroom mirror? Not me.

Guy and Hilda stayed for three weeks, during which time there were book signings, forays to Harvard and Brown, and a winter clambake sponsored by the Frome Literary Society.

On that occasion our poetess laureate, Shirley Joe Birdwell, schlepped all the way down to Watch Hill to terrorize Guy with a thirty-stanza encomium, upon which the heavens commented with cascades of icy rain, and the fire could be restarted only with gasoline, which pretty much ruined the clams.

The evening before their return to France was devoted, at Guy and Hilda's insistence, to the DeVilbiss Circle. Hilda and Abigail did most of the cooking, and Conrad and I, armed with a generous check from Guy, went out and bought enough wine, almost, to replenish the reserves of well-aged Médoc and Côtes du Rhône Guy was about to render up from his cellar. It was an Occasion. I got as drunk as I had at the Rational Tap with Conrad (we all did) but what remain in my mind aren't snapshots or slides but paintings, oils, deep-hued and tactile and candlelit. Caravaggio maybe.

Here we all are, arrayed around the oak table, holding hands and swaying to one side. Not saying grace, of course, though Guy did say something about the Muse of Invention, the "mother of us all." Guy looks, as he says this, not at his dutifully barren wife, but at my sister, who yawns, great-throated. Conrad looks arrows at me. Tim's carefully built fire throws our shadows on the ceiling. There ought to be an exquisite rat off in a corner sniffing the air.

In this small masterpiece, all of us but one incline solicitously toward Tim, who has sloshed burgundy all over his shirtfront and regards himself with comical alarm, his cheeks and nose ruddy with booze. Hilda's white arm extends toward him with a proffered napkin, neatly triangulating the central image, whatever that means. At the far left, in deep shadow, Conrad contemplates his ragged fingernails.

Here's the sofa-size one, or it would be if the table were long instead of round, with Guy standing in the center, a beatific smile on his face, arms outstretched, palms up, to formalize our fellowship. Apparently he's making a speech, although judging from the glazed upturned faces of his disciples not much of it is sinking in. Dorcas and Tim, from opposite sides of the table, spoon-launch croutons at the head of Our Blessed Lord.

Guy had Hilda print up a formal menu, which I still have, here, under the blotter on my desk.

During the interminable hors d'oeuvres section, Tim and I went out to the kitchen and attempted spontaneous Quahogs Étouffées, which spontaneously flambéed when Tim dropped his cigarette in a puddle of apple brandy. The flames were blue and quite beautiful, and cold, it seemed to us, or it must have, because after some experimentation we each dipped all ten fingertips in Calvados and lit them, then raced back into the dining room with our hands outstretched, shouting "Voilà!" We achieved a nice scream from Hilda, but by the time Guy turned to see our spectacle the flames had gone out, so we had to run back to the kitchen to try again. My sister came in and stopped us, actually calling me, for the one and only time in our lives, *childish.*

What she said was, "Grow up, Dorcas." I, who had done nothing but Grow Up for thirty-eight straitlaced years. "Oh ho," I said, drawing ineptly on four years of high school French, *"Comme le ver de terre a revolvé!"* and Tim told her to "Get bent," although only after she had left the kitchen. We cooled our fingertips, which we had in fact slightly burned, under the kitchen tap, and then trooped back to the table like chastened kids.

I remember that part clearly, the part when I played with matches. The rest of it, until we went outside, is pretty much lost to me, although I have the impression that by the time we reached Normandy Apple Tart with Calvados Crème Fraiche my ridiculous behavior had brought Abigail and Conrad closer together. I don't think he approved of my antics.

Hors d'oeuvres

Portuguese Artichoke Crowns
with Crab Pepper Mousse

Asparagus de Ruffey
in Fontina Phyllo Tartlets

Fritatta Niçoise DeVilbiss

Soup

Potage Dieppoise
with Narragansett Bay mussels

Salad

Champignons en Salade de Guy

Dual Entrée

Poulet Normand

Carpaccio of Normandy Beef
with Basil and Garlic Sauce

Baked Potatoes Abigail

Bread Basket

Dessert

Normandy Apple Tart with Calvados Crème Fraiche

I do seem to recall him advising Pilar to "rein in" her husband. Today that strikes me as jarringly strange, but at the time I didn't care. I was AWOL and enjoying myself; I was little and quicksilver among the Big People; I was not responsible. Let someone else clean up the mess. Let Abigail clean up the mess. Get bent!

One last painting. The viewer looks down from, say, a forty-five-degree angle at a round table artfully strewn with knocked-over goblets and crumpled serviettes, white linen blotched with grease and wine. The diners lean back, sated, porcine, their hands and faces shiny in candlelight, except the far center two, the artist's focus. Abigail and Conrad sit tall, backs straight, shadowed faces inclined toward each other, well-matched. It looks like some kind of goddamn allegory, with a one-word title, some abstract noun. *Fellowship. Gathering. Family.* Damned if I know. *Envy. Avarice. Gluttony.* I should probably mention, just in case it matters, ha ha, that I didn't see Abigail take a single bite all evening.

As it turned out, Hilda cleaned up the mess. Sober, cheerful, and bustling, she threw the rest of us out of the house, into the mild November night, to walk it off. "Also," she shouted after us, "Guy has a wonderful surprise for all of you!" We shuffled forward in the dark, arms outstretched against unseen obstacles, single- and double-file (I was single), with Conrad and Abigail in the lead, until they insisted that Guy go first, since, Conrad said, "Apparently you know where we're going."

"I can't wait," I told the person in front of me, who I assumed was Tim but turned out to be Tansy, "for the wonderful surprise." Tansy had been as subdued as Pilar all evening. She said she was going to vomit soon, which didn't sound too wonderful, plus she was ruining the surprise. I think her private life had gone seriously awry, and I had no interest in learning about it.

There are few streetlights in Watch Hill, and it took a while for my eyes to become accustomed to the dark. When I could see the sidewalk I ran ahead and tapped on Guy's shoulder, demanding to know what the deal was. I was starting to sober up, which wasn't good. "I have been given," said Guy, "the keys to the city."

"Are we going to loot the joint, or what?"

"They've opened up the carousel for me," Guy said.

And sure enough, we were at the end of Bay Street, in front of the Flying Horse Carousel. I could tell it by its squat cylindrical shape.

"In theory the switch is back here someplace," I heard Guy say, shuffling off, and in a short time we were assaulted by multicolored incandescent light.

"Wow," said my sister.

The Flying Horse Carousel is supposed to be the oldest carousel in the United States. According to legend, it arrived at its permanent resting place in Watch Hill purely by accident, abandoned there by traveling carnies in 1879. Tansy, roused from her secret sorrow, got very excited. "It came in on a wagon," she said, "drawn by one dray horse. That horse was so faithful that it refused to abandon the carousel. When it died, they attached its tail to one of the wooden horses. I wonder which." She began to examine each painted rump. It didn't take much to restore Tansy's equilibrium.

Each horse was carved from a single block of basswood and suspended by chain from a center frame. When the carousel ran, the horses flew out centrifugally, over the dirt floor. They were smaller than most merry-go-round horses, and, in fact, no one over the age of twelve was allowed to ride them. The safest maximum limit, Tansy said, was one hundred pounds.

"Dorcas," said my sister. "Do you remember this place?"

I remembered reading about it, but that was all. *"Reading about it?* Jeez, you're amazing. You *rode* on it, for God's sake. Father took us here one summer, when we were eleven. I didn't get to ride. I was too big."

"That's too bad," I said, "since obviously you wanted to, and I didn't. That's why I don't remember. They were always making me look out the car window, and go to the circus, whereas all I ever truly wanted—"

"That's terrible," Guy said. "You were under twelve. They should have let you on."

"It's a national monument," Tansy said, reprovingly.

"So is my wife," said Conrad.

"I'm thinner now," said Abigail, "than I was then."

I was startled to realize that this was true. She wasn't even plump anymore, really. Not thin, but this only because her skin hadn't tightened up. She looked drained, depleted, and small. I am taller than my twin by a good inch, but until this night had never been able, literally, to look down on her. She had been larger than life. But no more.

"This brings us," said Guy, "to the surprise. They're letting us turn it on. Just for a few minutes."

"What's the point?" I asked. "We still can't ride it. We're not—"

"We can if we choose to," Guy said. "I've been assured that a couple of minutes won't damage anything."

"Since when," asked Conrad, who looked terrifically annoyed, "have you given a shit about Americana, you Bicentennial-hating, frog-fucking snob? This isn't your speed, and it sure as hell isn't mine. I'm going to bed."

"And I am getting on one of these horses," said Abigail.

Conrad laughed an ugly laugh. "Well, I'll stick around for that. Tomorrow the Chamber of Commerce is going to get the big surprise."

"You'll just have to bear with me on this," said Guy. "It has to do with a work in progress."

"My wife?"

"In a way. The work in progress is my first novel, and your wife is its inspiration."

"You're writing a *novel*?" This really was a nasty shock to me. "You hate fiction." Guy had this thing about what he called, with venomous contempt, "mere psychological realism." He often bragged that he hadn't read a single novel since *Nightwood*.

"Hilda thinks it's time."

"Why?" What a pompous poop. "Jesus, Guy, why not build a suspension bridge? Write a symphony? You know as much about—"

"You're writing a novel about my wife? Have you lost your fucking mind?"

"How do you turn this thing on?" Abigail gazed raptly at a white horse with a worn leather saddle. Its neck and head were extended, so that it could crane its gaze upward at the sun. "I remember this one," she said. "It had its own name."

"They all do," said Tansy. "Look at the bridle. See, there's a gold nameplate."

"Fayton," Abigail read. "It's the same identical horse."

Meanwhile Conrad was beating up, verbally, on Guy, doing his Dominant Male routine, but it didn't have its usual effect. Guy stood up to him by ignoring him. He seemed *centered*, as Tansy would say, and his eyes remained upon my sister. No, Guy said, mildly, he wasn't interested in Abigail's life story, which Conrad colorfully assured him was a matter of public record anyway. He wasn't interested in "achieving a fictional replica."

"Mere psychological realism," I said. "Heaven forefend. The thing that kills me about you guys, you postmodernist hoo-hah pooh-bahs, is how little respect you have for character. You carry on as though the human personality were some trivial thing, and it's not, it's *not*, it's everything. It's the great mystery." I had Guy's attention. He regarded me with respect, which was thrilling in a way, because I was suddenly sober, energized, speaking up for Readers Everywhere. "Your character. Mine. What does it amount to? It's real, but we can't know it. We can make predictions about our own behavior based on what we've done in the past, and how we feel about it now, and what niggling horrors we come awake to at three o'clock in the morning, but they're only predictions.

"We don't even know if we're good, until it's all over, and then it's too late. We can be decent all our whole lives, and then at the last minute we can do some inexplicable unforgivable thing."

"You always get back to morality, Dorcas," said Guy. "We can all count on *that*. You're predictable. So am I. We're clockwork things."

"Not true!"

"And who," asked Tansy, "is winding the clock?"

"Tansy," I said, "could we try, just this once, not to let this debate turn into a cliché festival?"

I heard a metallic clunk and turned to see my sister astride her dream steed. Her feet barely cleared the ground, and the entire structure listed slightly to her side. She was holding fast to the gold-painted pole, her head thrown back, staring upward in the manner of Fayton, the carousel horse with the irritating, nonsensical name.

"Somebody," piped up Tim, "has to balance it. We need someone on the opposite horse."

"If you're going to make people up," I said, "which is what fiction writers do, Guy, storytellers, they create fictional human beings, then you have an impossible, holy task. You have to create characters as complex and unknowable as real people. The fact that you can't do that, that you can't even come close, is the very reason you should try. If you're not going to bother, then stick with your poetry."

"I can never realize what you people talk about," said Pilar.

"Dorcas," said Guy, "would you mind getting on the other horse?"

"Get on Pegasus, Dorcas," Tansy said.

"I'm talking here," I said. "I'm making a point. Excuse me. Would somebody please for one goddamn second pay attention—"

"Get on Pegasus," said Abigail.

"I heard you," said Guy. "I respect you. Now, please pay me the same respect. I'm looking," he said, reasonably, "for my central image."

"Well who the pluperfect fuck isn't," said Conrad.

I was crying when I got on the horse. Not out loud, but I don't think I bothered to hide my tears. When had I become such a baby? I saw Abigail and her horse rise up, so that we dangled an equal, short distance above the dirt. My horse was a palomino or something. I don't remember the details. Pegasus was Perseus's horse. He sprang from the spilled blood of Medusa. "Abigail," I called to her. "Spell the name of your horse."

"P-h-a-e-t-o-n. Fayton."

"Conrad," ordered Guy, "turn that key back there."

And Conrad did as he was told.

At first we flew in silence at a sedate speed, heads tilting slightly inward, and I could see faces as I passed, Guy gleaming like Buddha, Tim smiling like a kid, Conrad scowling furiously. Why, I wondered, are you so angry? I shouldn't have gotten on Pegasus. It was bad enough that Conrad couldn't intimidate Guy. The *ver de terre* had indeed *revolvé*ed, at least for this one night. On top of this I was somehow betraying him, and I found that this mattered to me. Where did my loyalties lie? Where indeed.

Phaeton, desirous of his father's glory, drove the sun chariot to ground, perishing in spectacular excess of ambition. The night wind, as we gathered speed, froze my eyes, the faces blurred, my tears dried, my ecstatic sister's hair streamed out long and straight behind her upturned head, and the carousel calliope came to life, sharp enough to wake the whole town. "I Wonder Who's Kissing Her Now." We flew faster, parallel to the ground it seemed, our heads close together, our feet outflung and dangerous. The rickety rumbling thing was going to break, we would careen out through picture windows into people's living rooms, we were raising a ruckus, we were out of control. *I wonder if she ever tells him of me.* We were objectified, observed, fiddled with, entertained, like juggler's balls, in the mind of the only postwar poet certain to survive the millennium. We were a central image, Apollo and Dionysus, churning into butter, and that was my last cogent thought, if you can call it that, before I was cut off from my world by pure sensation, and I had no thoughts at all, and what a vast and lonely place that was. No signposts, no template, no limits. I was in my sister's universe. How could she stand it here? *How could anybody stand it here?*

Time Out

The Tail

I still don't believe she's coming full force, but it looks pretty bad. I haven't spotted a single bird all day today. Where do they go? The electricity went an hour ago, but I don't need it to read, although the light through the window is rather nauseating, the color of an illuminating bruise. Not much rain, but a hell of a lot of wind. I finally broke down and masking-taped all my windows, so I must be taking this seriously.

The phone was still working the last time I checked, and Anna was enjoying herself. I don't worry for her safety: The trees around our house are small, mostly birches; even if all of them fall, which they're not likely to do, they can't effect any serious damage. She's rounded up all the candles in the house, and set out a pile of books to read: a Ruth Rendell, *Mansfield Park,* and one of her favorite Sherlock Holmes stories, "The Final Problem." She must be on an English kick.

Of course I didn't bring a transistor radio with me. That's the kind of prideful old bat I am.

There's no one out in the street, on the Mile. Ten cars sit abandoned in the Food Land parking lot, and around back I can just make out the rear of a single trailer truck, looks like an Eclipse Syrup truck, hopping from side to side in an irate fashion. Wind must be pretty strong.

Right across the street a big show is in the making. Some slob apparently started to offload boxes of junk at the Job Lot, then took off without closing up the truck, and already two boxes have come loose, banging up against the Tile World sign, taking out the W, and spilling their contents into the air. Anybody fool enough to step outside right now could get whanged by a bagful of defective dice, impaled by crooked golf tees. Some of it has already made it across the street; two of my cherry trees have been decorated with knee-high-hose eggs and what looks like a plastic (it must be) likeness of the Blessed Virgin.

My guess is that we're at the outer edge. Pandora is playing crack-the-whip with Frome, and her eye could be fifty miles away. A hundred perhaps. Or maybe not. I've never been in the Eye.

Mother and Father told us about the big one, the '38 hurricane, which came along three months before we did, on September 21. Father was in New London on business, and he saw the Eye. (Mother saw it, too, in Frome, but she was the only Rhode Islander who did.) He'd taken the train down, but couldn't very well take it back after a tidal wave deposited an enormous Coast Guard lighthouse tender, by the dainty name of *Tulip,* across its tracks. Father witnessed explosions, fire, and floods on that amazing day, but we could never get him to talk much about the devastation. I suspect he saw dead bodies; it was not like him to dwell upon the tragic. Besides, nothing he saw that day, he told us many times, compared to the experience of the Eye.

This was one of his favorite dinnertime topics. He was worried about Mother, he would begin, home alone and pregnant with us. He wasn't worried for her safety—she was inland, as I am today—but he knew she'd be anxious for him. And I *was*, she would chime in, but bad as the storm was, here at home, I had no idea that it was anything more than a bad storm. We didn't hear the word "hurricane" on the radio until the next day.

Nobody in New England knew what a hurricane was, Father said. I thought it was the end of the world. First the rain, and then the wind, sounded like a hundred trains, and from the second floor of the Mohican Hotel you could hear windows, hotel windows, department store windows, popping like corn.

Then it stopped, and the sun came out. Father ventured outside to help clean up. The sky was blue, he said, but the sea was the awfulest shade of yellow you ever saw. The shade the Devil's eyes would be, said Father, who was ordinarily no devotee of the supernatural. The main street was littered with boats of all sizes, dinghies, sailboats, part of someone's yacht, the *Amphitrite,* and not far from where he wandered the entire business section of the city was on fire, casting up clouds of pitch-black smoke, but he was drawn to the waterfront. It made no sense to go near it, he said, as the water so clearly meant to come for us, but none of us could help ourselves. The land was full of boats and the sea was full of piss ("Say 'urine,' Jabez"), and the sunshine was *wrong,* he realized, the wrong color, and the air felt wrong too. And looking far out over the evil sea, he saw a wall of white cloud, and when he turned around he thought he could just make it out, the white wall, way beyond what few rooftops remained, and gradually he came to realize that they stood in the middle of a huge circle of still light, and all around them the world wheeled.

We were in this cylinder of quiet, he said, and the walls were moving, slowly but perceptibly, counterclockwise. It was, he said, like standing in an inside-out merry-go-round. He wished with all his heart that he could stay in the circle forever, moving with it until he found our mother. But the walls were closing in, and there was nothing to do but face up to whatever was behind them.

Abigail always wanted details, sensory details, what did the upended cars look like, and the women, how were they dressed, and did the wind rip off people's clothes, and she always wanted to hear more about the fires, and the waves. She was disappointed to learn, I recall, that there was no lightning. Although I remember Father's words, dutifully, like a recording secretary, I remained imaginatively back in Frome with Mother, and those bafflingly obtuse radio bulletins. They called it a *storm,* a *nor'easter,* a *fierce blow*; by the time they came up with its proper term it was history. How could that happen? I would ask, how could people be so ignorant, and our parents would explain, again, about Neville Chamberlain, and Czechoslovakia, and how even on that terrible day the only history that mattered was happening in Europe.

It occurs to me today that the entire northeastern seaboard of America was like Icarus in my favorite Auden poem, a boy falling out of the sky, unmourned by a world that had somewhere important to get to. *About suffering they were never wrong, the Old Masters.*

I used to believe that conversations like this, seminal adult talk, drove me to books, the obvious best refuge and bulwark against a perilous world. Now I know this isn't true. I had no choice. My choice was made for me, and Abigail's for her, in the womb.

. . .

And I wonder what is really happening today, right now. My sister, safe inland at the ACI, must have fewer clues than I. The walls there are too solid for buffeting, and I'm not even sure she has access to a window. But if she does, if she can see out, she is in the storm, effortlessly, one with the wind and rain, ravenous, scouring the perceptible earth for every last detail. My sister knows what's really going on. My sister always knows where she is.

I see the ceiling lights flicker and dim, I hear the wind and the pitiful creaking of dying trees, my skin feels raw, hyper-sensitive, not like a fever but like something opposite, an enlivening chill; outside my library articles of evidence mount up, jitterbugging, smacking into one another, slapping up against my windows. Clearly something momentous is happening. But I cannot say what it is. I will not know until it is over, and I can name it. I can't help this. This is what I am.

Winged Hedgehog

Chapter 19

Work in Progress

Now the books really begin to pile up.

We're closing in on the shattering climax, yet Hilda stops the action to flog the dead nag of Guy's first and last novel. Guy's "work" was almost six years in the gestation and only half-term at the time of Conrad's death. After an entirely unconvincing crisis of conscience, Guy decided he had to finish it, and *Appetite* magically contrived to hit the stands the very week of Abigail's preliminary hearing, boosting the hell out of its initial sales. Perhaps Guy's agent, in collusion with Hilda, managed to shield unworldly Guy from their machinations. Perhaps not.

Guy's Abigail, Fanny Montaigne, is a grotesque character, of course Larger than Life, topping off at 8'6". Why do we take writers seriously when they do this? He subjects his Rabelaisian woman to picaresque adventures of dubious eroticism; congress with winos, dead people, bison; at the novel's end she fondles a small child, who turns out to be, *quel surprise,* her own baby self. Hilda affects to draw parallels between this creature and my sister, but really all she's doing is chiding the reading public for neglecting her husband. To understand Abigail, she actually says here, one need only read "aloud, to oneself, in any candlelit church" the saga of her husband's "most deeply felt" creation. I may be wrong about the bison. There was something both unspeakable and confusing with a beast.

Appetite's first reviews were respectful, if tentative, and initial sales quite robust, considering that their author had never sold respectably outside university walls (within which he was taught widely enough to keep him in Calvados and pearwood bread troughs). But after the first month sales began to plummet on word of mouth, and then came "Big Fat Fanny," Gore Vidal's public disemboweling of Guy in the *Review of Books,* a brilliant three-page stompfest so joyously vicious as to become an instant legend, and the DeVilbisses fled to the Old World in mortification. ("You know," said Abigail, wiping her eyes as she finished reading the review in the prison visiting room, "he really should have seen that one coming. Poor little booby." This was another occasion where we made such a racket that I was asked to leave.) *Appetite* still dominates remainder shelves and church rummage tables. I look forward, once the furor of the trial dies down, and with it any attendant curiosity about Guy's "work," to consigning our single copy to my basement morgue, alongside *Fun with Stunts* and *The Irritable Bowel Handbook.*

Conrad's work in progress will never make it into print. Abigail had the only copy of the manuscript, ten blue-lined sheets stained with gin and smeared ash, and she gave it to her lawyers, and sent a Xerox to me, across the top of which she wrote "Exhibit A!!!" It is, in fact, Defense Exhibit A, and on its strength alone Miles Minden is confident of acquittal. You could tell that the sheets had been pleated and crimped together at one end, like a child's homemade fan. Whether he did this, or Abigail, I have absolutely no idea. Yes I do. It was him.

It isn't really a manuscript at all, just ten handwritten pages of false starts, framed and punctuated by filthy cartoons, the pornography of a demented, ungifted child: naked women, all headless, all violated, mangled, rearranged, in a variety of ways, exhaustive rather than ingenious. Interspersed with these are what one might take to be abstract doodles, if one were not aware that their creator had the benefit of extensive medical training. Both text and illustration are accomplished with blue ballpoint ink. Each uterine triangle is darkened so thoroughly that the cheap paper bellies out beneath.

When these pages arrived in the mail here, three weeks after his death, I read them on my feet, unable to sit down or even lean back against the wall. I remember Gloria Gomes asking me if I was all right, and telling her, Just fine, thanks. I stood there and pretended, all to myself, that what shocked me was the *prose*. I knew he wrote garbage, I thought, but *really*. Then I went back and analyzed the text, observing clear evidence of his pathological view of women, his deteriorating self-control. There never would have been a book, not even if he had lived. He was too far gone to organize his fear and loathing into even the tritest narrative thread. Tsk, tsk, tsk.

Reading Conrad Lowe's de facto last will and testament was like the morning I woke up in the house I had shared with my sister for almost all of our lives and refused, for as long as I was able, to see the gaping breach in our wall. Just how plain *is* the nose on your face? Unless you're looking in a mirror?

I don't like to contemplate images. Even the most benign make me feel nervous and inadequate. Give me a thousand words any day.

Here was his ideal woman: fleshy, functional, mutilated, immortal, self-replicating. He'd probably been drawing her all his life. He had sketched them while we sat in our Agincourt "office" sparring and gossiping and playing word games and sipping Irish coffee and watching fat squares of sunlight inch across the wall. I admired his black leather notebook binder and his gold A.T. Cross pen, and I told him more than I had ever imagined telling anyone, even my sister. I showed him myself. And he did this.

And they are all Abigail.

Jason Mason Morgan Adam Bunyan Adam Heartstone stared up through slitted lids at the woman's sumptuous ~~flesh ass buttocks~~ plump back. He wasn't sure, but he thought she was his wife. But what was her name? There was something wrong with his mind. And where the hell *was* he? Stuffed into a white slip tight as a tourniquet, she sat in front of a huge chrome magnifying mirror, troweling orange pancake makeup ~~on her face~~ off her cheeks with thick slabs of cold cream. ~~Atop her head was~~ She was wearing a perky ~~A~~ nurse's hat ~~sat on her~~ What was she doing in that nurse's hat? "Don't even think about it," she said, without turning to look at him. "I know you're awak

He could remember only his name: Adam Heartstone. How he came to be here, in this glaringly white room, was ~~the $64 question~~ nagging mystery an awful mystery. *A hospital,* he thought, *must be a hospital room. Must have been in an accident! That explains why I can't feel my*

He couldn't move, except for his eyeballs Only his eyes Apparently he was paralyzed from the ne He couldn't move. No, wait—his eyeballs Why couldn't he move?

What was wrong? Frantically Adam Heartstone glanced around the sterile, steel-and-chrome enclosure, for some clue to his present condition.

Must be some sort of operating room, he reasoned, but then, what was that dining table doing If this was an operating room, it was a pretty weird Wait, this was no operating room! Across from his gurney was a small table covered in white linen, and on it, instead of surgical tools, was a carefully laid place setting. He counted two forks, two knives, and three spoons. Well, he thought, my eyes still move. That's something anyway.

Why couldn't he move? What was wrong? To his horror, Adam Heartstone soon realized that even his eyeballs were

"And anyway, Sweetie," she was purring, as she helped herself to what looked like a link of knockwurst in wine-dark gravy, "I'll be right here, in front of you. Everything you want is right here." He still couldn't move, but sensation was returning to his body, which should have been reassuring, except that the sensation was searing, cauterizing pain. The worst of it seemed to originate below his waist. If only he could look down. If only he could ask her who she was. He wanted so badly to speak. A tear formed in the corner of one eye. He could feel it roll down the length of his face. The familiar woman glanced up from her meal. "What's the matter, Darling?" She speared a piece of meat with her fork and twirled it in the gravy, then suddenly jabbed it toward his face. She grinned at him and her grin grew and grew until it split her face and she was all big square teeth and her lower jaw hung suspended in the air. "Hungry, honey?" she said. "Wanna bite?"

Abigail also sent me a box of cassette tapes, ten hours' worth. Her lawyers said these were of no use to her defense. The cassettes are neatly numbered, and on each side is printed

BIG BITCH

as this was apparently his working title. But of course they are his "interviews" of me. Deep background for a book he never intended to write. Whether my sister ever listened to them, I don't know. It wouldn't matter anyway.

There should be more than ten hours, much more. But Abigail, who doesn't withhold anything from me, wouldn't have hoarded these. Besides, they are numbered consecutively, and the handwriting is his. I have kept them here, in my locked drawer. I have listened to them so many times that they have blunted my memory, stunted my imagination, and although I know they reproduce only a fragment of our conversation, they have become, in effect, definitive. And yet, surely, not representative. These conversations are edgy, rancorous. I remember rising, mid-morning, and looking forward to the day. I remember laughing and laughing, and making him laugh too. I just can't recall specific occasions, and when you listen to the tapes, well, there really isn't that much to laugh about. He must have erased the ones I mean. Or perhaps, most of the time, he didn't bother to record. The evidence is gone. I know I didn't imagine it. The laughter.

What was your first time?
You know I'm a virgin.

I mean what was the first time you said no?

I was twenty-one, apprenticing at the Rumford Library. He was a volunteer tutor who used to come in on weekday afternoons to work with illiterate adults. His name was Abe Marx.

What did he look like?

Funny little man, retirement age, shorter than me. Furry. He saw me reading *Atlas Shrugged* and demanded to know why I was reading that fascist tripe. We used to go out for coffee at a diner right across the Seekonk. He claimed to be on the Hollywood blacklist. I was young enough to believe him. I thought of him as a cross between André Gide and Norman Mailer, and because we were always discussing books, and because of the great difference in our ages, I was caught completely flatfooted by his sexual advance. You will find this freeing, he said, as though he were about to indoctrinate me, on the corporeal plane. It was a horrible moment.

I was offered a permanent job in Rumford, but declined, because of Abe Marx. I can still hear the sound of my own voice when I ran away from him.

What did you say?

Next question.

Come on. What was so terrible about the sound of your voice?

It squeaked.

Like a mouse?

Like a mouse.

What exactly did you say to him? You remember the line, don't you?

I said, What do you think you're doing?

Imitate it.

No.

Come on.

No.

And he said . . .

He said, I'm liberating you from your bourgeois prison.

And you didn't laugh in his face?

I might have, if he had been looking at me. But he wasn't. He was looking at my blouse, the buttons on my blouse.

He was looking at your tits. That's looking at you.

No it's not. I'm not there.

Too true.

He was trying to unbutton my blouse, and his fingers were arthritic. He was concentrating so hard that the tip of his tongue stuck out the side of his mouth. He looked just stunningly exposed. I was paralyzed by pity.

Hold it. He did this in a diner?

Of course not, at a diner. He was walking me to a bus stop. It was nighttime.

A bus stop? Jesus.

Sordid, isn't it? Ludicrous, isn't it? This is tiresome.

He tried to rip your blouse off at a bus stop, and his pickup line was "I'm liberating you from your bourgeois prison"?

It isn't funny.

Abe Marx, studly bon vivant and Commie-about-town.

Actually, he didn't say "prison."

???

He said "oubliette."

What is that? Is that a bidet?

A medieval prison cell, a basement room with an opening in the top, for throwing down food scraps. If you were sent to an oubliette, you were forgotten forever. Hence the name.

He copped a feel at a bus stop and said, "I'm gonna liberate you from your bourgeois oubliette"?

May we please change the subject.

Gotcha.

It's not due to any wittiness on your part. You can forget about that.

You're laughing. A rare treat for me.

It's just the word. *Oubliette.* I always thought it would be a great name for one of Guy's epic heroines. You know, how he always gives them French names—

Oubliette LaVavoom.

"Oubliette Sansculottes, Whore of Lourdes."

Next.

"Oubliette Sans-Pitié."

Next up. What was your next time?

What?

Your next "no."

???

The next one you turned down, Dorcas.

There was no next time.

Not possible.

Necessary. Therefore possible. The episode with Abe Marx was so awful—

Come on. The guy was a klutz, he caught you off guard. Big deal.

It was a very large deal to me.

What were you afraid of? Rape?

I wasn't afraid of anything. It was . . . the exposure. His face was so naked. I was witnessing his inner life, his little soul. I shouldn't say that. I shouldn't comment on anyone's soul, it's not my business. Let's just say it was unpleasant.

Let's not.

. . . .

Dorcas.

. . . .

You are so very interesting.

There was no next time. I kept myself to myself. It was that easy.

But you go to bars a lot. There must have been opportunities.

I certainly don't go to bars a lot. I go to the Blue Moon and the Tap on occasion. I go to bars a lot with you.

No drunken passes?

Certainly not. Where I go, everybody knows me. Half of them think I'm a lesbian.

By design?

In a sense.

Ever been approached by a woman?

Yes, but women are so subtle that they don't make scenes.

For a full thirty minutes Conrad roots around after sapphic truffles. There was a woman once, on an overnight train to an ALA convention in Chicago. She made a discreet overture, I declined in kind, that was it. I could have told Conrad about it but saw no point in rewarding his effrontery. We were allies now, but he still could offend me, and he did on this occasion. Sex was, is, Abigail's territory. If he wanted to talk dirty he could talk to his wife.

Let's talk about power and dignity.

We did that one already.

Yes, but then I was just twitting you.

And you're not now?

I was curious then; I'm just as curious today. I acted

like a jerk because I had to get a rise out of you. You really hated my guts.

Yes.

And now you don't.

I guess not.

You announced, over a plate of greasy lobster, that your sister had power, but no dignity.

I don't remember saying that. That sounds pretty pompous. Why would I say that? I don't announce things.

You were explaining how you and she divided up the world. Sacred and profane, you said. Mind and body.

It's not that simple. I probably said all that—

You actually said all that.

Because I was upset. There's nothing wrong with Abigail's mind. She's just lazy. She takes everything in, the same as I do. Nothing gets past her. She just doesn't bother sorting it out.

We're talking about you.

I bother. That's it. That's the whole thing. You can put that on my tombstone. *She bothered.*

And is bothered. Everything bothers you.

You should talk.

What do you mean?

You're the angriest person I ever met. Everything sets you off. Do you know that sometimes you actually make me want to defend Guy DeVilbiss? What do you get out of batting him around?

It isn't what I get. It's what Guy gets. I'm just performing a service for my old chum.

Please.

What do you think he keeps me around for? He gets his loving from everyone else. I'm the anti-Hilda.

Guy's a masochist? I don't see that.

Guy's an artist. Artists are ruthless. He takes what he needs, and he needs my contempt. Plus I'm his model. I'm everything he despises.

Professes to despise. Underneath it all he doesn't have any more use for women than you do. You both look at us and see what you need to see.

Some day he's gonna cut me loose. I'm too much of a political liability.

Which brings up the obvious question: What do you keep *Guy* around for? What's in it for you?

. . .

What? Quit it.

. . .

I said knock it off.

How can you ask me that, Dorcas? Without Guy, there are no Gorgon Twins. There is no dark lady. I'd be out there in the void, snarling and gnashing away all by myself.

You were friends from college. It didn't have anything to do with us.

We were the kind of friends who got together once every couple of years, for a drink at the Plaza or at some international airport, and once for a lost weekend at a Famous Writers Retreat. I've seen more of Guy and Hilda in the past year than in all of the previous thirty.

Lower your voice.

They can't hear me. They never hear anybody.

His voice is suddenly petulant. In fact, throughout all the recordings he sounds twenty years younger than in real life. Everybody sounds young. I guess the cheap mike didn't pick up the lower register. We sound young and offhand and as if we have all the time in the world.

In the background there is never silence; always some sibilant scratchings, paper sounds, as though our "office" had been infested with little sheets of animated paper shuffling about by themselves. Sometimes you can hear my sister come in with refreshments, or a request from Hilda that we "keep it down, dears, Guy's trying to nap." (So Conrad was wrong about not being heard. Except he was right too: They heard us only as ambient noise, potential muse-blockers.)

Abigail says

Want a G and T, honey?

and

Hey, Baby, can I freshen that?

and

Damn, those two are driving me crazy. Could I just hang around you guys for a half hour or so?

and in my memory he answers her, and I do, of course, and we chat about this and that, and we thank her for her kind attentions. And of course we let her hang around us guys for a half hour or so. But on the Big Bitch tapes all you hear is glasses clinking, papers dancing, the soft click of a closing door.

Surely we at least made eye contact with her. Nodded thanks. Smiled in a friendly fashion. Surely we did that.

He wasted hours on my childhood, my adolescence, trying to find his way in there, the fool. Finally he asked me about my first book. My real first time.

The Hidden Staircase, the best (I was soon to discover) of the Nancy Drews, and though I soon outstripped them, even found them funny, I still have my copy of that first one, bound in blue and orange. I read for myself all the books my mother had read to me, and then I went to the Scituate Library, there being no Squanto yet, and took out every fairy tale collection I could find, Andersen and Grimm and then Perrault, the French tales, stories from all corners of Europe and Asia. Soon I graduated to world mythology. The Norse were unbearably depressing; even their gods were mortal; but the Greek gods and heroes gave me a bridge, a lens through which to view the people around me, the forgettable face in my bedroom mirror. I read about Io and Tantalus and Athena and Phaeton, and my world achieved solidity and color. The gods were both petty and divine; they acted just as the rest of us would if we had the power. Eventually of course I outgrew them too, put away my homemade paper dolls, but I can still recall how brightly they burnished my inner life. They were like Father's old View-Master, a favorite toy of my preliterate days, which when you held it up to lamplight flooded our ordinary rooms with exotica. King Beaudoin, the Oldevai Gorge, the Apollo Fountain at Versailles.

When we hit adolescence, our parents had their hands full with Abigail and couldn't stop to worry about me. Every now and then one of them would ask me, especially on long car trips, to please put down my book and look out the window at something, and once Mother burst into tears at the dinner table and observed that life was passing me by. A shocking moment: I think she was entering into the change. Later she apologized, and I assured her that life was doing no such thing. I don't think she ever truly understood, and this still hurts me, as she of all people should have appreciated what I was doing. There were a couple of years then, in my teens, when I wavered; when I wondered if indeed something were wrong with me, and when my life was going to start. One summer I went for a whole week without reading anything but cereal boxes and shampoo bottles. It was a grim ordeal, and to this day the phrase "lather, rinse, repeat" is a tiny Pavlovian trigger of anxious dread. Then my favorite high school teacher, Mr. Bliss, mentioned C. S. Lewis to me ("You might look into *Surprised by Joy*") and soon all was right again. Lewis never sold me on mere Christianity, but he did assure me that I wasn't neurotic. It was possible to live an imagined life, and to live it fully. To dwell within one's own mind and, through books, the minds of others.

You escape, said Abe Marx, into your books. I didn't have the wit then, quite, for the obvious riposte: I escape, when I feel the need, into what all you bullies insist is reality. I study birds, library patrons, local politicians. Sometimes I garden. Sometimes I watch the Sox. Sometimes I drink. I keep a neat house and I pay my taxes, all in the real world. But I don't live there.

Of course, Lewis was a scholar, and I am not. I do have a reputation, locally, as something of an intellectual, but this is wrong. I am simply an omnivorous reader, and like all good omnivores I take my pleasures where I find them. In my real life, my inner life, I am as great a sensualist as my sister.

How does that work, exactly?

What do you mean?

It's not that I don't believe you. I'm your greatest admirer. But most of us plebes do our sensing through our senses, if you get my meaning. Your sister, for instance. Me too, I must admit. Right now, for example, I'm looking at you. There you are. I'm not imagining you. I couldn't. I'm not that clever.

Well, of course, but what is your point? I'm not claiming to be a spiritual entity.

Your speech is clipped, precise, and low. I hear you clearly. You have a unique scent—

Aren't you cute.

—of Castile soap and lemon polish, and today . . .

Excuse me?

. . . don't panic . . . just checking . . . you've used a new shampoo. Your hair smells of almonds.

It's Hilda's. I ran out of Prell.

Did you.

Look, big deal, I'm a perceptible object.

You're wonderful.

I most certainly am not.

And I love your mind, I hold your inner self in the highest regard, but Dorcas baby, here you are. Look. See? There's your shadow.

. . .

Dorcas?

Six more weeks of winter.

Aren't *you* cute. I could never have gotten to your mind without my senses. So I ask again, how do you pull it off? Mental sensualism? [He burlesques this ridiculous word: *sssen-ssyooallism*. It is a gauntlet, a white-glove slap in the face.]

. . .

Now you're pissed at me.

I went to college too. You're just playing with words. You're wasting my time.

I'm sorry. Sit down. I'm truly sorry.

I was referring to the sensual experience of reading. The book is real, the chair I'm sitting in, the lightbulb is real, everything is three-D real. Whoopee. I read in time, okay? You win. The time is real. The time is gone. The time—

Take it easy.

I read Ray Bradbury when I was twelve years old, on a Congregational church retreat in Framingham, baby-sitting for the minister's children in a freezing cold log cabin, late at night, while the others were singing around the campfire. I read by the light of a kerosene lantern, and the lantern grew dimmer and dimmer, until I could barely see, and the darker it got the scarier the story became, and then, upon the last line, the light went out. *Something Wicked This Way Comes* was the greatest book I ever read in my whole life. It is more real than the minister's children, or Framingham, Massachusetts.

Ethan Frome. I was eighteen, a freshman at Bates, alone on my dormitory floor over Thanksgiving break. Snow fell in big wet clumps, four days in a row, you never heard such silence.

American Tragedy, I'm in the back seat of the car, we're driving to Franconia Notch to look at the flume, whatever that is, Abigail is hungry and bored, demands to stop every hour for one thing or another, Father lectures us all on passing landmarks, and I've caught the edge of our car blanket in my rolled-up window and made myself a little cave. They fry Clyde Griffiths for having entertained a criminal thought. I am rapt and appalled. "The Old Man in the Mountain, Dorcas," mourns my mother, "You're missing it all." The blanket is a tattered old strawberry quilt of our grandmother's, I can see it still, with my *eyes*.

Ditto *Hunchback,* same quilt, different destination, Quebec City, or Ausable Chasm, and when they pry Quasimodo from Esmerelda and his bones crumble into dust, I cry like a baby, a marble baby, Niobe. I don't make *one audible sound.*

All right.

See how it works?

I see. I do.

These are my memories. This was my youth. This is my life.

I believe you.

Go to hell.

In the end I suppose he did.

CHAPTER TWENTY

Purgatory

Hilda's antepenultimate chapter is called "Hunger." (A good plain title, for Hilda.) She covers over a year in fifteen pages, taking the story from their departure from Agincourt in late 1977 to the brink of February 13, 1979. The details are vague, because the DeVilbisses were absent most of that time, and Abigail apparently wasn't very forthcoming. I can actually sympathize; she didn't confide in me much, either.

What basically happened was that after Guy and Hilda left for France, things fell apart. I wasn't expecting that; I thought we would continue as before, only without the annoying hosts. There was no reason I could see to alter our daily routine. Yet immediately the atmosphere turned sour. Abigail and Conrad, returning from dropping them off at Logan, were at each other's throats as they slammed the Plymouth doors. Undoubtedly he had started it, whatever it was, but my sister was giving it back to him, and this was new. She wasn't going to bend any more. That night she sent us out to the Blue Moon, just to get a bit of peace. He was in a foul, uncommunicative mood. Not rude specifically, but cold, distracted. This had a shameful effect on me: I found myself trying to amuse him, and when I realized this, and even in my ethically compromised state, I was disgusted. Perhaps, I said, it's time for me to move back to my own home. This roused him to a semblance of his former charm, and the evening ended amicably. But it was the beginning of a new era, the last era. The Bad Time.

He was chronically nasty with Abigail, to little effect, which worsened his mood. He had always been able to hurt her. But now she was too busy exercising and starving to pay much attention to him.

Every morning before sunrise, she would jog to Fort Mansfield and back, and at lunchtime she would drag out the rowing machine she had ordered from Hammacher-Schlemmer and sweat through two soap operas. The rowing noise, a steady, rhythmic thunder, drove Conrad crazy, and he was always shouting at her to knock it off, Dorcas and I can't concentrate, as though we were engaged in some great creative National-Book-Award–winning endeavor, instead of playing In the Manner of the Adverb and debating whether rye or bourbon made the perfect boilermaker.

By Christmas she was truly thin. The exercise had tightened her skin, and for the first time since Anna she had a waist. She looked ten years older than me. Nobody was happy with the new Abigail. She took no pleasure that I could see in her hard-won slenderness. Instead of reveling in a new wardrobe she schlumped around the house in voluminous old clothes. Her hair was lank and often unwashed, and she didn't bother with makeup. She was totally focused on shedding weight, but as an end in itself, rather than a bridge to some idyllic future.

I was so worried about her that I surreptitiously made an appointment with Dockery Dick and tricked her into his office. When we pulled up she didn't want to go in ("What is this? Another intervention? Shame on you."), but went through with it anyway. I don't think she had the energy to kick up more of a fuss. The visit was a disaster. The Stooge was delighted with her weight loss, not to mention her monogamous state, both of which he took as the gifts of a benevolent, intervening Christ, and the beaming lunkhead actually followed her back out into the waiting room to ask me if I wasn't just so proud of my sister.

Unhappiest of all was Conrad. The man thought he had issued an impossible challenge, and now he didn't know what to do. That he could no longer insult her body drove him wild.

I remained with the H. C. at Watch Hill for almost three more months, commuting to Squanto on weekdays, spending the occasional night in my own home with Anna, but always returning for the weekend. I stuck it out through Thanksgiving and Christmas and into the New Year. Anna came down for the school Christmas break, during which time everyone was civil, and she and I saw a snowy owl late one afternoon, perched atop the Flying Horse Carousel. After she left, the atmosphere became so noxious that I threatened more than once to decamp, and each time they stopped me. Not together: It wasn't a concerted effort. They did nothing in concert. He always managed to behave agreeably for just as long as it took to change my mind. And Abigail needed me.

One especially acrimonious night she followed me out to the car, which I had loaded up with my original suitcase and six paper bags full of accumulated odds and ends. "Look," she said, "I know it's rough. But it'll just get worse if you leave." She looked so negligible. There were hollows under her eyes, and I could not remember the last time I had heard her make so much as a wisecrack.

"Come home with me," I said.

"You know I won't."

"But I don't know why."

"Sure you do."

"Whatever's going on here, it isn't love. It isn't even love-hate. I'm not just talking about him now. You too. The two of you loathe each other. I don't know how you can stand this."

"You don't know everything," she said, patiently.

"Did he send you out here?"

"Of course not," she said. "Yes," she said, "but I'd have stopped you anyway. *I* need you," she said.

And of course I helped her unpack the car. But from then on I slept poorly, and spent more time with my sister than with him. I refused to jog, but I did walk behind her in the early mornings, before leaving for the library, and trained my binoculars as often on her diminishing form as on the winter birds. I began to feel as though I were shepherding my sister through some long, serious, possibly final illness. I stopped drinking.

Probably of the three of us, Conrad suffered the most. He couldn't taunt his wife anymore, and he couldn't get lit up with me. And Guy and Hilda were gone. Despite his professed disregard for them, I think that in some odd way they functioned as his surrogate family. After his death we learned that he had mistresses stashed in all the major cities, three in southern California alone, but they were all more or less professionals, and not one seemed distraught at his passing. He simply had financial arrangements with them. In fact one of them wrote supportive letters to Abigail at the ACI, the gist of which was, the bastard had it coming to him. The point is, he had no friends. Only his literary agent came to the funeral, and he was just sniffing around after a fast postmortem buck. Guy and Hilda, as silly as they were, actually valued Conrad Lowe, and I think this meant more to him than he let himself believe.

Now he had no family, no punching bag, and no drinking buddy, and he was not doing well. Many nights he disappeared until two or three in the morning. Twice we got late-night calls from the local constabulary, and we had to drive down to the Westerly police station and collect him. Two weeks into the new year he wrapped the Plymouth around a copper beech, and after that he was stuck inside with us, as I refused to let him take my car.

One Sunday morning in early February I attempted to sneak out by myself for a solitary day at Squanto. I was halfway to the car when Abigail called to me from their bedroom window. I assured her that I'd be back by nightfall, but she insisted that I wait for her. I assumed Conrad was still asleep, but five minutes later they emerged together, too lightly dressed for the day. "Look," I said, practically begging, "I need some time to myself. I just have to be alone."

Abigail threw two satchels into the back seat and followed them in. Conrad rode shotgun. "Lead on," he said to me, and slammed the door.

I drove for an hour in silence. After I crossed the Massachusetts line, Conrad asked where we were going. Montreal, I wanted to tell him. Halifax. Nunavut. "Purgatory Chasm," I said, between my teeth.

"Hey!" Abigail said. "That's a great idea!" I could tell she was genuinely pleased. This might have placated me, had we been alone.

"The Bishop Berkeley place, right?" asked Conrad, yawning. "Where he got struck by lightning and realized that the universe was chock full of nothing?"

"That was the other Purgatory Chasm."

"There are *two*? What a magnificent state."

"You're thinking of the one in Middletown. This one isn't even in Rhode Island. And he did not hold that the universe was chock full of nothing."

"Essie S. Perkippy. I knew her well."

"We used to go to Purgatory Chasm all the time when we were kids," Abigail said. "I love it there."

"So what's the deal?" Conrad asked. "Is it an amusement park, or what?"

"It's just the Chasm," Abigail said.

"It's chock full of nothing," I said.

"Whatever you say, ladies."

The day was overcast, the temperature hovering just above freezing, and ours was one of only five cars in the lot. We could hear, from across the road, children playing on the swings and slides, and the push carousel, where my sister always threw up and I did not. Abigail led us through a pine needle-carpeted grove to an old picnic table beside a brick cookout oven, and immediately began to examine the table's underside. Sure enough, there was

A.M.
D.M.
6/16/1949

deeply etched with Father's boy scout knife. I remember being astonished that he would enable us to deface public property, and how he took me by the hand and showed me around the picnic grounds, pointing out all the old initials and avowals of constant love. When I was still skeptical, he said, "Think of it as a kind of library." Actually, it was more of an archaeological site, where you could piece together the mating habits and linguistic vagaries of vanished tribes. On the evidence of these tables and trees, it apparently hadn't occurred to the ancient scribes to etch obscenities until the early 1960s, at which point the quality of the printing itself suffered a downturn. Unless somewhere in Southern New England there's a "Robet Ahearn," it appears that some of them didn't know how to spell their own names. Or maybe they just grew fatigued.

Abigail and I were enjoying identical flashbacks. There was something timeless about this place. We used to come here on hot humid summer days, while everyone else fled to Scarborough Beach and Point Judith, and here it was always cool and dry, and the air smelled of pine. They never modernized the playground, or widened the parking lot, and the rest of it was just a big rocky hole in the ground that had resisted change for at least fourteen thousand years, when the last Ice Age ended and unleashed a glacial torrent on a tectonic fault plane. The resulting deep jumble of boulders, spilling in a quarter-mile-long scar, is a pleasing anomaly in the surrounding Puritan landscape, the mysterious flamboyant red jigsaw piece in a sepia puzzle.

I hadn't packed anything to eat, since I hadn't planned to come here in the first place. I had driven here because, in addition to being a childhood refuge, it was the longest day trip I could think of. As I watched them unpack their satchels I had a startlingly vivid mental picture of myself backing quietly away and driving off, abandoning them to their own devices in the primeval forest. It could be hours before they even realized I was gone. The way everything turned out, I probably should have gone ahead and done it.

Abigail unpacked her usual depressing assortment of rabbit food, which she proceeded to ignore. Conrad had of course brought with him only liquid sustenance. I told him this was a state park, no drinking allowed, and he pointed to one of the green-painted wooden signs nailed high on a number of trees. "Loophole," he said. The old signs read, as they always had,

NO BEERS, WINES OR LIQUEURS ALLOWED

For some reason, probably because "liqueur" is harder to spell than "liquor," this misspelling had never annoyed me. I loved that over the decades these signs had been periodically repainted, and no one had corrected them.

"Lucky for me," he said, tearing the seal off a pint of Jim Beam, "I decided, at the last minute, not to go with the crème de banana." He unpacked his leather binder, flattened it open on the picnic table, and regarded me expectantly.

"I'm going for a hike," I said.

"Wait for me," Abigail said.

Conrad began to extricate himself from the table.

"What are you people? Twelve? Five? Stupid?" Suddenly I was yelling. "Leave me alone! For pity's sake!" I stalked off toward the chasm, then whirled around, fully expecting them both to be three feet behind me. They remained seated, each looking off in a different direction, neither at me. I hate to raise my voice. Hate it.

At the north entrance the chasm descends abruptly, like a giant's stone staircase. There are alcoves along the way, which looked like caves to us when we were small, and if you look up you can read more romantic protestations scratched high on the sheer rock walls, chiseled deep, their authors hanging by a thread. You have to admire that. When we were kids we used to scamper fearlessly from rock to rock, even Abigail, who wasn't nearly as agile as I. On this day I found that I could still scamper here, fueled as I was by outrage and desperation. I went down and down, past Lovers' Leap, Devil's Pulpit, that unnamed crevice where Abigail had gotten her leg stuck and been rescued by a handsome park ranger.

The chasm was mine alone, all other visitors apparently opting for the playground, and as I descended I lambasted my tormentors in full voice, and they listened attentively to me. "It's time, people," I said, "to put up or shut up. Divorce or kill each other. Either way, leave me out of it." I said, "I quit," over and over and over again, and when I caught my breath I was at the base of the chasm, in the boulder field, where there was as much earth as stone. The ground was spongy, and stretched over much of it was a thin shroud of ice, fragile as a pressed leaf. I sat down on a mossy rock and immediately the damp cold entered my bones and I was shivering, and my throat was closing up again, as though I were about to sob, but I wasn't, not any more, no more of that nonsense. *I quit. I quit. I quit.*

Now they call them panic attacks. Maybe they were calling them that in 1978, but if so I had filed that term away with the Universal Choking Sign. To me a panic was a more or less rational response to a specific perceived threat. That day, at the bottom of Purgatory Chasm, I thought I was experiencing some sort of cardiac event. My heart, which should have slowed when I came to rest, banged in my ears, I was gulping for air for no good reason, and while attempting calmly to assess these symptoms I became terrified, again for no good reason. I had never been a fearful person, not even as a little child, but now I shuddered and gasped and whipped my head around, searching for the cause of my distress.

There are no tigers in my native habitat, no bears either, but I felt stalked, staked out, hunted down, exposed to some piercing merciless eye. I had to get out of there, and yet I couldn't move.

They call it "fight or flight" too, and I probably would never have flown, would have remained transfixed until I blended with the rock, had the word *vastation* not popped into my head like a cartoon mouse come to save the day, and I began to know what this was, I could name it!, the James boys had it, William and Henry, sought spiritual remedies for it, it was a real, comprehensible event, and I was not dying, probably.

Vastation. The word saved me, as words always have, and I could stir again, and stir I did, charging up the eastern loop of the trail back like a bat out of hell. I hiked uphill too fast for comfort, for I wasn't after comfort, I was outrunning the beast in the jungle. In no time I was thirty feet above the chasm floor, hastening up the rocky rim, actually looking forward to rejoining Abigail and Conrad, and then I heard them clearly, close by. I couldn't see them anywhere, yet their voices reverberated as though they were indoors, in a tiled room.

"I know what I'm doing," my sister was saying. "I told you. We came here all the time."

"What's on the other side?" he asked.

"Come and see. Come on."

There was a long silence. "Where's Dorcas?" he asked.

"She's fine. She knows her way around here. Come over here, with me."

"I'll just wait here. Take your time."

They sounded almost amiable. I pretended, briefly, that their constant poisonous animosity was an act for my benefit, to keep me busy; that they were secretly the fondest of lovers.

"You're scared," said my sister. "You're afraid to come in here with me."

"Don't be stupid."

"You're actually afraid."

"I'm bored stiff."

Abigail snickered. "Hardly *stiff*. Hardly that."

"Go to hell."

"What's the matter with you now? Claustrophobia?"

By the sound they were close enough to touch: I heard him take a deep drag on his Marlboro; I heard the flicked stub snap against stone. Were they underground, beneath my feet? I walked out to the edge of an overhanging rock and peered around. I couldn't spot them anywhere below, and they couldn't very well be hiding in the trees at my back.

"Did she stuff you in a closet? Bury you alive?" Abigail sighed heavily. "If you don't tell me, I won't know, will I?" Abigail's tone was remote, cool. She sounded like a therapist on autopilot.

"And just exactly why do you want to know?" His speech was beginning to slur. "You got a plan, sweetmeat?"

"I got a deal, lover. The deal is, you talk to me. We try to work through all your—"

"The deal is. The deal the deal the deal the deal. You kill me."

She swore under her breath. "All right, I'm coming back. Move out of the way, please."

There was a shuffling sound, the sound of nylon fabric whispering against stone, and I realized where they had to be: the Lemon Squeeze, a twenty-foot spherical rock split clean down the center, leaving just enough space for a child or a slender adult to edge through. At its far end was a sharp drop. When we were kids I used to slip through it all the time. Abigail never fit. In recent times they started calling it

"Fat Man's Misery," but that's a day-tripper name. It's the Lemon Squeeze.

They were indeed below where I stood. I'd have to walk ahead and double back under to see them. I really didn't want to do this.

"Do you mind? Would you please move? I can't get by."

"Fat-ass."

"Idiot. Twiggy couldn't get by you."

"Go the other way."

"The other end is impossible. It's just a sheer drop."

"What a fucking shame."

"Which you'd know already, if you'd just had the balls to—"

There was the sound of scuffling. Abigail grunted, and swore again. "Let me by, you—" More scuffling, then the splash of broken glass. From Conrad came a stream of vile oaths and vicious, specific threats, and I ran down toward the Squeeze. Since the wedding they had never to my knowledge laid hands on each other; if this was a first, it was happening in a dangerous place.

"I'm going to kill you," he said, "you evil, ugly, useless, ugly bitch."

Abigail laughed, a brand-new and terrible laugh. Had Medea ever laughed, she would have sounded just like Abigail. "You're on, champ," she announced, and I could hear her shuffling back through the Squeeze. "Come and get me," she said. Her voice no longer reverberated. She was standing on the tiny ledge, at the dropoff.

Then I could see her. I had made it down to their level and was facing the northern wall of the Squeeze, the western half of which jutted out over nothing. Abigail stood on tiptoe, way out beyond my reach, leaning into the narrow passage and taunting him, singing to him. Come and get me, Ramrodder, go ahead, kill me, you can do it, I'm right here. Come to Ma-ma.

I couldn't have stopped him. Unable even to open my mouth to scream I stood rooted and held my breath and waited to see his long arms emerge and propel my sister into space. Today, when I close my eyes, I can still see those arms, sweatered in threadbare gray wool, shoot out, his crabbed hands extended toward her throat, the image far more vivid and persuasive than actual memory. In drab memory I hesitate dully calculating the odds of my dashing into the passage and tackling him before he succeeds in killing her. The odds were bad, on top of which if I took my eyes off her I was sure she would die. I had once been a capable, rational woman.

Abigail glanced my way. "What are you doing here?" she asked, in an absurdly conversational tone, as though I had barged in on her in the bathroom. "Look, would you do me a favor? Captain Courageous is stuck in there. Would you help him out?"

"Help him what?" I had found my voice at last. "Help him kill you?"

Abigail smiled at me, in a superior way. "You always take everything so seriously. He's not going to do anything. He never does. Just get him out of there. He's such a fucking baby."

Numbly I went down to the entrance to the Squeeze, and there he was. Not stuck, but slumped down near the entrance, his back against one wall, his head in his hands. The air reeked of bourbon, and there were glass shards all over the ground. Thank God for that. It gave me myself back. "Pick that up," I said to him. "Pick up every single piece of glass."

"I'll cut myself," he said.

"Little children come to this place," I said. "Pick it up right this minute!"

And he did, every piece, and walked back to the park entrance with the broken glass cupped in his hands, and dumped it in a trash can, and he didn't cut himself. Nor did he say another word. We drove home in silence, as the short day waned and the sky got darker still, until, within a mile of Watch Hill, I told them that I would be leaving for good in the morning. Abigail said she understood. Conrad said nothing. A single tiny snowflake settled on my windshield, melting immediately, and just before I pulled into the driveway, another settled in its place. I'd have to get an early start tomorrow. With snow, you never know.

CHAPTER TWENTY-ONE

The Great Blizzard of 1978

Snow heavy at times tonight. Probable accumulations of 8 to 16 inches. Windy with drifting, Snow ending tomorrow. Low tonight in teens. High tomorrow in the 20s. Northeast winds 25 to 40 mph tonight and north winds 25 to 35 mph tomorrow.

I slept poorly Sunday night, partly out of guilt about my impending escape, but mostly because of those two tiny snowflakes on my windshield and the real possibility of coming awake to a storm and finding myself snowed in with George and Martha at Agincourt. I didn't achieve real sleep until four in the morning, and when I woke up it was almost noon. Of course they'd let me sleep. And it had indeed begun to snow, in big fat flakes. But the road outside my windows was reasonably clear, and I saw no good reason to change my plans.

It's worth noting that tens of thousands of Rhode Islanders took to the highways that day in the identical casual, can-do spirit. And in the intervening years those same people, when presented with the veriest dusting of snow, race to the nearest supermarket and strip its shelves of bread and milk. Since that day, nothing panics us, here in the Panic State, like snow.

Conrad stayed in bed. Abigail helped me carry my stuff to the car. She wouldn't come with me, and I was through arguing with her. I told her to get the Plymouth fixed, or else she'd be housebound. I promised to call her that night, from Frome. I started the car, and she leaned into the window and kissed me. "Tell Anna I love her," she said, and straightened up, her face expressionless. And still I backed out of the driveway as she waved me off, and headed off for home, her kiss still moist on my cold cheek.

We never kissed, ever. As I drove north on the Westerly road the drying kiss puckered my skin like paper glue. After two miles I thought I could feel it still, and I didn't raise my hand to rub it away. Abigail hadn't meant to make me worry; she was manipulative with everyone else, but not with me. She was not, is not, the suicidal type. True, at the Lemon Squeeze she had appeared bent on her own destruction, but appearances had deceived me. She was right about Conrad. He was no danger to her, at least not at that moment. I put the mystery of that kiss out of my mind, and concentrated upon enjoying my freedom.

There were quite a few cars on Watch Hill Road that day, parading north at a sedate pace, and at first I had no trouble following the navy blue Lincoln in front of me. I have always loved to drive in this kind of snow. It's not particularly slippery, and it puts a hush over the road, and the more thickly it closes in, the safer you feel, domed in white, as in a child's merry paperweight. I listened to the Jupiter Symphony on

'GBH, then turned it off for the silence, because they were prattling on too much about the foolish weather.

By the time I got to the Airport Road I couldn't see the outlines of the Lincoln anymore, just the red smudge of its lights, and the wind began to pick up. That there were still other cars on the road quickly became something I had to take on faith, because as far as I could see, there was me and that Lincoln, and I tried to recall if I had ever known anything as white as this day. We slowed to a belly-crawl. I had absolutely no idea where we were. After I had driven for an hour I checked the odometer: I had come seven miles.

Wherever that Lincoln was going, I was going too. It turned out that it was headed, not for Frome, which would have been way too much to hope for, but for Ashaway, at the outskirts of which we each came to a wheel-spinning stop. I tried rocking the car, but it was hopeless. After debating whether to take anything with me (no, I decided; if I have to, I can always come back), I emerged into the howling white, no boots on my sneakered feet, and made my way over to the Lincoln. An older couple emerged, and together, wordlessly, hunched forward at the waist, we descended into Ashaway.

We stopped at the first shelter we came to, an oblong concrete structure on the outskirts of town. We could see the outline of a sign on the roof, but couldn't begin to read it. All that mattered, anyway, was that you could see lights inside, and it looked warm. So it was that at one P.M. on February 6, 1978, I came to Rocco's Famous Sport & Trophy.

Rocco himself ushered us into a long room cluttered with duck decoys, waders, half-opened boxes of hunting boots, basketballs, pool cues, and eight other people, all of them clearly sheltering from the storm. Before the day was through six more straggled in. Rocco kept us all supplied with coffee and hot chocolate, and we gathered around a small black and white television set and listened to the day's events unfold, there being nothing to watch except talking heads and archived films of old blizzards. The announcers were snowed in too, as were mobile cameras, spy-in-the-sky helicopters, police cruisers, ambulances, fire trucks, and, most significantly, snowplows.

By suppertime I was ready to face the prospect of spending the night in a motel, at which I was informed by the Lincoln couple that there were no motels in Ashaway. They themselves lived in Ashaway, but on the other side of town. Fifteen of us, plus Rocco, would have to bed down at the Sport & Trophy. Our host, a prince among men, unpacked sleeping bags and army cots and inflatable rafts, and while we lined up to use his phone he grabbed a Coleman lantern and set out for a nearby convenience store. We stood in the open door and watched the swirling white swallow up Rocco and his brave little light.

Anna answered the phone on the second ring. She had two high school friends with her, stranded on what was supposed to be an afternoon visit, and they'd built a fire in the fireplace, cooked and eaten dinner, and washed up. They were having a fabulous time. She was happy to hear from me, but only because she'd been worried, and I gave her the number at Rocco's and promised to see her some time tomorrow.

Half an hour later, just when we were about to send out a rescue party, in blew Rocco, quilted in snow, bearing a plastic garbage bag full of plunder. "Sorry, folks," he said, "somebody else must have had the same idea. All I got is snack crap and stuff." There had been no one in the store, he told us, and the door was wide open, and there wasn't a loaf of bread or a carton of milk in the place.

Rocco had brought us a case of Spam, two jars of yellow

mustard, two boxes of cream-filled chocolate cupcakes, at least a hundred packages of peanut butter cheese crackers, and, sloshing in the bottom of the bag, a million packets of grape Kool-Aid with which to wash it all down. That night we dined like kings, the old kings, the ones who ate meat with their hands, and we regaled one another with tales of the strange lands from which we had journeyed, Hopkinton and Olneyville, Chepachet and Attleboro, and the singular quests which had brought us to this hospitable place. With the exception of the Lincoln couple, retirees returning from a stay with their daughter's family in Stonington, we were all working people, on the road to deliver auto parts and office supplies and olive oil, or on our way home from early closings. There was a schoolteacher, a hairdresser, a dental hygienist, and an insurance salesman (who assured us, chuckling, as we registered alarm, that he was off duty for the evening). There were two hunters on their day off. Some of us, including me, never revealed their occupations, and none of us exchanged full names, but we were good company that night. And later, bedding down on a hardwood floor, nestled snugly between a civics teacher and somebody named Bev, I slept more profoundly than I had in weeks.

And awoke the next morning to snow, snow, and snow. Breakfast was not quite as jolly as dinner had been, although most of us were still in a positive mood. We spent the first half of the morning trying to open the front door so that the men could go out and scavenge. High winds had blown a drift of epic proportions against the entire storefront, and the rear door was also unmanageable. Mid-morning the men left, smartly attired by Rocco in the latest Eskimo gear. We didn't see them again for more than two hours, the length of time it took them to locate the convenience store, which had effectively disappeared, and burrow into it. "You can all forget about your cars. You're never going to find them again," they announced upon their return, as they dumped on counter and floor every edible and semi-edible thing they had been able to find, including a frozen-solid block of saugies, five gallons of rainbow sherbet, a gross of spearmint gum packets, and a giant box of Bisquick.

We stared blankly at our comestible future, and then one of the women started laughing, triggering a tension-releasing group laugh, except that the woman who had started it kept going and seemed for a while unable to stop, and after she finally did a pall settled over us, and we went our separate ways to ponder our plight, which wasn't easy in a single twelve-by-fifteen room. Rocco assured us all that we'd be okay, it couldn't snow forever, and besides he had plenty of heating fuel, and if we were still here tomorrow (*"If,"* snorted two of the men) he'd break out his homemade jerky, of which he had an inexhaustible supply.

This triggered a run on the phone, as it occurred simultaneously to all of us to worry about the heating fuel status of our loved ones. It took me an hour to get through to Anna, because the phone lines were tied up statewide, but when I did she assured me that we'd had an oil delivery two days before, and she had plenty of stuff to eat. When I elaborated upon where I was, she laughed herself into hiccups. "Poor Dorcas," she said, "no place to hide and not a book in sight."

I asked her to call her mother, and then I hung up. *Poor Dorcas.* I didn't like the sound of that, especially coming from my girl. And I really hadn't needed reminding that there was nothing to read. For the rest of that dreary day I made a library out of Rocco's Famous Sport & Trophy, and to this day I can remember the address, down to the very zip code, of the factory in Worcester where his trophies were made, and the banal cover designs on each of his catalogues, and all six recipes on the back of the Bisquick box. The others exchanged life stories, commiserated about local politics, cursed the ancestry of all snow-removal personnel, while I studied Rocco's inventory list, read up on duck blind construction, and committed to memory "The Saga of Acme Quoits," which, to my sorrow, was only a mimeographed page and a half long. Late in the afternoon I was overjoyed to discover a pornographic paperback hidden in the bathroom behind the toweling and soap supplies. It was titled *Full Frontal Funhouse,* an odd choice for text-only, and the plot wasn't much, but just the heft of the book, the reassuring orderly march of words across the page, was enough to soothe me, and I only regretted having to read it in the bathroom.

So I was in decent spirits when the telephone rang shortly after supper (saugies off a hotplate: really delicious) and it was Anna, and she was worried about Abigail. "Mother sounds funny," she said.

I hadn't given Abigail an extended thought since the blizzard began. "In what way funny?"

"I don't know. She says she's okay but I don't believe it. She kept telling me she loved me. She *never* does that."

"Just please tell me exactly what she said."

"I called her, and the phone rang and rang, and when she picked it up, or *he* did, there was this clunking sound like it was dropped on the floor, and then somebody hung up. I called right back and *he* answered, right away, and he thought it was you. He said, 'Dorcas?' And when I told him I wanted to speak to Mother he just dropped the phone, and after a while she was on the line. She started crying. She said she was a bad mother, because she hadn't called to see how I was, and you know, she *never* does that. It took me a while to calm her down. Then she said everything was just fine. Which is bullshit. I'm sorry, Dorcas, but that's what it is."

"Don't worry," I told Anna. "I'll take care of it. It'll be okay."

"Dorcas," Anna said, "*he* wanted your number there in Ashaway. I wouldn't give it to him."

When I put the phone down everybody was looking at me. "You got troubles?" asked Rocco.

No, no, I assured him, everything was perfectly fine, but I needed to make a phone call. I didn't know how I was going to talk to my sister in such a public place, but right then everybody pretended to be engrossed in some urgent enterprise, reminding grateful me that Rhode Islanders can be, in their own odd way, the most gracious people in the world. I took a deep breath and called Watch Hill.

After ten rings he picked up. "There you are," he said. "Whooping it up in Ash Wednesday, I hear. How's doings? The kid said you were—"

"Put my sister on."

"Hey, that's kind of rude. So's leaving without saying good-bye."

"Put my sister on."

"All righty." He set the phone down. *Sweetcheeks!* he called, *Honeybun! Your sister's on the line!*

"Dorcas?" Her voice was small and breathy.

"Tell me yes or no. Are you alone right now?"

"Yes."

I had to believe her. "What's happening? Anna said you weren't yourself."

For a full minute she just breathed. Finally she spoke so softly that I couldn't hear her. She had to repeat herself twice until I heard: "I'm so hungry, Dorcas. I'm so goddamn hungry."

"What?" I practically shouted into the phone. Bev, boning up on French's mustard vinaigrette suggestions, glanced at me in alarm, then looked quickly away. "Then eat something, for God's sake. The pantry's full, the refrigerator too, I checked it before I left. You ought to be stuck here with me. All we've got here is—"

"It's all gone. There's nothing left."

"What? How on earth? It's only been twenty-four hours."

"He's done something with it. He's hidden it. I can't get out the door."

"Put him back on."

"You don't know," she said. "You just have no idea how hungry I am."

"Put him back on the goddamn phone," I hissed, cupping my hand around my mouth, although basically I didn't give a damn whether anybody heard me or not.

Again, there was a long, scary silence.

"Abigail! Go next door. If nobody's home, just keep looking until you find somebody."

"I told you. We're snowed in. I just don't have the strength to shovel."

"Well, *he* does. Put him on *now*. Right *now*."

"I have to go." *Click.*

I stared at the phone for a good five minutes, thinking, calculating, and then I called back and told whoever picked up and refused to speak that I'd be there as soon as possible. "And if that's you," I said, "you miserable worthless sadistic bastard, you'd better be gone when I get there."

"I'm leaving in the morning," I told Rocco and the others.

"But what if—"

"As soon as it clears. One way or the other I'm leaving. I've got an emergency in Watch Hill."

Instead of arguing with me like the rest of them, Rocco thought for a while. "Do you cross-country?" he asked me.

"Cross-country what?"

"Guess not. Hold on." He rummaged around in the stock-room and emerged with a big flat box. "They're yours," he said, presenting it to me. Snowshoes, brand-new. He wouldn't hear of taking money. Just bring them back, he said, when you're through.

I didn't think I'd sleep at all that night, but I did, awakening refreshed before the others, and when I opened the door, there, above a neck-high snowdrift, was the rising sun, raying pinkly across an innocent sky. Rocco had put together for me a fantastic snow outfit, warm enough for Greenland, and while I got myself ready he heated up the last of the hot chocolate for me. Whispering together we went over the necessary maps, until I was clear in my mind how to proceed. He showed me how to wear the snowshoes, and how to use the compass he pressed into my mittened hand. He loaded me down with venison jerky, a canteen of Kool-Aid and an ingenious folding shovel, and he wished me luck. Give us a call when you get there, he said, and waved good-bye to me behind the closing door.

A prince among men. And not once did he, or any of them, ask me what the emergency was about. I love Rhode Island. I really do.

The trek was arduous and long and absolutely the best time I ever had. I am not the outdoor type; nor was I changed by this experience. It was just the sort of thing everybody should do once. To have the sparkling world all to yourself, free of landmarks, grids, and signs; to walk for miles and hear nothing but the sound of your own breathing. I didn't see another living creature, not even a bird, until the day was half gone. It is nine miles from Ashaway to Watch Hill as the crow flies, which is pretty much the path I took. I dreaded my destination, but that dread didn't spoil the day; if anything it sharpened it up. I was going to save my sister. How, I didn't know, nor did I worry about it. Who could worry on such a day?

And who would clutter it up with thought? On that beautiful day I lived in the moment, in pure sensation; in, I suppose, my sister's world. And this time I was ready for it. I thought for a fleeting moment of Henry David Thoreau, and then I put him out of my mind. He would have done the same for me.

By the time I got to Westerly, people had begun digging out in earnest, and on the outskirts of Watch Hill I actually found a Dunkin' Donuts, manned by a cheerful old crone named Olivia, who, in exchange for the story of my journey there, loaded me down with day-old doughnut holes and two dozen freshly baked jelly doughnuts. Now I knew I could save Abigail, and, with the sun beginning to fade, I marched on to Agincourt.

The sun was setting when I arrived. There was a lot less accumulated snow down there than at Ashaway, but evidently the wind had been fierce off the water, and I had a terrible time finding the cottage, hidden as it was behind a huge drift satiny with ice. They really were trapped inside. I was suddenly exhausted, my ankles were killing me, and the thought of battering my way inside was daunting. I wanted to stand there and bellow until one of them opened a window. Damn the neighbors, if indeed there were any. I didn't see any signs of one. But after summoning what remained of my strength I got out Rocco's little shovel and set to work.

It was dark in there, and it smelled stale, moldy, as though the place had been deserted suddenly, and abandoned for years; as though it were inhabited only by ghosts and mice. Long minutes passed, before my eyes, burned by snow sparkle, could make out even large shapes, the coat tree, the telephone table. Plumply suited and hooded in goose down and lambs' wool, I stood in the front hall like a wary space traveler, calculating whether to remove his helmet and test the air. Was there sentient life on this planet? And did it mean us harm?

Where were they? I hadn't called out, but I had certainly made enough commotion getting in the door to alert them of my presence. At least, I thought, it doesn't smell downright bad. At least there isn't what the horror books and police procedurals always describe as "the sweet odor of rotting meat." This was an unwise thought.

I untied my hood and listened very hard, breathing shallowly, and then at last, thank heaven, came shuffling sounds from the master bedroom upstairs. I imagined Abigail in her pig slippers (a Christmas present from her husband, which she defiantly wore all the time) slouching toward the top of the stairs. She moved like an invalid, and she didn't call my name. Surely she had heard me come in. She had to know it was me, come to help her. I opened my mouth to announce myself, and found that I couldn't speak. It wasn't fear exactly; more a profound unwillingness to affect the moment, as unsettling as that moment was; to set in motion whatever was going to happen next. I had come to save her, but I didn't want, right then, to see her.

The kitchen, I thought, that's it, I'll go to the kitchen and find out just how bare those cupboards actually are. Surely something's left. I turned to go, and there he was, inches away. "I knew you'd come," he said. He put his hands on me, unzipped my parka, slid it off me while my arms dangled straight down, like a child's. He touched my cold face with a colder fingertip. "You are," he said, "one amazing piece of work. Look how far you've come." His smile was admiring. "You're mad at me," he said. "But you'll get over it."

I backed away, circling him until my back was to the kitchen. Behind him, my sister loomed up from the murk, and came to stand beside him, rubbing sleep from her eyes.

She looked unwashed, apathetic, as though drugged. He put his arm around her puny shoulders. "Look who's come to save us, honey," he said.

I fled to the kitchen, where things got even worse. The shelves were anything but bare, and the refrigerator was still stocked with milk, cheese, English muffins. In the freezer was even new stuff, acquired since I left, a Sara Lee cheesecake, a gallon of vanilla ice cream. Was my sister delusional? There was enough here to feed everybody at Rocco's for a week.

"Do you see?" she asked me. "It's all gone." She leaned against the door frame.

What do you say then? "Abigail," I finally said, "you're frightening me."

"Did you bring me anything?"

"Of course I did. It's in my backpack, in the hall." I wasn't going to go back there for it.

She left, and returned after a long while, dragging the open backpack behind her. She regarded me with horror. "How could you?" she said. There were tears in her eyes. She'd never looked at me like that in her life.

"What are you talking about?" Oh, God, he must have stolen the doughnuts, and I grabbed for the backpack to confirm this, and there they were, the cardboard box, the cheery pink and white bag of doughnut holes. I wanted to shake her, to smack her face, to pummel her old self back into her, but there'd already been too much of that. "Abigail," I said, slowly, "look here. Look at what I brought you. It's all right here."

"Is that supposed to be *funny*?" she screamed hoarsely. "Are you in on it *too*?"

"In on what?" Did she think the doughnuts were poisoned? This was some kind of psychotic break. How could I have left her alone at such a time?

"You know I can't eat *that*!"

"Can't eat what?"

"I. Can't. Eat. That."

Slowly, keeping my eyes on her, I reached into the bag and retrieved a doughnut hole. "Look, Abigail," I said, holding it up to my mouth and biting into it. "See? It's perfectly–"

She slapped it out of my hand. "I hate you!" she screamed. "I hate both of you!"

I was shaking now, with anxiety and exhaustion. "Listen to me," I said. "There's no way I can get an ambulance here today. Probably not even tomorrow. They're saying we can't dig out until the army comes, and the army can't fly in before the weekend. You have to calm down. You have to start making sense. That's all there is to it."

"Fat chance," said Conrad. He stood right in back of her, his head right above hers, so that it looked disembodied, perched, like the Cheshire cat, on top of hers. "She hasn't made sense for quite some time. I was hoping–praying, really–that between the two of us we could straighten her out." He grinned widely, just like the cat, showing me all his teeth.

"Do you have any idea," she whispered, "how much fat and processed sugar is in just one of these?" She held up the bag of holes as though it were a dead rat.

"See what I mean?"

"Do you know what the caloric count is for a jelly doughnut? No, of course you don't. You never had to count a single calorie in your life."

"Wait a minute," I said. "Are you saying you–"

"Yup," said Conrad. "Sad, isn't it? If you only knew how hard I've tried to get her to eat just a little sliver of cheese, for Christ's sake, a slice of toast, without butter, even. She simply won't listen to reason."

"You bastard hypocrite," she said, over her shoulder, not bothering to turn and face him. "Ask him what he did with my chicken bouillon. Ask him what he did with all my zwieback crackers and my cottage cheese and my celery and carrots and my Tab, I had two six-packs left, and all my cans of spinach and green beans. Ask him."

"See, she's flipped. Where on earth would I—"

"I know where you hid them. They're out there someplace under the snow where I'll never get to them, until it's too late!"

"What difference does it make anyway?" He sounded reasonable, exasperated, as though he had been trying to teach long division to a slow child. "Clearly," he said to me, "she needs something more substantial than zwieback. She's wasting away. She's gone too far. I've tried and tried to convince her, but she just won't listen to me."

"*Liar!* He wants me to quit! He's been sabotaging me for weeks! I'm winning, and he can't stand it!"

I was so tired. I had traversed the frozen waste alone for this: two lunatics locked in some stupid love-death spiral, with me utterly, laughably irrelevant. Whatever else was going on, I was off the hook. They didn't need me at all. "Have you been drinking water?" I asked her.

"Well, of course," she said. "What does that have to do with anything?"

"It means you're not dehydrated. You're not going to die, at least not tonight. I can go to bed now, and in the morning I can get up and leave, and in the meantime you two psychos can stay the hell out of my way. Thank you so much."

It took me a half hour to haul the convertible settee from the frigid back porch into the living room, and another half hour to find clean bedding, and in my quest to do so I didn't run into either of them. It was so cold in the house, despite the constant rumble of the basement furnace, that I went down there to check on it. There seemed to be plenty of heating oil. The old furnace just hadn't been able to keep up with the freezing gale. I collected an armful of maple logs from Guy's tidy firewood stack, and brought them upstairs. Kindling was a problem, until I remembered where Conrad kept his precious blue-lined three-hole notebook paper, and for good measure I dumped the jelly doughnuts onto Hilda's big cutting board over the kitchen sink and tore the greasy cardboard box into three pieces. Soon I had a good fire going. The fire calmed me down. It had been, I decided, a real Jack London sort of day.

I got in bed and stared into the flames and pretended I was back in civilization with Rocco and Bev and the civics teacher, and that I had never been forced to see my sister, my Warrior Bawd twin, reduced, perhaps for good, to a pathetic, whining mantis-creature. At the end of the day, all we have, any of us, is pride. At least I still had mine, and it would have to do for us both. In the morning I would get her out of here if I had to kick her all the way to the county line. I was saddened, but temperately so, and full of clean resolve. I did not allow him space in my conscious mind. These were my thoughts as I drifted off.

And opened my eyes at midnight to a dying fire and he was there, sitting on the floor beside my bed, stroking my head with a gentle hand. I had been dreaming the sort of dream I hadn't had since I was young, and I came awake smiling. He put his other hand over my mouth, light as a wink, and whispered, "Shhhhhhh. She's sleeping." And then he put his lips on mine, and they were dry, and his breath was whiskey and smoke and some tantalizing third scent, like cloves, only it wasn't cloves, and I opened my mouth to his tongue, and his fingertips traced my brow, my throat, my collarbone. This was joy. I rose up against him hard, my arms strong around his back, and he held still, and I hung suspended, breathing him in; and then he pressed me back down and leaned in close and whispered, "Perfect. Don't move. Wait right here." And then he was gone.

It happens just that fast. No rhythm to it, no inexorable buildup, no shrieking violins. You slip through an open door you didn't know was there. It closes behind you, sealing you off forever from everything you knew and all you were. You are in the void, and all directions are down. What else are you capable of? How far can you fall?

I listened for the answer while the fire died, my mind perfectly white, untracked, alert as any dog to all sounds real and imagined. I listened to the pop of unseasoned firewood, the final shift as it crumbled into embers, the emptied silence. I waited without moving until I could see in my mind's eye the shape of this day, not at all a Jack London sort of day, and then the shape of my entire life, the hard bright ruined arrow of my life, and I arrived at the spot where I had been led, and then I understood. Endgame.

Well played.

And I had known all along, hadn't I, that it *was* a game, that he was a terrible man, one who simply *loved* bad weather. I had been given every clue, every chance. The only thing I hadn't known was my own weakness. But he had. Because, apparently, we really are all alike, and there is not and never has been anything special about me. I am of no consequence. I am not an honorable woman. I am not a contradiction in terms.

You would think that, having arrived at a place where there was nothing to hope for, and so nothing, really, to fear, you might just close your eyes. But even with nowhere to go I had to wander. I stood up, creaking and sore like the old woman I soon enough would be, wrapped my blanket around my shoulders, and roamed, like my own ghost, about the first-floor rooms, settling for a time on the parlor window seat, searching the moonless sky for the promise of light. When day came I would have to do some pointless thing.

"It doesn't matter," said Abigail. I couldn't see her in the dark, but she was somewhere close to me. I hadn't heard her come down. When had she come down? How long had she been here? "He's passed out now. He won't bother you anymore."

She sounded like a mother apologizing for an unruly toddler.

"Abigail," I said.

"Dorcas," she said, "I'm so hungry."

I could make out her outline now. She was sitting on my bed. I couldn't speak.

"Dorcas," she said. "I have to eat something."

Just like that, so did I. I had hardly eaten all day. I was starving.

She rose and took my hand and we went into the kitchen, where she turned on the light. "You'll really eat now?" I asked, and she said yes, she was ready. Hunger gave me momentary purpose, rescued me, for a time I understood would be finite, from the numb horror of this night. While she rummaged purposefully through drawers and cabinets, I got out six eggs and scrambled them with cream, and made us each an omelet with cheese and ham, and served them up on Hilda's best stoneware, and set us each a place across from each other at the kitchen table, and between us, as a centerpiece, I arranged twelve doughnuts on a white platter. I poured us orange juice and milk both, and started the coffee. Through the kitchen window I fancied I could see first light. "We'll leave as soon as we're finished here," I said. "I'll figure out something." When she didn't answer I turned around and she wasn't there.

She wasn't in the living room either, and the front door was still closed and locked. I stood for a long time at the base of the stairs, and then went back to the kitchen table. Wherever she had gone, she was lost to me. I was of no use here. I was a profoundly useless human being. The eggs were cold and I scraped them into the garbage with the doughnuts, and I dumped out the juice and milk, and I cried and cried into the kitchen sink.

"Dorcas," I heard her call from far away. "Come here."

She was upstairs. "No," I said.

"You have to come up here. I need you."

"I can't. Please don't ask me."

"I'm not asking," she said then, in a new voice, a cold, dry voice. My voice.

I don't remember climbing the stairs. Sometimes I am able to not remember the entire night. I can go for days at a time. The only light on the second floor was a night-light in their bedroom, where, of course, she was. She stood by the bed, her back to me. "Come here," she said. She was holding something in her hand.

She had uncovered him. He was lying on his back, legs drawn up toward our side of the bed, the palm of his right hand resting on his narrow upturned hip. He faced slightly away from us, with no dreams rolling behind his closed lids, you knew he was asleep and not dead only by the barest rise and fall of his hairless chest. She leaned over him, so that I couldn't see his body anymore or what she was doing, and then sharply there were fumes, and when she straightened up, his nakedness gleamed in the soft night-light as though oiled, like a painting, an Old Master, they were never wrong, and she put a bottle in my hand, Calvados, empty. Then she lit a match. Blue flame raced across his body, sluiced over his flat belly, his soft nestled sex, down his long legs, and he was all bone, no fat on him at all, his body was young, younger than us, younger than him, and on he slept, like some enchanted knight, beautiful licked in the blue, no heat but such a basking light that I could see, in profile, the Giaconda smile on my sister's face.

"Let's eat him," she said.

CHAPTER TWENTY-TWO

The Eye

Hilda's final chapter, "Tragedy," focuses on the "tragedy," which took place a full year after the Great Blizzard of 1978, about which she actually knows nothing, except what she and Guy read in the *International Herald Tribune*. She plods along through the months leading up to Abigail's "savage act of assertive self-realization" on Route 6, where the H. C. had gotten themselves stuck in a snowbank during a much more modest storm, and Conrad, too plastered to think through the ramifications of what he was about to do, got out and knelt down behind the rear bumper, to give it a push. She makes a big deal out of the fact that he was kneeling ("Perhaps he said a short prayer." Sure he did, Hilda.) She makes an even bigger deal out of Abigail's two black eyes and broken nose. Well, I can't blame her for that.

Hilda knows nothing of the Great Blizzard, or of its immediate aftermath, when Conrad woke up on a bright, digging-out morning with what looked to him like a full-body sunburn. "What the hell happened to me?" he asked, and Abigail, successfully snorting back a horselaugh, spun an elaborate tale about how he had staggered out naked into the howling wind, and she hadn't found him for the longest time, and it was lucky for him he didn't have frostbite on his thing.

"Isn't he, Dorcas?" she asked me, carving off another wedge of cheesecake. We were all in the kitchen, he in an open robe and boxer shorts, his chest and stomach as red as a tomato. He looked so confused, so credulous, standing there. Whatever magic he had exerted over me was gone. He had done me terrible and lasting damage, and it had taken all his power to do it.

"Indeed," I said. "He's very lucky."

He made eye contact then and I could see him remember, not the flambeau, but what had gone before, the endgame. He smiled foully and asked me if I had slept well, and I said, Just fine, thank you. I was standing at the kitchen sink, in which still reposed a sticky mass of jelly doughnuts wetted down with my own tears, and I informed him that I had slept like a veritable baby. All that day he used his arsenal of grins and winks and nasty glances to goad me into an acknowledgment of defeat, and in the end he had to give up. If the English make the finest actors, then perhaps the New English aren't too shabby at it either, at least at one little thespian trick, the one where you are convincingly oblivious to the immense outrageous object galloping around and around you. He never knew if I remembered. Perhaps he believed I had convinced myself it was a dream. Perhaps he even wondered if the dream had been his. I'll never know, and I don't give a rat's ass.

The story should have ended that day, when Abigail and I left him alone at Agincourt and took up three days' residence at a local inn. Or a month later, when he showed up drunk at our house in Frome, demanding to see his wife, and we called the police on him. He should have died drunk in bed, from smoking, or throwing up, or just from being too awful to live.

A well-wrought piece of fiction, I used to lecture Guy, helps us make sense out of the chaos of our lives. Why be deliberately obscure when real life is so impossibly fractured and opaque? In a novel, Conrad Lowe would have died, or disappeared, after we declined to eat him. In reality he stayed around, slinking in and out of our lives until late the following fall, when my sister took him back.

"I'm strong now," she said, and she certainly looked it. She wasn't yet up to her fighting weight, but she had regained much of what she had lost, and was beginning to look like herself again, as though she could mop up the floor with any man, even Conrad Lowe. He had lately been affecting heart-felt remorse, calling her every night, and when she got her job back, he took to following her on her postal rounds, and once inveigled her into the back of her mail truck for what she told me, before I could stop her, was the best sex they had ever had. "Look," she told me, "whatever his problem was, he seems to be over it. I know it probably won't work, but it's worth a try." No, it certainly wasn't, but nothing I could say would stop her.

The DeVilbisses had returned from France, but Guy was too preoccupied with his "work" to spend much time with Conrad and Abigail, and they ended up living two miles down the road from Anna and me, in a rundown rental, and by year's end the honeymoon was over. They fought constantly, often with their fists and whatever heavy objects were handy. Both of them spent about the same amount of time in the local emergency room. She never called on me for help, and when I telephoned her, which I did once a week, she never sounded in the least pathetic. She was not, in those last months anyway, a victim.

I think now that she hated him from the time we left Agincourt, and that she took as much pleasure in the battle as in the bed, and that she intended all along to kill him. I don't mean that she provoked the final fight just so she could run him over. My sister is not a sneak. But she's no fool either, and when the opportunity presented itself, she took it.

She called me right afterward, from a private house a block from the site of what Miles Minden calls "the reckoning." It was mid-February, almost exactly a year after our last night at Agincourt, and it was snowing, and midnight, and she was on my mind. I picked up on the first ring. "It's over," she said, and instantly I knew, more or less, what this meant. I remember that as she began to explain her voice shook, and that I closed my eyes and steadied myself against the kitchen wall. He was gone. It was an accident, she said. I backed over him.

We were twins. I could ask her anything. I took a breath, but before I could put the question, she said, "Eight times."

Did we laugh then, in perfect unison? Barking like harpies? I don't remember. Yes, I do.

On her final page Hilda manages to drag Shakespeare into it, and she ends with my sister as Mistress Quickly, and so Conrad Lowe is not in hell, but "in Arthur's bosom; if ever man went to Arthur's bosom." Which, if no man ever went to Arthur's bosom, is certainly true; though it's pushing it to imagine that he spent his final moments babbling of green fields. Yet, I am moved, despite Hilda's foolishness, or perhaps on account of it. She is true to her silly self. In the end, who deserves mercy? Everyone or no one.

My sister, who is much smarter than Mistress Quickly and measurably less soft of heart, never talks directly about Conrad Lowe. As far as I have been able to tell, she misses only her old life, which she plans to resume as soon as she's acquitted—or, more likely, freed without trial, charges dropped: lately Miles has hinted that the D.A. seems ready to throw in the towel. She has wallowed in all the attention, to a degree that has threatened to drive me mad, but in the end I think she will quit the national stage, and content herself with local notoriety. Rhode Islanders tend to stay put. Everything we know is here.

Hilda mourns him; Abigail does not. I wonder if she misses her love for him, if indeed that was what it was. She surprised me once, in the early days of her strategic sojourn at the ACI, when I offered to argue Miles out of keeping her there. She had just spent fifteen minutes railing against the narrow lumpy mattress and the goddamn chicken à la king and the nerve of her lawyers warning to keep her hands off the prison guards, "As *if,*" she huffed, rolling her eyes toward the especially unappetizing specimen stationed in the visiting room. Say the word, I told her, and I'll figure out a way to take you home. For a while she was silent, her face impassive, and then she said, "Let it go. I'll be home soon enough." But you hate it here, I said. "Well," she said, meeting my eyes. "That's the point, isn't it?"

The lights have come back on. I've finished Hilda's book, and catalogued it, and after some internal debate placed it on the New Non-Fiction shelf, in True Crime, under D for DeVilbiss. Really it belongs with the other Bios, under M or L. When you read a biography you know you're getting a more or less inspired guess; less, in this case. True Crime should be, well, true. But there it is, eye-level, between a cheap compendium of serial killer lore and yet another unnecessary look at Lizzie Borden, the dusty old sphinx of Fall River. I can't wait for Moriarty's review.

Outside, the late afternoon sky is an optimistic, ladylike shade of gray. The low clouds have blown away, as have half the branches on my cherry trees. It's a mess out there, but a manageable one. Apparently, Pandora has, just as I feared, taken one good look around and flounced off with her nose in the air. More fool she.

When I was seventeen years old I set out to write an answer to Molly Bloom. Molly Bloom had not, in fact, asked me anything; Molly Bloom was a fictional character, and one not famous for asking questions. But fictional women are real, and this one was famous for saying yes, and that bothered the hell out of earnest me. I began an epic monologue, for my eyes only, and my speaker was, so help me God, Mary Budd, and my idea was to make *no* every bit as beautiful as *yes*. I failed. I put down my pen and every year or so I'd pick it up again and fail again, and for a long time I thought I was just too young, that the failure was all mine, that some day it could be done, and that I would do it. *No* is not a plump round word, it doesn't sing like a serpent, there's nothing cheap and alluring about *no*. Therein, I believed, lay its promise. *No* is slender, steely, unadorned. *No* is an arrow, bright and shining. I was Mary Budd, and I would say *No*. And I did, off and on for ten years, and each attempt was lamer than the one before. In the end I threw it all away, but I can still remember bits of it, *I left him under the Moorish wall* and, of course, *I will not put the rose in my hair like the Andalusian girls,* . . . but no matter how hard you try, *his heart was going like mad and no I said no I won't NO I said forget it Charlie absolutely NOT no way José N-O Means NO*—well, it just isn't art. It isn't even true. *No* is a necessary word; but not, I think, sufficient. You need them both: *yes* and *no*.

I miss my sister.

I'm going to lock up and go home now. If we have electricity, Anna and I are going to bake her a cake, as we do every Saturday, for our Sunday visitation. This time maybe devil's food with butter frosting. Or maybe—who knows?—on my journey home I'll see, on every side, way out behind the rooftops of my town, a white cloud wall a mile high, a great revolving cylinder of white. Well, probably not, of course not; the storm has left us far behind. But even so, it's there, all right, whether we see it or not. The Eye. Always. And my sister is in it. And I am in it too.